INVITATION TO THE BLUES

SMALL CHANGE #2

ROAN PARRISH

Published by Monster Press

Edited by Julia Ganis, JuliaEdits.com

Cover design by Natasha Snow, natashasnow.com

NOTE ON CONTENT

This book contains explicit discussion of depression, anxiety, attempted suicide, and feelings of worthlessness.

For everyone doing battle

CHAPTER ONE

SO THERE I WAS, working in my younger brother's sandwich shop to make rent after moving out of my parents' house, where I'd gone to temporarily lie low when I was released from the hospital I ended up in after trying to kill myself.

No, it's not the start of a grim joke. Just my grim fucking life.

See, if you start with "So there I was," it sounds like you're setting up the story with something meaningful. Something that will spin out into a metaphor. As if me making sandwiches was actually about me putting the pieces of my life back together.

Sure. If my life was made up of smoked turkey and ham. God, please don't let my life have been made up of smoked turkey and ham. I loathed deli meat.

Christopher slid the next ticket along the counter to me. It was my third week working at Melt, Christopher's sandwich and coffee joint off South Street, and my fourth day on sandwich-making duty. Christopher had gone through all the sandwiches with me for the second time after closing yesterday, hands moving in a conductor's effortless flicks and sweeps.

Scoop, spread, pile, slice, wrap. Mustard and mayo to seal the bread from the moisture of the other ingredients, veggies enrobed in meat or cheese so the layers wouldn't slide, every choice mathematical, down to a sprinkle of salt or a grind of pepper. This was his symphony.

"Hey, where are we with the Rueben, bro?"

Corned beef gleamed pink on the counter before me and my stomach lurched. The rubber gloves I wore did just enough to separate me from the meat that I could touch it if I unfocused my eyes enough that I couldn't see the webbing of fat that marbled the meat or the places where the slicer had torn at flesh.

Nausea washed over me and I levered the slices onto the rye bread.

"Coming up," I said. If I didn't breathe through my nose, I couldn't smell the rancid stink of sauerkraut or the sweaty odor of the Swiss cheese. I shoved the thing onto the grill and peered at the ticket Christopher had just passed me.

"Hey." His hand landed on my shoulder and I startled. "You wanna switch out and take orders instead?"

I eyed the neat slices of tomato and onion that I'd prepared in the morning dark before opening, wishing that could be my whole job. If only I could slice things into perfect pieces of themselves instead of touching dead flesh or speaking to living people, I'd be fine.

"No, I'll stay here."

"Okay." Christopher lingered at my side for a moment and I could feel him not saying something. I turned toward him a little, eyes still on the onion. "If you could go just a little bit faster, that would be awesome."

His voice was so gentle I almost couldn't hurt myself on it.

"Sure," I said.

I hummed the Minuetto of Mozart's Symphony No. 41 to give myself a rhythm, and tried to work accordingly. But although my hands moved in perfect time, the music swelled so large it blotted out everything else. At the end of the movement, I surfaced to the sandwich half-made in front of me and finger smears of mayonnaise dotting the countertop where I'd begun to play the part I knew as well as I knew my own name.

"Why don't you take a break," Christopher said, his voice strained.

I'm sorry.

I said it in my head but didn't let it out. I'm sorry was a trap, a pit of quicksand that seemed easy until you slid all the way down to *Sorry for what?* Or, worse: *That's okay*, when what they really meant was *You're always sorry but you always do it again*, or *I feel sorry for you*, or *I didn't expect anything more*, or *Sometimes when I look at you my skin crawls with how pathetic you are*, or, *There but for the grace of whatever go I.*

How could I be so damn good at playing music, and so damn bad at making a sandwich?

Outside, I lit a cigarette and closed my eyes against the glare. I could feel the sun in the red I saw behind my eyelids and the prickle of sweat it brought out under my arms, but the heat didn't register. I smoked one cigarette and then another, hoping the smoke would dull my sense of smell to the food, and then it was time to go back in.

I briefly indulged the fantasy of not going. Of walking away. Of walking forever. Then I unstuck myself from the alley wall and forced myself back inside.

I said what I was doing low, under my breath, to keep myself on track. The sandwiches got made. Christopher smiled at me tentatively. The shop closed. When I peeled off the gloves, talc clung to my skin in scabrous patches and I scrabbled at the faucet to wash my hands before I puked.

Floor swept and mopped, counters gleaming, I finally looked at Christopher. I'd felt his eyes on me as I cleaned. He was worrying his lip and running a hand through his hair and I decided to put him out of his misery.

"I'm crap at this," I said. "You have twenty-year-olds who are better at making sandwiches than me."

My brother smiled sadly. "Ten-year-olds are better at making sandwiches than you."

I shrugged. "I get it."

"Jude..." The way he lingered over my name said everything I already knew. He'd let me stay if I really wanted to. He wished he could do more to help me. He wished things were different. He wished I were different.

"You have to do what's good for Melt," I told him. "Don't be an idiot. I'll be fine."

Hey, it could be true.

Christopher pushed himself up to sit on the counter I'd just washed, powerful arms lifting his weight easily, powerful legs swinging. My little brother had been bigger than me since he was twelve.

"What're you gonna do?"

Music was all I'd ever wanted to do. It was what I'd worked for my whole life. The one place I felt good in my own skin. But since leaving Boston, I didn't even have that.

"I could...give piano lessons," I offered.

"Good, great!" Christopher would never believe me if I told him, but he reminds me so much of our mother when he's like this. They spread their desperate enthusiasm over my tiniest victory as thick as mayonnaise. And just like mayonnaise it makes me want to gag.

They meant well. They always meant well. Especially Christopher. He didn't even want anything from me. He only wanted things for me.

I swallowed hard and forced a smile. My muscles moved as if through tar. "Yeah, I'll...ask around."

"If you make a flyer, I'll post it on the bulletin board," Christopher said, gesturing toward the board packed with community activities, fundraisers, and job postings. "And Ginger'd post one in Small Change, I'm sure." He paused. "Well, I'm pretty sure, but ask her, since it's not my shop. Obviously."

My smile at that was genuine. Christopher was one of the most confident, self-assured people I knew, but every once in a while self-assuredness slid over the line into entitlement and bossiness, and Christopher's partner Ginger had no problem pointing out when he'd crossed the line.

"Maybe I'll tell her you promised me she'd say okay," I teased, just to watch his eyes go wide. I winked and relief spread over his face. He passed me some paper and a pen.

Christopher had moved into Ginger's apartment above her tattoo shop last month and I'd never seen him happier. It was small, but most of what Christopher had was kitchen gear, and since Ginger would rather floss with razor wire than do anything involving a pan, that seemed to work out pretty well.

She liked to play a game where she texted me pictures of Christopher doing complicated things in the kitchen with captions like, "BROWNING BUTTER: cooking technique or 16th century torture?" and "BROASTING: cooking technique or what happens when dudes get together and brag about shit?"

I'd taken over Christopher's lease because if I spent one more month in my parents' house I was concerned that I might expire from the weight of disappointing two people who loved me dearly. It wasn't their fault, but my parents were fixers. They wanted to make things okay for me, as if cooking the right dinner or renting the right movie might fundamentally change the way my brain worked. It was painful to watch. Painful to see them flounder over and over to turn the world into a place I could fit.

So I had to leave, because I couldn't fail any more.

Christopher moving in with Ginger had presented the perfect opportunity. I took over his lease and he offered me the job at Melt, because that was what Christopher did: he helped people.

I took it because that was what I did: I let people do the work for me because I didn't have the energy to do it myself.

———

WALKING into Small Change usually grated on my every nerve. There was always loud music playing, and people talking, and underlying it all was the hum of tattoo machines and the sharp scent of disinfectant. It was a riot of color, with every inch of wall space full of art or shelves of supplies so there was no blank place for the eye to land. Taken together it was a war waged on my senses.

Tonight, the shop was mercifully calmer than usual. Marcus was tattooing a lady in silence as she sat with her eyes closed, and Ginger was glaring at the front desk computer like it had offended her.

Neither of them looked up when I walked in, but when I stood in front of Ginger she tuned back in. She grinned when she saw it was me.

"Hey, bro. How goes the world of sandwich artistry?"

"Ugh, I am not long for that world, alas."

"Huh? Did Christopher do something to you? What did he do?" Her expression turned fierce, like if I said her partner had been mean to me she might march over there and threaten to beat him up.

"He fired me."

"He what!?" She pawed around the desk for her phone and didn't find it. I let it go on for a minute, the warmth of her outrage warming me more than the summer sun had.

"I told him to. I'm bad at that job. It was sweet of Christopher to give it to me, but it'll never work." Ginger opened her mouth like she was going to argue with me but I waved her off. "It's fine, really. Touching and smelling meat and cheese makes me want to puke anyway."

"Okay, not the best quality in a food service professional, true. Still, you want me to...?" She raised her eyebrows and made a gesture that could've meant anything from *talk to him* to *slowly remove his fingernails until he agrees to give you your job back.*

"Nah, really, it's okay. I wondered if you'd do me a favor though."

"Course."

"Would you put up one of these flyers here? Piano lessons."

The last time I'd cadged piano lessons was more than ten years ago. The words tasted like failure.

I slid the flyer I'd made at Melt across the counter.

"Sure, I'll just put it... Uh. Jude?"

She was making a decidedly unhappy face.

"You don't have to."

"No, it's just. Dude, this flyer. It's so awful."

"What?" It had all the necessary information: my name, my qualifications, the words *piano lessons*. "It's fine," I said.

"Um, no. This flyer is the paper equivalent of a busted-ass white van with puppies in the back driving around a school zone. Good lord, no one's going to hire someone to teach their children from this flyer."

I looked at it again. It was nothing fancy but it didn't look that bad, did it?

"Hey, I know," Ginger said. "We'll help you make a way better one. Faron!" she called out. "You still back there?"

She smiled at me sweetly and I knew just what she was going to do.

From one of the private rooms came Faron Locklear. He moved like he was gliding an inch above the floor. He made no sound and hardly even seemed to disturb the air around him.

"What's up?" he asked softly. Of course he'd never yell from the private room.

"You're done for the day, right?" He nodded, then he looked past Ginger and saw me. He inclined his head and smiled and something about the way he did it seemed regal. Even just standing there, I felt clumsy by comparison.

"Hi," I said.

"Hello, Jude."

Always hello or hi. Never *hey*. Never *Hey, Jude*, not even without a joke involved. A slight New York accent bent his vowels and elided his Gs.

"If you have time, I thought you could maybe help Jude with this flyer since your fonts are so great. It's the saddest thing I've ever seen and I don't wanna have to feel sad every time I look at something in my own shop, ya know?"

She smirked at me and winked.

"You're extremely unsubtle," I muttered.

"Subtlety's for suckers and hand models," she said, and went back to glaring at the computer.

Faron took the flyer and led me to his station, which was in the back corner of the shop. He liked to be as far from the door as possible. He gestured me into the stool and sat in the chair, spreading out his long legs so his knees didn't bump the drawing table. While his expression wasn't as horrified as Ginger's, he examined my flyer with narrowed eyes.

"I think we can do better than this," he said finally, and raised an eyebrow at me.

"Sure, great, thank you."

He slid a clean sheet of paper onto the table and gazed at it for a while, then began to sketch.

My problem with Faron was that he was stunning.

He was tall and taut, with broad shoulders and an elegant neck. His tawny brown skin was flawless and he had dreamy, gray-brown eyes that always seemed to focus on something in a plane beyond this one. His riot of corkscrew curls was sometimes loose, but today was caught up in a topknot. It had been bleached nearly white when I first met him and was now growing out. His cheekbones were high and broad, casting shadows that made him look like he was candlelit from every angle. His mouth was lush and full, and his rare smiles turned his chiseled beauty to a warmth so engaging that you didn't ever want him to look away from you.

His beauty was a problem because it made me want him and I hated wanting anything. Desire was the beginning of disappointment.

It wasn't just his looks though. I could've handled that. I'd known a lot of beautiful people.

No, it was everything.

He was graceful and forceful at the same time. His focus was intense, whether it was on the things that only he saw or on whoever he was listening to. And he made me feel calm—as if he held the whole world in his hands and slowed it down or sped it up to whatever speed I was going.

It was intoxicating: a promise of peace as long as I was in his presence.

A hope.

And hope was even worse than desire.

Yup. I had a crush on Faron. A cringeworthy, blush-inducing, heart-hammering crush on a man so glorious that I likely looked like a wisp of tatty shadow beside him. God knew I hid away like one.

"What colors would you like?" Faron asked.

"I, uh... Can you choose?"

"Okay. What mood do you want it to have?" Faron asked. His eyes searched mine and I felt like he was looking inside me. I must've been staring for a while because he raised his eyebrows in question.

"Mood? Oh. Well, it's to appeal to parents."

That was not a mood. I thought more in terms of music, so I tried to imagine the mood of a piece about piano lessons, but I just started to hear "Twinkle Twinkle Little Star" in my mind. Jesus Christ, I couldn't believe I was back to teaching piano lessons. All those scales played badly. The irregularity, the dissonance. I'd forgotten how much I'd hated it until this moment.

I would stand next to the bench and flinch every time a student hit a wrong note, like a cartoon hammer swinging out of midair.

"Fuck me," I muttered.

Faron was still looking at me. He held himself still, his only movement the occasional blink and the slow, regular rise and fall of his ribs as he breathed in perfect rhythm. He was in perfect rhythm.

"What does it feel like to play the piano really well?" he asked, voice low and hypnotic.

I let my eyes flutter closed and imagined the feeling of being onstage, with the darkness of a concert hall spreading around me. The rustle of skirts and shoes and programs from the audience and the last-minute shuffle of backstage fading away to a perfect silence that came from within. The moment before my fingers touched the keys dilating as peace flowed through me.

"It feels like I'm three steps ahead of myself rolling out a perfect road to walk along. Effortless. Complicated but effortless, like pronouncing a long word that you're intimately familiar with. It feels like flying. It feels like always being on the edge of falling but never falling. It feels like perfect control and perfect release."

And then it was over. And you had to be in the world again.

I'd pretty much blown any chance I had of playing with the Boston Symphony Orchestra again. Antonio had started using someone else and I'd been too full of dread to call him and see if there was any chance of going back.

I hadn't even played much in the months since I'd been living with my parents. A few times when they were both out, I'd snuck into the small living room where the piano I'd learned on as a child still stood, viciously out of tune and sticky-pedaled. I'd played small, tentative things and they'd all sounded terrible.

Practically, I knew it was because the instrument was out of tune. Aurally, though? There were just the sounds coming from my hands. And those sounds were terrible. Tuneless. Wrenching.

I was scared to open my eyes because I could feel that they were damp. A hand landed lightly on my knee and I almost fell off the stool. It was Faron's left hand, and he didn't move it when I startled. He wasn't even looking at me. He was still sketching with his right hand, but as his warmth seeped into me it was like he saw me even without looking. He saw me with his hand.

I watched the words appear on the paper like they weren't even words, but shapes in the form of letters. Then he moved on to markers and I looked away, wanting to be surprised.

I'd grayed out the rest of the shop while I focused on Faron, and now, as he took his hand off my knee, it came back into focus.

Marcus finished his client's tattoo and spoke to her softly before she left. He waved at me but made no move to come talk. I liked Marcus but it was a relief not to have to summon the energy for polite conversation. I'd used up all of that for the day.

People didn't usually approach me. I had it on good authority that with my pale skin and black clothes, I looked remote and standoffish. ("You look like a skinny, redheaded Batman," Ginger had told me once. And, later, "Daniel said you look like the cover of *Wuthering Heights*.")

"Okay." Faron turned the sign to face me. It was simple, but somehow he'd managed to capture the mood I felt while I was playing. It was maroon and navy blue—dark, formal, velvety colors against the white background. The letters were bold, but he'd laid them in an arc so that they seemed to curve around the top of the page, drawing your eye down to the piano he'd rendered in a few clean lines. More the idea of a piano than the form of one.

Each line led to the next line, guiding your eye down the page, just as each note of a piece as I was playing led directly into the next note.

It was music on paper and I felt my breath catch. It was perfect.

My eyes shot up to Faron's. "How did you do that?"

"I did what you described."

"But…how?"

He smiled a little, and shrugged. "It's what I do. You play. I draw. It's what we do."

I dropped my eyes to the floor. It was poured cement, shades of gray swirling around and around each other.

"I don't, really. Not anymore."

There was a lump in my throat and I tried to swallow around it. My ears hummed with the Doppler *wah wah wah* of heartbeat and blood and panic. I made a fist and released it to the count of five.

"Thank you," I said. "It's perfect. Maybe I'll go somewhere and make a copy for Melt…"

I trailed off as I imagined finding a copy shop, going there, making the copy, bringing it to Melt. Probably the twin to the terrible, sad flyer Ginger had banished would be fine on Christopher's bulletin board.

"Here." Faron stood in a fluid flex of thighs and calves, and walked into the back of the shop. I followed like he was the Pied Piper. A curtain hanging in the back doorway separated the shop from a small back room, with a table, a defunct kitchen, and a large copy machine.

Faron pushed buttons and adjusted paper, and the machine began spitting out copies on regular-sized paper.

"You can put these up other places."

He handed me a stack of a dozen or so color flyers, everything still perfectly readable even when sized down.

The weight of the flyers was the weight of responsibility. Now that Faron had done this for me, I had to put up these flyers. I was exhausted just thinking about it. Where would I put them? Would I have to ask for permission?

"Thank you," I said, because what else could I say? I leaned against the wall and held the flyers to my chest.

"I could help you," he said softly.

I should've said no. He'd already done me a favor with the flyer. But the possibility of spending time with him was a shining beacon. It was appealing. And so little was actually appealing these days.

"That would be so great," I heard myself say, and relief coursed through me.

Faron's smile was warm, but casual. It was nothing for him to offer. It was easy. My stomach felt hollow.

"Do you have to work tomorrow morning?" he asked.

"No, I...I kind of got fired. Well, I fired myself. It was better for all involved." Faron's brows furrowed. "Hence the piano lessons," I added.

"All right. Tomorrow morning, then. Around ten?"

"Okay. Here?"

I realized I didn't know where Faron lived. I didn't know anything practical about him. After all, what did it matter what street someone's apartment was on when they could slow time?

Faron said, "Sure," and squeezed my shoulder as I left with the flyers. I left the one he'd drawn on the front desk for Ginger to hang wherever she saw fit. She winked at me again as I left and I didn't meet her eyes. It was like I could feel the drag of the wink scraping over my entire body.

I really, really needed to get home.

CHAPTER TWO

THE ALARM on my phone blared for minutes before I could drag myself out of bed to silence it. When I finally did, I made myself take my meds and then get right into the shower. That was key: make every transition as quick as possible, each activity moving straight into the next. If I stopped—if I sat down or lay down—it took a monumental effort to get moving again. It was always hard to make myself get into the shower—all that nakedness, the harsh pricks of water slamming into unprotected skin.

I washed my hair, scratching at my scalp to wake myself up. I lathered my body up as quickly as possible and closed my eyes as I did it. I could feel every rib, every knob of my spine.

I cringed away from my own touch and let the water rinse me clean, moving back to my hair. It was the only thing about my body that I didn't hate to touch, so I kept it long.

I dressed in black jeans and a thin, black long-sleeved T-shirt. I wore black because it made people think that I looked so pale *because* I was wearing black. It was all about the small deflections.

When the steam had cleared from the mirror, I combed my damp hair and put it up in a ponytail. I rubbed moisturizer with sunblock all over my face because I burned in minutes if I didn't.

As it was, walking around in the sun would add even more freckles to the mess I already had. Some days when I looked in the mirror I didn't even see discrete features, just a chaos of dots, like a horrible optical illusion.

I stared at myself, wondering what Faron saw. I was so pale you could see blue veins under my skin in certain places, even through the freckles. My eyes were an odd orangey color shot through with flecks of greenish blue. Cat eyes, my ex, Kaspar, used to call them. My lashes were blond. Sometimes I tinted them with a little brown stain applied with a mascara wand. It made me look less like an alien. That's what Kaspar always said, anyway. He liked when I darkened my eyebrows too. And when I wore foundation to camouflage my freckles.

When I closed my eyes I could see the way Kaspar looked at me sometimes, as if he couldn't quite understand how he had ended up with me. As if he wished someone else were there with us so he could fully express the extent of his shock that I existed at all.

———

I SAW the dog before I saw that Faron was the one walking it. It was a big dog, with golden fur that looked long in some places and short in others. Its ears were floppy and pointing in two different directions, and it walked like it was drunk, legs everywhere, and tail wagging constantly.

It was a ridiculous creature, as silly-looking and clumsy as Faron was elegant and poised.

"Good morning, Jude," Faron said as they got close.

"Morning," I said. It never did to qualify things too early.

"I hope you're not allergic. I didn't have your number or I would've texted you to ask."

The idea of Faron texting struck me as so absurd that I didn't answer right away.

"Oh, no. I'm not. It's fine." Then I realized the idea of Faron texting me seemed doubly absurd, but I couldn't let the opportunity pass. "I suppose I should give you my number in case you have any more questions."

"I suppose you should," he said seriously.

"So, who's this?" I asked, after we'd exchanged numbers.

"This is Waffle. She wanted to come with us." Faron rested a hand gently on the dog's head and she squirmed to arch into his touch. I knew how she felt.

"She is about the color of a waffle," I mused, reaching down to stroke her fur. It was softer than it looked. She snuffled around to try and smell my crotch and I stepped back.

"She is, but I named her that because when I first got her she could never decide whether or not she wanted to do something. Whether to come with me or not. Whether she wanted to sit on the couch or the floor. Whether she liked it when I pet her or not. She'd squirm away, then come back, then leave again."

Sounds like me, I thought. Then I gave myself a stern talking to not to compare myself to an internally conflicted mutt.

As I was lecturing myself, Waffle was attempting to access my crotch again. Talk about squirming away.

"Not a dog person?" Faron asked.

"Not a fan of faces shoved in my crotch." His eyebrow went up and he smirked, just for a moment, and I realized that from someone else it might almost be flirtatious. "Not uninvited, anyway," I added in a cheap attempt to distract myself from any sliver of hope that Faron might ever flirt with me in a hundred years.

"I get it," he said. "You're a cat."

"I do like cats," I mused.

Kaspar had gotten custody of our cat, Rimsky-Korsakov, by default when I'd landed in the hospital and then fled to Philly without even collecting my belongings. Kaspar named her, the pretentious fuck.

Faron raised his eyebrows in acknowledgment. "That's not what I said."

"I know," I muttered. "My ex used to say I was like a cat," I added grimly.

"It's not bad. Cats want what they want and they don't suffer fools." He looked me up and down. "Its not cats' fault that they're soft and pretty so people want to pet them even when they don't want to be pet."

I was lost for a while in a world in which Faron might have just called me pretty.

"Do you want to get some coffee before we head out?" he asked, and I must have nodded because I found myself on the front step of Melt a minute later.

Christopher looked up from behind the counter and his neutral smile dropped off his face for a second, to be replaced by a grin.

"Hey, bro! I thought I fired your ass."

"I believe I fired my own ass."

Christopher snorted and then saw Faron. "Hey, man." He reached out to shake hands in a gesture so natural and easy that it made me positive that some people were born to interact with others and some were not.

Faron toasted me with an iced coffee as I replaced my terrible flyer with one of his on Christopher's bulletin board, and claimed a table in the corner. Waffle settled at his feet. We sipped our coffee in silence for a few minutes and Christopher brought a bowl of water for Waffle.

When he slid a plate with two muffins, each cut in half, onto the table between us, though, I leaned back in my seat.

"It's a blueberry and a corn," Christopher told Faron. I was quite familiar with the muffins he served from my brief food service career. "Eat, Jude," he said before I could say anything. I looked at my hands in my lap, pale fingers twisted together like something that lived underwater.

"You don't like muffins?" Faron asked, taking half the blueberry muffin.

"He doesn't like anything," Christopher said, and escaped back behind the counter. I glared at him.

I broke off a corner of corn muffin. I could feel the individual grains of cornmeal between my thumb and finger, and I could imagine them choking me. I put it back down.

"Do you want the blueberry instead?" Faron asked, offering me his half. I shook my head quickly, stomach churning at the thought of biting into one of the soft, squirmy blueberries studding the thing like landmines.

"No thanks," I added. My mouth was bone dry and I gulped some more coffee.

Faron ate half the blueberry muffin and half the corn muffin in easy bites as he gazed out the window.

I didn't feel like I had to think of things to say to him. He didn't watch me nervously the way my parents did. And he didn't try just a little too hard to be casual the way Ginger did. He just *was*, as if I weren't even there. It was such a relief to simply coexist with someone.

I got a few bites of my half of the corn muffin down and then gave up. It tasted like sand in my mouth even though I knew it must taste like corn. I broke the rest into a pile of crumbs so Christopher might not notice and swallowed the last of my coffee so I wouldn't feel the mealiness on my tongue. Faron looked at me for a moment. Then he ate my half of the blueberry muffin and dumped my crumbs in the trash as we walked outside.

"What kind of places do you think I should put these? I haven't lived in Philly in a while, and I don't know this area that well."

"Hmm. Who gets piano lessons?" Faron asked, leaning against the brick wall like he had all the time in the world.

I ticked them off on my fingers.

"The children of people with disposable income and retro-grade bourgeois notions of what high culture is. The children of people who play the piano and don't want to teach their kids themselves. Adults whose parents never got them piano lessons and they feel like if only they had, then probably their whole lives would've been different."

Faron smiled.

"Uh, retirees who suddenly realize they have a lot of time on their hands and need to fill it with hobbies. People going through midlife crises who want to redefine themselves. Um, people whose therapists told them to externalize their feelings through art or music... And maybe teenagers who want to play in a band that already has a guitarist?"

He nodded and started walking down South Street. I trailed after him. He was wearing tight, bleached jeans that rode low on his hips, pale pink Nike high tops, and a loose grayish-lavender tank top that made his brown skin glow like it was brushed with gold. Scrolling black ink covered his muscled arms, the line work as graceful and flowing as he was, and when he raised his arms, the shirt flashed glimpses of his lean ribs.

He walked like it was a dance between him and the sidewalk, with rolling hips and swaying shoulders and I was so distracted by watching him that I almost bumped into his back when he stopped in front of a comic shop.

His expectant look indicated that I was now supposed to go inside and ask a stranger if I could post a sign in their store. I stared at the pale pink leather of his sneakers. He looked like he'd just stepped off a runway.

It wasn't that I was shy, exactly. It was just that the prospect of talking to people required so many dozens of decisions that I preemptively felt exhausted at having to make them. What to say, how to say it, how to arrange my face, how long to maintain eye contact, how to stand, et cetera.

Interaction with another person was so sudden and violent,

like a wave of cold water crashing over me from behind. It drained me faster than almost anything else.

"I hate talking to people," I said when Faron's shoes began to swim in front of my eyes. "It's so exhausting."

I wished that he would offer to do it for me, even though I knew I'd feel shitty for accepting the offer if he made it. But feeling shitty was par for the course, and therefore far less exhausting than doing the thing itself.

"I can go with you," Faron offered. "I can ask. But they should see you so they know who the sign is about."

"Okay," I muttered, and fixed my eyes on his back as we walked inside.

"Hey, man," Faron said to the guy behind the front desk. He was a big white guy in his thirties with complicated facial hair and a maroon beanie on his head despite the heat. "This is Jude. He's a piano teacher."

Faron placed a warm hand high on my back and pressed me slightly forward. I smiled my most easily consumable smile.

"We were wondering if y'all would mind posting this sign. He's looking for new clients."

I held up Faron's perfect sign in front of my face as if I could blot myself out and replace myself with something beautiful and informative.

The guy behind the counter shrugged. "Sure. Board's over there." He pointed to a wall just inside the door littered with flyers and signs and handed me a tape dispenser in the shape of a cassette tape and waved me toward the wall.

Flyer posted, we repeated the drill a handful of times, Faron leading us into coffee shops and a music store, and various other businesses. Most said yes, a few said no, and the barista working at one coffee shop said, "I didn't know people even took piano lessons anymore."

When we'd hung the last flyer, Faron sank down onto a bench

in the park outside Independence Hall and Waffle collapsed at his feet, chin on his shoe.

It was warm and the breeze smelled of cut grass and fried dough. We sat in peaceful silence for a while. I closed my eyes and tipped my head back.

"Do you mind?" I asked, taking out a cigarette. Faron raised an eyebrow but shook his head. "Thanks for helping me," I said after a while. "I can't believe my email address is on a bunch of posters now."

"You're welcome."

We sat for a while longer.

"I don't even want to give piano lessons," I said finally.

"How come?"

I could've told him about how parents always wanted to hear that their child playing Chopsticks showed some kind of innate, overlooked spark of genius. Or how the kids whose parents stuck them in piano lessons usually didn't want to be taking them so they didn't care. Or how mind-numbing it was to hear the same beginner pieces over and over again. Everyone understood those complaints.

But for some reason, I told him the truth.

"When things are played with the right notes and the correct rhythm, they just exist. They pour out of the instrument as a whole being. When I hear someone play a piece wrong—when they play a note too early or mash two keys at once...it feels like they're tearing something to pieces. Like watching someone break a bone or get slapped. I can't stand it. It makes me cringe. It makes me feel physically sick. And it makes me want to kill them for taking something so beautiful and torturing it."

I opened my eyes to find Faron looking at me seriously. "That's not ideal," he said.

No. No, it wasn't.

———

HAVING FIRED MYSELF FROM MELT, I now had nowhere I had to be and nothing I had to do. This was both positive, in that I didn't much want to go anywhere or do anything, and problematic, in that I didn't much want to go anywhere or do anything.

I spent the day and evening after Faron helped me hang up posters watching movies and deleting all the emails from Kaspar that had accumulated over the last few months, unread.

My mom called around eight and I didn't answer. Since I'd moved out last month, she'd called me every night to check in. I was thirty-six years old and my mother called me because she didn't think I could function on my own. Pathetic. I dumped my phone onto the coffee table and went to bed.

When I woke up the next day, it was noon, and I swore as I stumbled into the kitchen to take my meds. I hadn't heard the alarm for them and when I looked at my phone I saw I'd missed three calls from Christopher too.

When I saw his text, I realized why.

Just making sure you remember it's ma's bday today, he'd written hours ago. *I'll pick you up around 5 unless you wanna meet me at SC?*

"Fuck, fuck, fuck," I muttered. I, of course, had forgotten that it was our mother's birthday and now I felt terrible that I hadn't answered her call the night before. I put the teakettle on as I listened to her message and felt even worse.

"Hi, sweetie, it's Mom. I just wanted to say I hope you had a good day at the shop and that everything's going well. And I wondered what you'd like for dinner tomorrow? Ham, maybe? Or that...what did you boys used to call it? Italian chicken? Let me know, sweetie. I can't wait to see you. Bye bye!"

"Oh god," I groaned, and dialed Christopher.

"Our mother is cooking her own birthday dinner and wants to cook it based on what I would like to eat," I told him. "Should we...do something?"

Christopher snorted. "Yeah, okay. You try and tell her she shouldn't cook. I'll just be over here."

"Yeah, yeah." I knew how well that would go over. I bit my nail, trying to figure out what I should tell her. "What's her favorite, do you think?"

I could hear the sounds of Melt in the background, and it sounded like things were going smoother without me there.

"You know she just wants to make something you'll actually wanna eat," he said gently.

Anger washed through me.

"It's not my fucking job to be an eating machine to make Ma happy," I snapped.

"I know that."

"She should make whatever she wants!"

"I know, bro."

The teakettle started to scream.

I forced myself to breathe in and out. *I am in the kitchen. I boiled water. Now I'll make tea. Then I'll drink it. That's what's happening. That's where I am and what I'm doing.*

"I assume you got her a thoughtful gift already?" I asked evenly.

"I got her a gift pass to that Russian spa that Mrs. Bauman is always talking about. And Ginger painted her something but she wouldn't let me see."

"God damn it." That was perfect. I was a terrible son.

"The spa thing can be from both of us," he said. "You can just sign the card tonight. So, I gotta get back to work—do you want to meet me at Small Change or get picked up?"

"I'll meet you. Thanks."

"Okay, great. I'll see you around five, okay?"

"Okay," I echoed.

I couldn't be the son who forgot my mom's birthday and didn't get her a gift after she'd let me live with them for months when I had nowhere else to go. I couldn't be that person.

I'd just go out and find my mom a gift, and end up at Small Change in time to go to dinner. And if that meant that I might get to see Faron at the shop...well, that had nothing to do with my decision.

———

I SUPPOSE I'd felt confident about nearby stores because of touring them with Faron the day before. But after two hours of wandering in and out of shops between my apartment and Small Change, I was irritated, exhausted, and vaguely nauseated at the state of consumer capitalism in America.

None of which was unusual, but all of which made me disappointed that all I had to show for my efforts was a blank notebook with a flowered cover that vaguely reminded me of stationery my mother had used to write notes to her sister when I was a child. I didn't know whether my mother had any use for a notebook, but it was going to have to do.

I'd considered earrings made from various found materials, but dismissed them since my mother had worn the same plain gold studs for as long as I could remember. I'd considered several cutesy kitchen things like an apron with eggbeaters on it and tea balls in the shapes of animals, but since she was cooking her own birthday dinner—not out of a deep love of cooking, like Christopher's, but simply because that was The Way Things Were Done—I didn't want to seem like I thought all she did was cook.

As I got to Small Change, I realized I should've had them gift wrap the notebook at the store. I slunk in and found Morgan, Small Change's piercer, near the front of the store.

I found Morgan's cutting sense of humor amusing and refreshing but I never knew what to say to her, so I was pretty sure she thought I was useless.

"Hey, Morgan," I said.

Morgan jerked her chin in greeting. "You here for Christopher?"

"Yeah. I don't suppose you guys have...wrapping paper in here?"

Morgan raised one perfectly painted eyebrow and looked around like maybe the tattoo shop would turn into a party store around her.

"Hey, Jude!" Ginger called from her station. She was tattooing what looked like a bone on a white guy's thigh as he lay in the chair with his eyes closed. "Just decorate some paper from the back." She nodded toward the back room. Morgan winked at me.

I grabbed a sheet of oversized paper from the copier and took it back to the front of the shop so Christopher'd see me when he came down.

"That for your mom?" Ginger asked as I passed her.

"Yeah. Kind of last minute, but." I shrugged and held up the notebook.

Ginger's eyes narrowed and she pursed her lips.

"What?"

"Uh. Nothing. Well. Just, your mom works at a stationery shop..." Ginger said slowly.

"Oh my god."

I was such a fucking idiot. Of course I knew where my mother worked. She'd worked there for ten years. I just didn't think about it.

"Hi, Jude."

Faron's soothing voice spun me around to where he'd come in from one of the private rooms.

"Hey," I said. Then, when he just smiled at me, I added, "Could I use your markers for a minute?"

He gestured toward his work station and I spread out the sheet of oversized paper and stared at it blankly. I couldn't draw for shit. I tugged at my hair as I stared at it. Finally, I drew some yellow stars on it. They looked like something from a children's birthday party and I made a sound of disgust and put the marker away.

Faron put a hand on my shoulder lightly, and leaned over me to look.

"May I?"

"God, please," I said, and made to get out of his chair. But he kept his hand on my shoulder, and slid a marker from the pack. With a dark blue marker, he drew crescent moons of different sizes. Then he took a silver marker and drew trails shooting from my stars, and added clusters of dots. Now it looked like some cool woodblock print of the night sky.

I shook my head. "Jesus. Thank you. Again."

My brain started to scream at me about how I was pathetic and kept needing to be rescued, but I was about at the end of my patience and I told it to shut the fuck up because doing art was Faron's literal job and not mine.

I wrapped the notebook, though now that Ginger had pointed out where my mom worked I realized what a stupid gift it was. Too late now.

Christopher came down the stairs as I taped the last corner and grinned at me. He was carrying a covered pie plate. He must've baked something for dessert. God damn it.

Ginger turned her face up and Christopher kissed her mouth and smoothed her hair back, then let her return to tattooing.

My stomach lurched, like a stone had dropped down a deep, empty well.

Christopher was wearing a blue and gray plaid shirt tucked into dark jeans. He was bigger than me, and broader. We looked a bit alike, but everything about him was stronger and handsomer. His hair and eyes and skin were all a shade or two darker than mine so he looked like a hot redhead instead of an alien. As often happened when I looked at his familiar features, I felt like a ghost of Christopher. The smaller, faded copy, even though I was older.

I put a hand to my hair self-consciously as I felt a wisp of it brush my cheek.

"In case you were wondering if you should do something about that," Morgan drawled, "you should."

I fixed her with a blank look and tugged the elastic band from my hair, but I stopped when I realized they were all looking at me, and so was Ginger's client and two girls on the couch by the door. Morgan was shaking her perfectly coiffed head at me and tapping her immaculately manicured nails on the desk.

I knew she didn't mean to be insulting. She loved doing people's hair and makeup; it was what she'd done for a living before piercing, even. But all I could feel were everyone's eyes on my glaringly orange hair and freckles and skinny, pale body, and I wanted to disappear. Anger flared my nostrils.

"You ready?" I asked Christopher flatly, looking anywhere but at him.

In the process of not looking at Christopher or Morgan or the girls by the door, my eyes accidentally met Faron's. He was looking at me curiously, like he wondered what I'd do next. Probably hoping that whatever it was wouldn't involve him.

Once I'd locked eyes with him it was hard to look away. Everything about his appearance drew me in. It wasn't lust. It was the sense of a safe landing for my eyes. The way my fingers would drift into playing certain pieces of music over and over because they were my favorite combination of notes. Faron was beautiful, but it was also how he dressed and the way he moved so gracefully and the way he held himself. Everything about him just flowed together and my eyes got stuck running over him again and again.

Of course, then I made myself look away, because my staring problem was probably making him uncomfortable. But he took a step toward me and said, "May I?" It was what he'd said a few minutes before about the wrapping paper so it took me a second to realize he was looking at my hair.

Ginger's eyes were narrowed and Morgan was staring.

I nodded. I couldn't seem to do anything except say yes to anything involving Faron.

He was four or five inches taller than me, and when he moved behind me I could feel him all along my back. Then his fingers sank into my hair and my eyes fluttered shut. I held perfectly still. His graceful fingers combed through my hair and I squeezed my eyes shut even tighter. Usually, I didn't like being touched. It didn't feel good and it made me aware of a body I'd rather forget.

But when Faron touched me it felt amazing. Now, every instinct told me to pull away because it already felt like he owned me. Every instinct was desperate for him to touch more than my hair.

I wanted him to pull me flush against his chest and hold me there. I didn't get any further in the fantasy than that. Partly because these days my fantasies seemed to top out at the level of a Victorian promenade and partly because Faron began braiding my hair.

He smoothed and braided, holding my hair firmly but never pulling. Every nerve ending in my scalp was lit up like a Christmas tree and when he held his palm out for the hair tie I wished for a sudden thunderclap that would startle him into dropping the braid so he had to do it all over again.

Faron smoothed a hand down the braid and then moved away and my hand went to my hair where he'd made a thick braid that started at the crown of my head.

"Thanks," I said, and he smiled and inclined his head.

"Okay," Ginger said, breaking the tension. "You guys better get going. Say happy birthday to Ann for me, and tell Ron I said hey."

Christopher kissed her goodbye and waved to everyone else. I felt Faron's eyes on me as I followed Christopher out of the shop.

"Can you hold this?" Christopher handed me the pie plate and shifted a wrapped package that must've been Ginger's painting to the dashboard of his truck.

The smell hit my nose and I cringed, turning my head so Christopher wouldn't see.

"What is it?"

"Almond tart. I made it a few years ago for Christmas and now it's all Ma wants me to make."

He turned on the iffy air conditioning and I flipped down the sun visor.

"So, what's up with you and Faron?" he asked after a few minutes.

There was an unfamiliar little thrum in my chest at *You and Faron*.

"Nothing, what do you mean?"

"Bro. He just braided your hair."

I shrugged but ran a hand down the neat braid.

"He's a good guy," Christopher said. When I didn't respond, he asked, "Heard from Kaspar lately?"

"He emailed me a bunch but I deleted them."

"Sounds like he still cares. Maybe you could still make it work with him, if you apologize."

In the five years I was with Kaspar, I'd apologized more times than I could count. I'd apologized for hurting him and for being unkind. For bailing on plans because I couldn't get out of bed. For not being in the mood to fuck. For embarrassing him in front of his friends by being antisocial. For being a better musician than him. I'd apologized for my entire existence and personality. For my looks, my desires, my brain chemistry. I didn't think I had many more apologies in me, even if he would accept them.

"Just because you moved in with the woman of your dreams doesn't mean you need to marry me off now," I snapped.

It probably would be easier for Christopher if I was dating someone though. At least then maybe he wouldn't feel like he had to be on suicide watch. I sank into the seat and stared out the window.

"What'd you end up getting for Ma?" he asked, good humor still in place.

Ugh. "Notebook."

"Oh. Uh."

"I know."

"You wanna sign the card for the spa and it can be from both of us?"

I sighed. "No, it's okay."

The sunlight was harsh and the air through the truck's ancient A/C smelled like mildew. My chest tightened as we got to our old neighborhood. It was the house we'd grown up in. The house that for the past half a year had been my refuge and my prison.

When I'd come back here after checking out of the hospital in Boston, I'd thought it would be for a couple of weeks. I'd been desperate to get away and everything in Boston just reminded me of Kaspar and of how I'd probably thrown away my career once and for all.

I took some deep breaths as we parked, trying to perk myself up for the evening to come. Christopher easily juggled the pie plate and painting and my father opened the door before I could ring the bell.

He smiled and shuffled us inside with a firm rub to Christopher's back and a tentative pat to my shoulder.

I made my father uncomfortable. He loved me, no doubt. But love without intimacy is lonelier than indifference.

"Hey, Ma, happy birthday!" Christopher called as my mother came into the foyer. He held out the pie plate and she pulled off the foil and clapped at the almond tart.

"Thank you, sweetie."

"Happy birthday," I said, and she turned to me, smiling just a little too wide.

"Isn't your hair interesting like that," she enthused, hand hovering near my head but never making contact.

Dinner was uneventful until my mom asked how working at Melt was going. Christopher looked guilty, as if he should have tanked his business to keep employing his loser older brother who wasn't qualified to do anything but play piano.

"It's fine," I said before he could say anything. "I think I'm going to try and start giving piano lessons again, though, so I can ease out of the sandwich biz. Not exactly my one true calling."

Christopher's jaw tightened but he nodded.

After dinner, we sat in the living room and had almond tart and tea. I'd choked down most of my broccoli and a few bites of chicken, though I'd tried to breathe through my mouth to avoid the acrid smell of broccoli, but one bite of the almond tart sent me booking it upstairs to the bathroom. The cloying sweetness of almond shot up the back of my nose like I'd snorted saltwater.

I knelt in front of the toilet for a while, unable to tell if I was going to puke or not. Finally, when it was pretty clear I wasn't, I made my way into my bedroom and lay down.

This room had been the backdrop my whole childhood played out against and everywhere I looked was saturated with memories. From the time I was fourteen until I moved out, it had been my hiding place and my sanctuary—but a flimsy one. No matter how many blankets I wrapped myself in or how loud the music was, my parents still knocked on the door, still put plates of food inside, still ushered me from doctor to doctor and placed cups of pills next to my water. Christopher had sat outside that door and talked to me through it, my onetime best friend turned invader.

This room was where I learned who I was, and where I learned that who I was would be a problem for everyone who tried to love me.

Fuck. I buried my face in the pillow. I'd left my sheets on the bed when I took over Christopher's apartment and I could still smell myself on the pillowcase—a hint of shampoo and several days unwashed hair.

A tap at the door and Christopher said softly, "Hey, wanna give Ma her presents?"

"Yeah I'll be right down," I said into the pillow.

I could feel him lingering at the door and my whole body screamed for him to leave, muscles rigid. When he was gone, I went back into the bathroom to splash cold water on my face and chanced a look in the mirror.

I looked different with my hair braided like this. My sharp cheekbones and pointy chin looked more prominent than usual, and my freckles looked…neater? Like an organized pattern instead of a messy spattering. I rolled my eyes at myself in the mirror and went back downstairs.

"Sorry," I muttered, sinking into the corner of the couch Christopher sat on.

"Feeling any better, sweetie?" my mother asked, concern etched deep around her mouth.

"I'm fine. Just felt a little sick for a minute."

"Happy birthday, Ma," Christopher said, and handed her an envelope. She oohed and ahed over the gift pass, and told him how much she was looking forward to going.

I handed her my present, swallowing down the apology for it.

"What beautiful paper," she said. "Did you make that?"

"No, not really. One of Ginger's co-workers."

"Well it's lovely," she insisted. She unwrapped it so she didn't tear the paper. The flowered notebook looked even sadder as I saw it for the second time.

"I thought maybe you could…write in it," I finished weakly. My mother's eyes gleamed wetly as she thanked me.

"I will! I'll write…lots of things in it."

Her determination to make the most of my paltry gift was painful. This was where we were. She expected so little from me that giving her something she probably sold fifty of a day had her near tears. I gave her a tight smile and looked away so I didn't choke. Shame and resentment were a nasty cocktail coming back up.

Christopher cleared his throat and passed her the wrapped canvas.

"This is from Ginger. She's sorry she couldn't make it tonight, but she says happy birthday."

My mother untaped the newsprint as carefully as she had my wrapping paper. Inside was a canvas a little larger than a hardcover book. It was a painting of Christopher and me, in Ginger's stark style. I recognized the scene immediately.

I'd gone to dinner at their apartment right after Christopher moved in. Christopher had been in the kitchen and I'd peered over his shoulder to see what he was making. He'd tugged my hair and I'd ducked under his arm to twist away, but I'd slipped and he'd grabbed me. We'd both ended up falling clumsily to the floor, laughing. When we looked up, Ginger had snapped a photo with her phone.

Christopher had his arm around me, my hair was mussed, and we were both grinning. Christopher looked strong and happy, and I looked...free. Usually, Ginger's portraits were high contrast and gutting. Here, though, she'd made us look better than we really did. Christopher's hair was in place though it'd been a mess that night, and I had color in my cheeks. It was truly beautiful. I hardly even recognized myself.

"Oh my goodness," my mom said, and my dad leaned in, murmuring over the painting too.

I caught Christopher's eye and could tell this was the first time he was seeing it too. He was clearly moved. They all were. I was too.

All of us sat there together, wishing I was the person in the painting instead of who I was in real life.

CHAPTER THREE

—————

MAGGIE TEXTED me the next afternoon and demanded I watch a movie with her.

I'd met Maggie in the hospital in Boston. She was in the room across from mine and her meds adjustment made her hyper during the day and unable to sleep at night. She wandered into my room the night after I'd gotten there.

"Is that guy who just left your boyfriend?" she asked. She looked young, but I knew she had to be over eighteen because this was an adult ward. She was tall, with curly blonde hair, light brown skin, and blue eyes. It was an unusual combination and her direct stare was unusual too. I tended to make people look away when I didn't make an effort to fix my face.

I intended to just look at her blankly and silently reflect on how rude it was to just speak to someone uninvited, or allow her to think I didn't speak, a tactic which had saved me a lot of trouble in the past. Instead, I found myself telling her the truth.

"Not anymore," I said flatly, since I'd just told Kaspar it was over.

"He was hot," she said. "But clearly slimy. I'm Maggie."

"Jude," I said. Because most people didn't realize Kaspar was slimy until they'd known him for a while, and attention to detail deserved to be rewarded.

"You seem un-boring," she said. "Can I please hang out here for a while? I can't sleep and I'm fucking bored and my mom dropped off a stack of books I loved when I was a kid as if maybe retreading my childhood mental state will cause me to go into a trance and be that person again, only she must not have looked that closely because one of them is about a girl who was like literally conceived to be spare parts for her sister which is kind of the most depressing thing ever, and another one is about a girl who tried to kill herself, so, oops, Mom."

She bounced on her toes and tugged at her hair as she talked, and scanned my room, taking in the flowers that Kaspar had brought. White roses. Even his flower choices were passive aggressive.

"So why are you here?" she asked.

"I tried to kill myself, oops, Mom."

"Oh shit, sorry," she said, then laughed. "You tried to kill yourself and your boyfriend brought you funeral flowers? Oh, man. Is that supposed to be, like, a dark joke?"

"Unfortunately not."

"Well then you clearly dodged a bullet. Plus what kind of douchebag dumps someone in the hospital after a suicide attempt, Jesus."

"He didn't. I dumped him. It won't stick though. It never does."

"That's fucking grim, dude."

It was.

"Why are you here?" I asked. "Also reassure me that you're over eighteen because I feel like I'm contributing to the corruption of a minor or something."

"Manic episode, blah blah blah, more later because it's too boring to talk about right now. And I'm twenty-two, so never fear. Will you tell me more about sleazy guy? Please, I'm so fucking bored."

And I did. Over the next few weeks I told her all about Kaspar. How when I met him I thought I'd finally found someone who liked me even when I was a train wreck. How we moved in together and he didn't seem to mind taking care of me sometimes. How he liked that I could get lost in the music and didn't really care if I couldn't go out with everyone after rehearsal.

How I realized after a while that he didn't want me to come anyway because he liked to be the center of attention. And that his care came at the cost of letting him tell me what to do and having all my mistakes pointed out. That all the people I'd thought were our friends were actually his friends and he told them all about how he took care of me, did everything for me, was single-handedly responsible for my successes and deeply wounded by my failures.

Maggie had gone home before me, but she'd put her number in my phone and we'd started texting regularly. Once I left the hospital and fled the city, Maggie was the only friend I had left.

I'd lost track of people from my past over the years, and all my friends from the orchestra were busy having careers and lives —not to mention that Kaspar seemed to have told them a story of my departure that was even more lurid than the truth (and, no doubt, featured him as a martyr).

When the battered box had arrived at my parents' house with Kaspar's and my Boston return address, that held my laptop along with a random tangle of clothes and a few personal effects, we'd switched to chatting instead of texting.

It was great for Maggie because she liked to be doing three things at once and it was great for me because while I ran out of energy for talking in about twenty minutes, I could chat for hours if all I had to do was type.

She was more than a decade younger than me, but she had a kind of impatient insight that really resonated with me, like lying or sugarcoating were annoying wastes of time. I appreciated it, since my family seemed hell-bent on spinning a protective web around me so they didn't have to see me experience discomfort.

Now, I messaged her back saying I could watch a movie if she'd choose. My laptop pinged with a chat message and I moved to the couch and turned on the TV.

Christopher had left me his furniture when he moved into Ginger's place, so everything in it was his. He'd left plates and cups and silverware in the kitchen, claiming that he only needed half of his since Ginger already had some. Since I knew firsthand that Ginger's dishes and cups had been stolen individually from diners and bars when she was first living on her own, I knew he just did it so I didn't have to buy my own stuff. Fair enough, since I didn't have a job. But it was strange to be living in Christopher's apartment, drinking tea out of a mug Christopher bought, sleeping in a bed Christopher had inherited from his ex-girl-friend years before.

I did feel lucky that he'd left his TV, though, because it meant I could chat with Maggie on my computer as we watched movies.

Maggie: *now that you got fired by your own brother (still hilarious) does that mean you can watch netflix all the time???*

Jude: *I fired myself, as you well know, and yes.*

Maggie: *ok gimme 3 keywords of what mood you want*

Jude: *Ummmm. I seriously don't care.*

Maggie: *oh my GOD not even KEYWORDS?*

Jude: *Fine. Magical, Distracting, Cute.*

Maggie: *you want to watch harry potter literally 60 times a day*

Jude: *You caught me.*

Maggie: *whats yr time like today*

Jude: *I have nowhere on the planet that I have to be and not a single thing in the world that will be affected in any way by my existence on it.*

Maggie: *ok great so marathon!*

I smiled despite myself.

Jude: *Ok.*

Maggie: *ok sign into my dad's hbo and lez do this bitch*

Maggie's father was very rich and very shitty and while I felt pathetic being a thirty-six-year-old stealing someone's pay-TV access with my friend, it made Maggie really happy to feel like she was getting one over on him. And, all right, given the stories she'd told about him I didn't hate it either.

Jude: *The eagle has landed.*

Maggie: *hedwig is a fucking owl jude NO SPOILERS*

We pressed play at her countdown and I settled in. In a way, I was envious of Maggie and everyone younger than me who got to have this growing up. I felt more like myself when I was just words than when I was words and a voice, and watching a movie with someone else was wonderful when I didn't have to worry about them needing me to talk or wanting me to share snacks with them.

We were halfway through the second movie when I got a text. I glanced at it absently, assuming it was Christopher, since I was chatting with Maggie already, and I nearly pitched the computer off my lap when I saw that it was Faron.

Hi Jude, he'd written. *Want to grab a drink tonight? I'm done with work around 6.*

Jude: *Holy shit.*

Maggie: *srsly I wanna slap moaning myrtle every time*

Maggie: *what*

Maggie: *jude*

I stared at the message, waiting for it to disappear before my eyes.

Maggie: *juuuuuuuuude what*

Jude: *This guy just asked me to go for a drink.*

Maggie: *"this guy"? don't make me murder you bc not a court in the land will convict me. everyone knows a lack of details in a story is totally valid motive*

Jude: *I have a pathetic crush on him and I think he just feels sorry for me. Ginger probably told him that I have no friends and no life so he's decided to be my friend.*

I cringed just typing it.

Maggie: *yeah that's probably what's going on YAWN come on*

Jude: *He's stunning and talented and poised and cool. I'd probably spontaneously combust if he kissed me, like a vampire walking into a church.*

Maggie: *lol a+ comparison*

Maggie: *YOU are great looking and talented. not poised. cool hmmmm...depends.*

Maggie: *yr like...anti-cool cool. like when something's so cold it feels like burning*

Jude: *Wow. Well, let me just tell him that I'm so cold it feels like burning, thanks for the pickup line.*

Maggie: *LOL i dare you to try and work that into conversation i will give you a thousand dollars.*

Jude: *Should I go???*

Maggie: *yes*

Jude: *Oh now is when you suddenly don't have much to say?*

Maggie: *i told you yes!!!! you should absolutely go. what more do you want me to say?*

Jude: *It'll probably be a disaster.*

Maggie: *there are worse things than a bad date, and even if its terrible then at least you know*

Jude: *Fine.*

I opened the text message and stared at it.

Maggie: *what did you say what did he say whats happening!*

Jude: *Hang on, I can't converse on 17 devices simultaneously, I am not a child.*

Maggie: *screenshot it!*

Jude: *NO omg, boundaries.*

Maggie sent a string of crying laughing faces but gave me time to think.

I texted Faron, *Okay, sure. Should I meet you at SC or somewhere else?*

I wanted to turn the phone off so I didn't keep checking it, but Faron responded right away: *Want to meet me at Tavern on Camac around 6.30?*

Tavern on Camac was a queer piano bar that I'd gone to a million years ago but hadn't been back to since I'd moved back.

Sure, sounds good, I wrote.

When nothing else was forthcoming, I let out the breath I'd been holding.

Jude: *I'm meeting him later.*

Maggie: *yay!!! i'll totally forgive you for bailing mid-movie to go get ready*

If I wanted to have time for my hair to dry all the way so I didn't look like I'd spent the day holding an electric fence, I needed to shower now, so I took the out.

Jude: *Thanks for the pep talk :)*

Maggie: *obvi i'll be here desperately awaiting every single detail! good luck!!!*

———

TAVERN ON CAMAC was tucked away on a cobblestone street just wide enough for one car to navigate slowly. The last time I'd been there I was in my early twenties, meeting up with some friends while visiting home. It had been dimly lit and catered to a much older crowd, but when the men in their forties and fifties realized we weren't just there cruising but knew all the old standards and could sing along, they bought us a round and encouraged us up to the microphone.

Now, more than ten years later, it was still dimly lit, but the whole layout was flipped around and a sign pointing up the stairs where once bathroom hookups spilled out into the hallway suggested that the second floor was now a club. A few groups of men clustered around high-tops in the corner, and the bartender was a young white guy rather than the older black guy who'd tended bar years before.

The piano was still there, though on the other side of the room, but no one was playing. It was probably too early. I sat at a small table near the piano so I could see Faron when he came in. It was a little shabby but perfectly serviceable despite probably having more than one drink spilled on it.

Pianos look different when they're lit from above. The piano at my parents' house or those in practice rooms look like boxy furniture with keyboards inside them. I know what they do but they're unassuming and clunky. A piano lit from above glows like the whole instrument is a home for the music. Even though the spotlight focused on this piano was cheap and harsh, it lit up the keys like they were vibrating. My fingers yearned for them.

The next thing I knew, I was standing next to the piano, palm resting on the wood.

"You can play if you want. Marly's on break for a half hour or so."

The bartender had a tray of empty glasses balanced on one hand and he gave me an absent smile.

"Thanks."

I couldn't though. It had been way too long. And there were people around.

The bartender was still lingering, his expression serious. "People do it all the time," he said, like he could see my hesitation.

I glanced around. No one was paying any attention to me or the piano. I sat down and ran my fingers over the keys. Eyes closed against the harsh light and so I couldn't see if anyone was watching, I started to play. Soft at first—pianissimo. I played Chopin's Nocturne in E Flat Major and let it morph into a Shostakovich waltz. Then I was just playing. My fingers walked the paths of pieces I knew, and I let myself disappear.

I came to a natural pause and let my eyes flutter open.

Standing on the other side of the piano, one hand resting lightly on the instrument, was Faron. For a moment as we made eye contact I remembered what it was like to be myself.

Myself as a musician, as a performer, as someone who could do something instead of nothing.

"Hi," I said, standing up.

"Hi. That was incredible." He was looking at me with wonder. "I've never heard you play before."

"Thanks," I muttered, and sank back down at the table.

Faron was wearing those tight bleached jeans again, and a dove gray linen shirt with black lines stamped all over one sleeve. His hair was loose tonight, curls held back from his face by a headband of rolled bandanna, and spilling around his shoulders. "Can I get you a drink?"

It wasn't great to drink with my medication, but a drink or two would probably be okay.

"Okay, thanks. I'll have a gin and soda."

Faron slid my drink in front of me and sipped from his beer.

"Thanks for inviting me." I clinked my glass to his bottle.

"I'm glad you came. I thought the piano bar was a natural choice. Have you been here before?"

"Yeah I was just thinking about that when I came in. It's all different from the last time I was here, but I used to come with friends a long time ago. We were the only ones under forty, but the other patrons were nice to us—well, nice-ish—because we were such old standards geeks."

He raised an eyebrow.

"Like torch songs and jazz standards and classics from old musicals. It was pretty cliquish but once the other guys realized what nerds we were they liked having us around. They'd try to shock us or titillate us with stories of escapades from their younger days. Usually that meant talking about barebacking in the seventies and eighties. You haven't lived until you've heard about fucking some guy in the stairwell during intermission of

The Wiz when it came to Philly and both singing while you screwed."

Faron smiled. "You look different when you play."

The ice in my glass rattled.

"I feel different when I play."

"I was thinking about what you said. How when things are played right they exist as a whole. That's how you play. No uncertainty, no deliberation. It's how I feel when I'm painting."

He sipped his beer and I couldn't tear my eyes away from the movement of his throat as he swallowed.

"When I'm in it it's like it just comes through me. Like it's already there and I'm filling it in."

His eyes got dreamy, like he was imagining the canvas.

"Do you like painting better than tattooing?"

"Not better. It's different. Tattooing's a job. I try to be professional. And no matter that it's me making art, it's about the client. It's their choice, on their skin. Painting's for me." A shadow crossed his face. "Ideally."

"What are your paintings like?"

He frowned.

"Bad question?"

"No. It's hard to describe. The things I would say don't give you a real idea of what things look like, if that's what you want to know."

I shrugged. "I want to know whatever you want to tell me."

He leaned back and looked at me, then his gaze fixed high over my shoulder.

"I used to play ball. Around the neighborhood and in school. I was pretty good, not great. I loved the way the ball felt in my hands. The texture of it and the weight. I loved the way it arced through the air when I shot. Interplay of heft and weightlessness. The first time I held a paintbrush it felt that same way. The feel of it in my hand, the swipe of the brush onto the paper. I didn't care what I painted, I cared about the shape my hand made and the pressure I applied."

His elegant hands moved as he spoke.

"As I kept painting I found things I liked to paint. Subjects. A style. But it's never detached from the physical act of holding the brush and moving the paint from point A to point B."

Given how graceful Faron's movements were and how he dressed like clothing was a mode of applying color and form to himself, it made sense that there would be a tactile component to his art.

"The textures of things, the particularities of the colors. Contrast. It's what I'm most interested in painting. Contrast and particularity. It's what I find most beautiful."

He refocused on me and then he smiled. A real smile. Warm and slow.

"Your contrasts. Your particularities. Truly beautiful," he said, and his eyes moved from my face to my hair.

I couldn't help smiling. "I feel that way about music too. Like certain instruments make swoops and arcs and others make booms and thumps. Some of their sounds are heavy and some are light and I see the shapes and weights and lines of the sounds as I hear them."

I finished my drink and Faron got us another round almost before my glass touched the table.

"I was going to get this round," I said when he brought the drinks. "Thank you though."

"You're welcome. You can get the next round."

I cringed internally, but I was long past attempting graceful lies, and Faron didn't seem the type to appreciate them anyway.

"I should really stop at two. Too much doesn't mix well with my medications. But I'll get your next round."

"Understood," was all he said. "Cheers, then."

"Cheers. I've never heard you talk this much. I wasn't sure if you did. Much." Then, realizing that was the kind of comment that probably made people really self-conscious, I added, "I'm glad you do."

"I'm down to talk if I have something to say."

I nodded. "I hate the feeling of being expected to talk. Sometimes I have a lot to say and other times…" I bit my lip, trying to decide how honest I was feeling. Fuck it, my brain weighed in. "Other times I can't talk at all. I have thoughts about things but it's like there's no delivery mechanism. They just exist with no way out."

"What do you do if you're around people and you stop being able to talk?"

"Seem really rude, probably. Uh, I nod a lot."

The lights dimmed, then, and a short woman with a toothy grin slid behind the piano. Marly, presumably, back from her break. She didn't announce herself or look around, just began to play. It was "This Can't Be Love" with an extended intro. She played easy, confident piano, the kind of piano that spoke of years of casual accompaniment. When she began "I Am What I Am," the men in the corner began to sing along. Marly's voice was smoky and low and when she finished, I clapped loudly.

People came up to chat with her and put money in the fishbowl on the piano. She'd spin out the piano part as she talked with regulars, and get back to singing when they left. She loved it, I could tell.

Envy speared through me so sharply I pressed my palm to my breastbone like I could rub away the pain, and I turned away from the piano.

"Do you want another beer?" I asked Faron.

"Okay."

I practically bolted from the table to get away from the instrument. But then as I waited for Faron's beer, she started playing "Skylark" and my breath caught. It felt like she was singing right to me and I didn't move until the song ended.

Faron thanked me when I passed him the beer, but I felt raw and the music haunted me.

"Do you want to leave?" Faron asked. I blinked at him. I didn't want to leave because I didn't want to be alone again. I didn't want to be away from Faron. But I was afraid if I stayed here any longer I might start to cry.

Faron stood in one fluid move and folded some bills into the fishbowl.

"Thank you," he told Marly, and offered her the beer.

She took it with a wink and drank as she played with one hand, and Faron put a hand lightly on my back to direct me to the door.

Outside, I fumbled to light a cigarette, trying to avoid any discussion. Trying to cloak myself in my own private atmosphere.

"Want to walk for a bit?" Faron asked.

"Yeah."

His fingers slid against mine and he took the cigarette. I thought he was going to throw it away or tell me it was bad for me, but he just took a long drag and gave it back.

"You care where we go?" he asked.

I shook my head. "You decide, okay?"

We walked in silence for a while and when I realized he wasn't going to ask why I freaked out, I relaxed. It was a beautiful night. The sun was just about set and the air was warm but the heat of the day had burned off.

"I'm glad I got to talk to you again," Faron said after we'd been walking for ten or fifteen minutes. "After we talked at Ginger's art show, I wasn't sure I'd ever see you again."

"You wanted to?"

"Yeah, Jude. I wanted to."

That night, I'd gone to the show with Christopher for moral support. He and Ginger had fought and he was concerned she might throw him out of the show. I was pretty sure he had nothing to worry about, but after everything Christopher had done for me, sticking around seemed like the least I could do.

Faron had come up next to me as I looked at one of Ginger's paintings. I'd met him at the shop, but we'd never talked. He'd said that Christopher looked nervous and we'd gotten to talking. When I went outside to smoke a cigarette, he'd come with me, and we'd talked for a few more minutes.

I'd had to duck out pretty soon after because I could feel my energy was about to crash. But I'd never stopped thinking about him. I'd wondered too many times to count if he'd ever thought about me.

"Why?" I asked softly.

He didn't answer right away and I lit another cigarette.

"There was something about you," he said finally. "You were self-possessed. But weary. Like you were there to support your brother, but it was costing you something. It made you seem strong. But then when we talked, you were...softer than I expected. That interested me. The contrast."

That was illuminating.

"Thank you," I said, not sure what else to say. "I...yeah, I wanted to be there for Christopher."

"Were you and Christopher always close?"

"We were really close when we were little. He used to follow me around everywhere."

It was all flashes. Chubby-faced Christopher bringing me buckets of sand and handfuls of shells for a castle down the shore. Christopher begging me to read him a story in the hotel room, sunburned skin livid against the bleach-stiff white sheets. Christopher falling asleep in the backseat of the car, his head lolling toward me and his dimpled hand open to mine.

"Then I...couldn't really do anything with him anymore. As a teenager. But he still wanted to be around me. God knows why. When I wasn't at school or lessons, I stayed in bed unless my parents dragged me out. He'd sit outside my door and tell me

about his day. Ordinary stuff. About his soccer game or something shitty a teacher did. Sometimes about a crush he had. I
loved it. I wanted him to just keep talking to me."

Faron and I were walking side by side, but I could feel the
weight of his attention.

"The best was when he'd just talk until he was done and then
leave. Then I didn't have to feel too bad. Sometimes, though, at
the end he'd try to get me to answer. He'd ask my opinion or if I
was okay."

I shook my head and my heart gave a lurch. Even all these
years later, this was one of the memories that still cut me to the
bone. My brother camped outside my door, his voice cracking
awkwardly when he said my name as a question. Hearing everything he said and yearning to be able to answer, but not being
able to open my mouth.

"And after a while when I didn't answer I could hear him give
this little sigh. Soft. Like he didn't even know he'd been waiting
for something until I hadn't given it to him. He'd get up and leave
and I'd cry because I'd hurt my little brother and because I
wanted him to have better than me, and… And because I wanted
him to come back and do it all over again because at least he still
tried."

My own voice cracked and I let my eyes go unfocused so all I
saw were the different textures of the city.

"And he did. He never stopped. There was a while when we
weren't in touch much, when he was moving around a lot and I
was in school. But now here we are again. Back in Philly. Alone
in my room again while Christopher has a life and sometimes
tells me about it."

A wave of disgust washed over me and I squeezed my
eyes shut.

"Fuck, I'm sorry. I think I'm a little drunk. I didn't mean to say
all that."

Faron turned down an alley and sat on the cement stoop of a

loading bay. He was looking at me, but not with the reproach I expected.

"Brothers, man," Faron said. "I think love and anger are closer together with brothers than with other relationships."

"You have brothers, I assume."

He nodded. "Three. And a sister."

I sat down next to him on the stoop and drew my knees up so I could wrap my arms around them. High above us, someone was listening to Tárrega's "Recuerdos de la Alhambra" and on Sansom the bar cycled through early nineties dance hits.

Faron glanced at me, like he was checking that I wanted to hear about his siblings and I raised my eyebrows in encouragement, remembering how he'd said he was happy to talk if he had something to say. I got the feeling that though he might be willing to talk, he'd just as soon stay silent if he thought he could get away with it.

In the dim light, his clean, strong profile and the halo of his hair belonged in a photo shoot.

"My two brothers and my sister are a lot older. Then my parents got pregnant again when Amo was fifteen. That's my sister. Kalil was eighteen and Syrus was twenty. It was a total accident. So when Sabien and I were born, Syrus and Kalil were out of the house and Mo finished high school and left before I really remember."

"You're a twin?"

"Yeah. I'm the youngest in my family by seventeen minutes." He smiled a faraway smile. "Technically, though, Sabien was born right before midnight and I was born right after, so our birthdays are on different days."

"Wow, that sounds like something that would happen in a medical show, only it would be on New Year's Eve so you were technically a year apart."

"Sabien would probably have liked that." Faron nodded.

"Did you not get along?"

Faron didn't say something for long enough that I thought he wasn't going to answer. When he did, I realized this was just his way. He considered what he wanted to say before he spoke, like he wanted to make sure he expressed himself accurately.

"We did everything together. But we were very different so we disagreed a lot. Sabien was loud and energetic. He was always talking, always telling stories. Always wanted to be the center of attention, even when it wasn't good attention. Which was fine with me since it meant I could be quiet and let him talk for us both."

"What about now?" I asked when he'd been quiet for a while.

"We haven't been in touch in a while. He's in the army. I haven't seen him in three years."

"Do you miss him?"

Faron tipped his head back and swallowed hard.

"I've never been close to someone the way I was with him. Never...shared things that way. I miss what if felt like to be around him when he liked me."

"Does he not like you anymore?"

He sighed like maybe he didn't want to tell me, but I kept looking at him, hoping he would. I didn't want to be the only one getting personal. The only one risking something.

"Sabien used to get in trouble, when we were younger. Small stuff, nothing terrible. He was just restless and curious and thought he could talk his way out of anything. My parents worried about him a lot. It wasn't like he was a white, trust fund baby. They knew if he kept going the way he was going, it was only a matter of time until he got himself in a lot of trouble. Or worse."

He rubbed his jaw absently, a faraway look in his eyes.

"I don't know what they said to him, but when we turned eighteen, Sabien joined the army. He didn't even tell me he was going to do it. He... He'd never made a big decision without talking to me about it first. I was furious. And terrified. I told him he couldn't leave, that he'd get himself killed. And he just gave me this cocky smile and said he'd be the one doing the killing."

Faron shook his head, hands fisting at his sides.

"I told him that was worse. That I didn't want a... That I didn't want a murderer for a brother. He was furious. Hurt. That's how we left things. That's how I let him go off."

Faron looked guilty, even all these years later.

"When he came back after a year, I thought he was home to stay. I thought we could both apologize. Make up. I thought we'd get an apartment together like we'd always planned. Somewhere I could paint and he could do whatever he decided to do. I had a lot going on then. I really needed him."

He bit his lip.

"But he was just visiting. And he was different. Every word out of his mouth was army this and country that and we got into it bad. He said if I was against the military, I was against the country. I told him I didn't know how he could have loyalty to a country that wanted him dead. It got heated."

Faron's eyes refocused on me and I could see the pain there.

"Things have never been the same since. He's been in nine years now. We've emailed a few times, but every time we've seen each other, if it comes up, it comes between us. And it always comes up. We see it really differently."

He stood and offered me his hand and I let him tug me back to the ground because it was clear he didn't want to talk about his brother or the army anymore. But he didn't let go of my hand right away once I had my feet under me. His skin was warm and his hand was bigger than mine.

I looked up at him, wishing that he would draw me close and kiss me. Run his fingers through my hair and down my spine and kiss me until both of us forgot what it felt like not to be kissing. Then he pulled gently at my hand and we walked out of the alley. And I felt the heave of disappointment in my stomach that said *Of course he doesn't want to kiss you. No one wants to kiss you.*

"You're in Christopher's old place, right?"

I nodded as we turned back on to the street, the magical interlude where Faron might kiss me swallowed up by the reality of the city and my life.

We began walking in that direction and I saw Faron look over at me a few times out of the corner of my eye, but neither of us said anything. I smoked another cigarette, the familiar burn in my chest and my mouth comforting.

Faron was leading us on a meandering route, cutting through alleys and small side streets and looping back around. I wasn't sure if he just liked to walk, or if he could tell that I didn't want to be alone.

It was one of the most frustrating feelings. When I was by myself I was often so lonely it was physically painful. When I was around people, though, I was desperate to get away from them and be alone.

But there were a few people, sometimes, who felt suspended between being alone and being in company. Apparently, Faron was one of those people.

"Look," he said, pulling me from zoning out. He was pointing at a hulking shadow half on and half off the sidewalk. When I focused on it, the moonlight just let me pick up the glint of white keys.

"Oh wow."

I walked over to the piano. Even at first glance it was a shambles, the wood deeply scarred and the top coated in something sticky. Sitting lopsided like this would have the tuning out of whack quickly too. I plunked a few keys. Some resonated, but most were gummed up. The pedals stuck and there was a deep gouge out of the front left leg.

Taped to the side of the piano was a note in messy all caps: *GARBAGE*.

It tugged at my heart, the idea of a piano being crushed in a dump somewhere. It was like potential music being snuffed out.

"Shame," I said. "I wonder if there's a school or something that needs a piano and we could call them to get it instead." But I trailed off. I doubted many high school music teachers had the time or the knowledge to refurbish a piano.

"Is it still good?" Faron asked.

"It looks pretty bad off," I admitted. "But maybe it could be fixed. That sucks."

I walked away so I didn't have to look at it anymore, and after a minute Faron fell into step beside me again.

"Kind of an inconvenient instrument to play, I guess," Faron murmured. "You can't carry it around with you."

I nodded. All through school, when everyone else practiced at home, I'd been stuck in practice rooms. Sometimes it felt like I'd spent all of my twenties in practice rooms. I'd moved far too often to even think of buying a piano. Living with five people in a small apartment, there hadn't been room for one even if I'd been willing to deal with the inconvenience.

In the midst of a bitter fight, Kaspar had once told me he thought the only reason I agreed to move in with him was so I could have a place to put a piano. I'd never been entirely sure he was wrong.

"There are keyboards, but it's not the same," I said. I hated the way they sounded. I'd always rather practice with nothing than a keyboard.

When we got to my front door, Faron asked if he could use my bathroom, and I felt a zing of excitement that he would be inside my apartment, even if only for a minute.

I'd left the lights on because I hated coming home to darkness. I stuck my keys on the hook and toed my shoes off and Faron stood there looking around.

Seen through his eyes, I supposed it probably looked sad and bare. Just basic furniture and no decoration, since Christopher had taken his things with him.

"Spartan," he said with a smile, and crossed to the bathroom.

I put on water for tea and listened to Faron peeing, trying not to picture him holding his cock just ten feet away, and failed. It was probably as gorgeous as the rest of him.

"Do you want some tea?" I asked when he came out.

"Sure, thanks." He looked around again as I poured it and we sat at the small kitchen table. "But you don't have a piano."

"Nope. It's in Boston with everything else." There really wasn't much else, since when I'd moved in with Kaspar his apartment had been fully stocked. Some clothes and shoes, a few books, my music, and some souvenirs from touring that I'd gotten because I'd thought I was supposed to have souvenirs.

Just my piano and the cat. I shook my head because thinking of Rimsky-Korsakov made me too sad. Maybe I should get another cat. It felt disloyal to even think it, but I highly doubted that Kaspar would let me have her, since she'd been his before he'd even met me. Even if she did like me better.

"Jude."

I jerked away at a gentle touch on my wrist.

"Sorry," I muttered. "You just startled me."

Faron just watched me for a minute and I felt my cheeks get hot. I had an unflatteringly blotchy way of blushing on my throat and my ears that was probably happening.

"Do you not like being touched?" he asked softly.

I shook my head and looked down.

"It's not that. I...I don't like it from people I don't know. Or sometimes, I guess I don't like it at all. But then sometimes I like it a lot. And I want it too much."

I swung wildly between cringing from touch and craving it.

I sealed my mouth shut. Memories of Kaspar whispering how hot it was that I was so sensitive, that I was so responsive to his touch, butted up against memories of him untangling my fingers from his, telling me I was too needy, too clingy, too changeable. Memories of wanting him to wrap me in his arms and hold me all night slammed into memories of nights I couldn't bear even to feel him brush up against my skin in his sleep.

Tease.

Faron's expression was neutral. Not disinterested, I didn't think, but actually neutral, as if any answer I gave would've been equally okay with him. He put his hand on the table, palm up, offering it to me if I wanted it, but not imposing if I didn't.

I slid my hand into his, heart racing, and he curled his fingers around mine.

"I wanted to ask you something," he said. The heat from his hand settled into me and I realized it must've been the hand he'd wrapped around the tea.

"Okay?"

He looked a little self-conscious. "Would you ever let me paint you?" His eyes roamed my face and my hair the way they had in the bar when he'd mentioned the contrast of my coloring.

In another context it would've sounded like the worst kind of come-on. A pretentious *Would you like to listen to my original recording* kind of come-on. The kind of come-on I'd heard more times than I could count over the years, from other guest soloists, conductors, wealthy donors, and everyone in between.

But there was nothing sleazy or flirtatious about Faron. Just the opposite. His appeal was in his sincerity, his quiet confidence. And I'd be damned if I could imagine why he'd want a painting of pale, skinny me, but if it meant I could spend more time in his presence—in the presence of someone who made me feel like maybe my entire being wasn't just an inconvenience—then there was only one possible answer.

"If you really want to, yeah."

"I really want to," he said, and he squeezed my hand.

CHAPTER FOUR

I RANG the bell of the McMastersons' house just before ten on Saturday morning, with my stomach in a knot. When Kira McMasterson had emailed me about piano lessons, it had taken me a moment to remember I'd posted those signs. The woman who had been giving her son Nate lessons for years had taken a new job unexpectedly, and left town.

It was an attached house on a tree-lined, cobblestone street in Old City, where every stoop had wrought-iron railings and flowers spilling from window boxes. The fixed shutters were painted a glossy forest green that set off the deep red brick of the buildings and variegated terra cotta and brown brick laid in a fishtail pattern on the sidewalk. Gas lamps burned above the doors even on a warm, sunny morning, and the historic street-lamps arched gracefully.

These houses had probably sold for a cool million at the absolute lowest, which made me feel much better about quoting the McMastersons what I was actually worth an hour. Kira had seemed pretty stoked about having a member of the Boston Symphony give her eleven-year-old lessons, so either Nate was a prodigy or the McMastersons were in it for the bragging rights. And I kind of doubted the kid was a prodigy.

The door opened to reveal a blonde woman in her forties who'd tried to moisturize herself back to twenty-five. She was dressed in the kind of jeans that looked like a casually perfect fit but were probably tailored just for her, and her oversized blue-and-white striped shirt was cut to reveal the hollows beneath her clavicle. She wore delicate gold jewelry and white leather loafers, and her handshake was us grinding our bones together.

"Mr. Lucen, welcome. I'm so glad to have you."

"Hi, thanks. Jude, please."

She smiled at me like I was doing her a favor.

"Jude. All right, then. I'm Kira. Welcome to our home."

I resisted the urge to glance behind me and check for whatever camera she seemed to be speaking for.

It was a rather beautiful home, in the same way that she was rather beautiful: everything was expensive, well cared for, and hewed so close to neutral that you couldn't find anything specific to critique. It was the elevator music of decor, and it made me fidget.

"Can I get you anything to drink? Coffee, tea, lemonade, kombucha?"

She said "kombucha" like someone who'd been told what it was by an employee at the Whole Foods a few blocks west when she was studying the seven-dollar glass bottles.

"I'm fine, thank you."

"Water?"

"No, no, thank you."

As she reconciled her disappointment at my rejection of her hospitality with keeping her smile on, her husband came downstairs. I did a double-take because he was also wearing spotless jeans, a blue and white button-down shirt, and a gold watch. Had they come from some kind of family picture that required matching outfits? His grin was toothy and when he shook my hand I could tell that they shared a moisturizing habit as well as a couturier.

"I'm Bart McMasterson," he said. "Good to meet you." People who introduced themselves with their full names always seemed like they were selling something. Like they lived lives where they had to introduce themselves by their full names all the time. But Bart's toothy smile was firmly plastered on his face, and at least he hadn't tried to crush my hand in dominance.

"Nate," Bart called behind him, still smiling at me.

A kid slunk into the room like he had been called to the gallows. He was the most ordinary-looking child I had ever seen. Light brown hair, blue eyes…a mouth. I stared at him for a moment because it was like looking at a picture frame insert.

"Hey," he said.

And that pretty much set the tone for the lesson.

Once the pleasantries were out of the way, I spent the hour seeing where Nate was at—looking at the pieces he'd played with his previous instructor, and running him through simple skill drills, and asking him about what music he liked to play.

Unshockingly, he didn't. Like to play. And my wager about him probably not being a virtuoso? Yeah, I won that.

But teaching piano was all I was qualified to do, since I'd fucked up actually playing piano, so I couldn't really turn my nose up at giving lessons to an apathetic rich kid.

I shook Kira and Bart's hands and agreed to Tuesdays and Thursdays at four. They didn't even blink when I named my price.

———

FARON CALLED as I was sitting on a bench in a small park near the McMastersons' house. It really was a beautiful neighborhood.

"Good morning," he said. His specificity charmed me. "What are you doing today?"

"I just had a lesson. One of the people who saw your sign. But I'm done now. Nothing else."

"Oh, that's great. Well, I wondered if you want to come over. If you still feel good about me painting you?"

Despite how genuine Faron always seemed, about ninety percent of me had assumed that the painting me thing wasn't for real. But it was becoming clear that I would jump at the chance to spend time around Faron, no matter what we were doing.

Pathetic dog.

"Okay. Should I, like, wear something particular or do anything?"

"No, just be you."

I sniffed under my arm tentatively. Not too terrible.

"Okay. When do you want me?" I hadn't meant to phrase it quite like that.

"Mm, anytime. I have a friend coming by to pick up some supplies, but I'll be here."

I hated the kind of uncertainty where someone said "any time." I just ended up agonizing over when in "any time" was the best, and it stressed me out.

"Um. Any time like now, even? Or is it too soon? Because I'm out already." *And if I go home it'll be that much harder to leave again,* I added silently. I shook my head at myself for sounding desperate.

"Now is great." He gave me his address, mentioned something about a garage door, and said he'd see me soon.

I briefly considered going home to reapply deodorant, but I truly did hate going home between things. I lost momentum and found a hundred excuses for why I couldn't go out again. I couldn't risk it. I compromised by stopping at a drug store and buying deodorant. Since I was there, I bought a pack of gum, cigarettes, and dental floss, which I'd been transferring from grocery list to grocery list every time I forgot to get it. On a whim, I also grabbed a loop of sturdy rope that the tag promised dogs would love.

The entrance to Faron's place was tucked away on a side street I passed twice and finally had to look up on my phone. No surprise I'd passed it, because it was really just a half-block-long strip of one-way street that terminated in a chain-link fence—what probably used to be one of the maze of footpaths that had originally been used to move goods from the ships that docked on the bank of the Delaware to the shops of the neighborhood and the market that Market Street was named for.

I realized what he'd meant about the garage door when I saw it. It was the side entrance of what must have been a warehouse until the seventies, when the district converted many of the old warehouses into commercial and residential properties.

On the other side of the chain-link fence at the end of the road was a small field overgrown with tall grass and wildflowers. A weather-blasted sign on the fence suggested that it had been bought years ago and never developed.

There was no doorbell that I could see, so I texted Faron to say I was outside and after a couple minutes of standing outside like I was casing the joint, the garage door rolled up.

"Hello, Jude," Faron said. He took a deep breath and turned his face to the sun, then gestured me inside. He rolled the door down and locked it at the bottom. It seemed like a rather inconvenient entry.

It would be hard to imagine a space more in contrast with the house I was invited into a few hours before. The door had opened onto a large, open space with a concrete floor. Not the kind of poured, sealed cement that made up the floors at Small Change or modern industrial lofts, but the cold, unfinished concrete of a warehouse.

It was dark and cool, though the sun shone brightly outside, and along the far wall were stacks of wood and rolls of canvas.

Boxes and a jumble of tools rounded out the corner, and a blue tarp covered something to our right.

I followed Faron through an arched doorway and found myself in a kind of loft space, except the apartment was still on ground level. The ceiling soared, some thirty feet up, and the interior walls were brick. Three thick, iron-strapped wooden beams shot from ceiling to floor like trees.

It was an open floor plan with a small kitchen and what I assumed was a bathroom off to the right. In the center of the space was a huge, brightly colored rug, and on it were arranged a shabby couch, a leather armchair, and a coffee table of wooden pallets resting on cinderblocks. Waffle was splayed out on the rug as well, one back foot twitching in sleep.

A box spring and mattress were set up on a fluffy white rug next to the back wall, along with a clothes rack and a folding screen for privacy.

The other wall held a row of windows, and the light spilled down on the space where Faron painted. There was a huge easel-like frame with a stretched canvas on it, and painting supplies all around it.

"Holy shit," I said. "This place is amazing."

Faron nodded. "I'm subletting it from a friend who's away for the year. Maybe longer. I really lucked out."

The toilet flushed and a man came out of the bathroom.

"This is my friend Winston," Faron said. "This is Jude."

Winston was taller than me and shorter than Faron, and probably in his mid- to late thirties. He was bulky with muscle, but had kind, sad eyes. His white T-shirt made his dark brown skin glow and he flashed me a smile with perfect teeth as white as his shirt.

"Hey, Jude," Winston said with a wink. "You probably get that a lot, huh?"

"Yup. Take it up with my parents who have no excuse, considering they weren't even Beatles fans."

Winston smiled again and pointed at himself. "Winston was John Lennon's middle name, turns out. My parents weren't fans either, but I served with a cat who was the biggest Beatles fan you ever met. He knew everything about them."

Winston put a coffee mug in the sink and shuffled some papers into a notebook on the counter. He clapped hands with Faron and drew him in for a hug and back pat firm enough it would've knocked the wind out of me.

"Thanks, bro. As always. I'll see you next week. Jude." He turned to me and nodded. "A pleasure. Hope I'll see you again."

"You too," I said.

Faron walked with him, presumably to let him out, and they talked softly and embraced again before Faron closed the door after him.

"He seems nice," I said. He did seem nice. He also seemed handsome and cool and he'd gotten to hug Faron twice in two minutes when I'd never gotten to hug him even once. Not that I was keeping score. "Have you, uh, known him long?" *Wow, could you be less subtle, Jude?*

"Six months or so." Faron moved around the kitchen straightening things up. "I'm part of this program called Mightier Than The Sword. It's about working with veterans to use art as a way of dealing with their experiences and healing. We do workshops and meet-ups and stuff. I teach painting, mostly. I met Winston at the first one I went to. We started hanging out."

"That's amazing. Did you start doing that because of Sabien?"

He bit his lip. "Kind of."

He was quiet for a while.

"Maybe working with other vets feels like a way I can help him. Even if he never knows. The military's a horrible bully, preying on poor people and people of color and making them feel like they have no other options than being cannon fodder. They depend on xenophobia and fear to remain untouchable. They perpetuate harm in the name of peace. Everything about them is a horror. But a lot of the people who get caught up in the machine aren't to blame for that. Some of them really didn't have better choices. Some wanted to do good, or thought they were. They need a way to cope with everything, and art seems to help a lot of people."

Faron stopped talking abruptly, almost like he'd forgotten I was there. He looked strangely uncertain, standing in the middle of this huge space.

I nodded. "Do you know if they want any musicians? Or, maybe that's a whole other kind of program."

"I'll ask," Faron said. He shook off whatever had tripped him up a moment before. "Do you want some tea?"

I snorted. "Okay. That's the second time today I've been offered. My new student's parents are like a *Better Homes and Gardens* ad and I sincerely hoped that Nate never gets kidnapped, because he's so generic that trying to describe him to the police would be useless."

Faron smiled and put the kettle on. I put my bag on the counter and remembered the toy I'd bought.

"Oh, I forgot. I brought this for Waffle."

I fished the toy out and tried to pull off the tag. Waffle came bounding over, apparently awakened by the sound of her name. The plastic loop holding the tag on was stubborn and Faron took the toy from me as I went for it with my teeth. He slit it with a bread knife on the counter and handed it back to me.

"That's really sweet, Jude. Thank you." His voice was so warm it kind of felt like an aural hug. I allowed myself to feel slightly less jealous of Winston.

"Sit, Waffle," Faron said. Waffle slid to the ground like she was on ice. Apparently it was the proper interpretation of the command because Faron patted her head and nodded to me. I held out the rope and Waffle tugged at it excitedly. I pulled back, pleased that my gift was a success. Then, with another tug, Waffle yanked me off my feet and sent me sprawling. I caught at the counter to try and stay standing, but it was no use.

"Wow," I said from the floor, as Waffle tried to lick my face. "Coulda just said you wanted me to sit with you, bud," I told the dog.

Faron held out a hand, and I could tell he was trying not to smile.

"All right?"

"Yeah. Just apparently weaker than the mouth of a medium-sized dog. No problem," I grumbled.

Faron pulled me to my feet easily but didn't let go of my hand. He drew me to him slowly—so slowly that I had time to pull away a dozen times.

My heart pounded as my chest drew flush with his and he wrapped his arms around me. It felt like sighing with my entire body. I hugged him back, pressing my palms against the musculature of his back. We stood there, entwined, just breathing, and I wanted to stay like that forever.

Tears pricked my eyes. It had been so damned long since anyone had held me, just held me, with nothing else at stake.

When Faron eased off like he might let go, I squeezed him back to me. Often, my sensitive sense of smell made me recoil from human scents. But he smelled good. Something fresh like grass and something warm like amber, and beneath it something dark and musky. The second I pulled him tight, his hand went to my hair. He tugged the elastic out and ran his fingers through it. I only heard his breath catch faintly because my ear was pressed close to his chest.

"Is this okay?" he murmured, one hand on my back and the other combing through my hair.

"Feels good."

I kept my eyes closed as he worked the tangles out of my messy hair. I let it wash over me that, no matter how affectionate Faron was, this was probably more than a hug of friendship. I told myself that over and over, since I was capable of finding any of a hundred reasons to excuse the intimacy of his fingers in my hair and his arms around me. My stomach fluttered and I made myself breathe deeply in rhythm with the rise and fall of Faron's chest.

There was a whistling noise, and then the scream of the teakettle, and Faron broke away, moving quickly to the stove as Waffle started snarling and my heart pounded.

Well. So much for the most peaceful I'd felt in years.

Faron turned the stove off but didn't make the tea. He came back to me and looked at me intently. His eyes were intense. Searching.

I held my hand out, not even sure what I was reaching for, and he tangled his fingers with mine.

"Can I kiss you?" His voice was so soft I thought I'd imagined it for a moment. But when I nodded, he squeezed my hand and cupped my cheek with his other palm. Then he leaned in and kissed me. His mouth was luscious and my heart was racing at the first touch. The closeness of him, the press of his lips, was so intimate that I felt dizzy. He stroked my cheekbone with his thumb and eased back, thick lashes half lowered over his beautiful gray-brown eyes.

I felt drunk with the taste of his mouth. It was the only explanation I had for saying what I said.

"I've thought about you a lot," I blurted. "Since we talked at Ginger's art show. A *lot*." Faron's eyes went wide. "I know it was only for a few minutes. But I've—jeez, never mind."

I shook my head and tried to pull away, mortified, but Faron didn't let go.

"I'm honored," he said. Probably from anyone else I would've taken it as a blow-off. But Faron's thumb was back on my cheekbone, and trailing over my skin to my neck. "I've thought about you too, Jude."

"You have?"

He nodded and kissed me again. Just the soft press of his mouth against mine, but it was overwhelming. The feel of his strong body against mine, the smell of his skin. The taste of his breath. Desire swirled in the pit of my stomach and the muscles of my thighs and I let my eyes drift shut as he learned my face with his fingers.

I've never been a casual person. I've never done things half-way. I've had my share of random sex, and I've had people I loved, and I've had people I hated. I've never felt much of anything in between. I could already tell that, if I let them, my feelings for Faron would be a lot more than a crush. If I kept spending time with him, if he kept touching me like this? Yeah. Hell of a lot more.

And look how well that's worked out for you in the past. You say you've had people you loved and people you hated, but you failed to mention that they're the same people. You stayed with Scott for a year longer than you wanted to, and you pretty much hated Kaspar for as much of the relationship as you loved him. What the fuck are you thinking even considering another relationship when you don't know how to love anyone without hating them or hating yourself?

My heart started to pound and I took a deep breath. Faron eased away and I opened my eyes. His burned. Interest, passion, desire—maybe all of the above? I wasn't sure. But the way he was looking at me said that he'd been holding back in that kiss. He'd been holding back a lot.

A smile quirked at the corner of his mouth and he kissed my hand, then untangled our fingers and moved into the kitchen.

"I have green tea, mint, yerba mate, jasmine, dandelion, chamomile, and a few blends for specific things."

He'd lost me at yerba mate, so I went with mint.

He put a mug of tea on the counter and tucked an errant curl behind his ear. His hair was up in a topknot today but a few strands drifted around his face. "I have something for you," he said. "In the garage. You shouldn't feel any pressure to accept it, though, okay?"

"I— Okay?"

Faron slid a hand into mine again and led me to the corner of the dim garage. He tugged the corner of the blue tarp like a magician with a tablecloth. Underneath was a piano. No, *the* piano. The one from the other night on the street.

"Holy shit," I murmured.

"You said it could be fixed. I thought you might want to fix it."

I have never been good at receiving gifts. I always feel vaguely guilty, which makes me irritated at the gift-giver for making me feel guilty. But I didn't feel guilty now. I felt overwhelmed.

"How did you…?"

"Winston and another friend helped me. Winston has a truck." My mind was racing. "I didn't want to dump it at your house if you didn't want it. And since the floor is flush here it was easy to get it inside. And if you don't want it, it's easy to get rid of again."

Even in the dim light I could see Faron bite his lip.

"So if I fixed it…I'd do it here?"

"You could. There's plenty of room."

I wanted it so much. A project. A way to feel useful. And the chance to spend more time with Faron? Yes, a thousand times yes.

"It could take a while," I warned.

He nodded.

"I don't know exactly what I'm doing."

"That's fine."

"I'm…not always the easiest to be around."

He didn't say anything and his expression didn't change. I sighed. Chances were that he knew things about me from working at Small Change. I'd had a therapist once, years ago, who'd told me it would easier if I just "came out" to people about my depression so all my cards were on the table. It was bullshit, of course: depression wasn't "all my cards" any more than my sexuality was, and it certainly wasn't some warning label I was required to stamp across my forehead to disclose myself as a threat to everyone I saw.

Still, while most of me believed that, I had felt like a threat for so long that part of me wondered if it wasn't the kind thing to warn people off. To give them a chance to protect themselves by steering as clear of me as possible.

All you have to do is answer the question of whether you want to fix a damned piano, I told myself.

"Okay," I said. "Thank you."

Faron's smile about lit up the dark.

Back inside, we lost hours watching video tutorials about how to fix the piano and googling supplies, and then digging through the pile of tools that Ramona, the friend he was subletting from, had in the garage.

By that time it was late, and when Faron asked if I wanted to stay for dinner, I bowed out. I was amped up and tired and I was pretty sure I wouldn't be able to eat anything, and I didn't want to offend Faron by rejecting his food. It was a battle for another day.

He hadn't even gotten to paint me, which was why he'd invited me over in the first place. But presumably if I was going to be here to work on the piano, he'd get another chance.

At the door, he ran his knuckles along my cheek and handed me back the elastic he'd taken from my hair earlier. I stood awkwardly, wanting to hug him again. Given how much I hate being touched when I don't want to, though, I was always loath to initiate any contact in case I was doing that to someone else. Faron leaned in and pressed a soft kiss to my mouth.

"Good night, Jude," he murmured. And it sounded like a promise.

CHAPTER FIVE

MY FIRST OFFICIAL lesson with Nate was on Tuesday, and it revealed exactly what I'd suspected. Nate had no interest in the piano or in learning to play it. Which was normal for a kid and not any real affront to me, except that the ebony Steinway in the living room was going to waste.

I ached to play it. The whole lesson, I stared at Nate's clumsy hands and wished they were mine. Wished I could go back to being eleven, when the instrument felt like a grand discovery and the world was just a backdrop.

My first piano teacher, Ms. Merchant, had been the one to see potential in me. Not that she'd admit approval with much more than a nod before moving on to dissect the places I'd erred. But I came to value those nods more than my mother's unconditional approval or my father's easy smiles because they meant something. They indicated that I'd done well. They were only given to me when I earned them. And when you earned something, you weren't obligated to repay it.

My parents hadn't liked her. After their initial pride that I was sticking with lessons and that Ms. Merchant was taking me to recitals and entering me in competitions, they grew leery of her discipline, her impossibly high standards, her expectations. I heard them talking one night when they thought I was asleep.

"He's a kid," my father had said. "He should be playing outside, having fun with other kids. Merchant's turning him into a piano-playing zombie."

My mother had agreed. "I don't like the way he talks about it now. Is he even enjoying piano anymore? When he comes home from lessons or recitals all he says are the things he didn't get right. It's too much pressure."

When they'd tried to suggest I ease off, take fewer lessons, I'd just practiced harder. When my mother tried to broach the topic of another teacher, I panicked. No one could understand me the way Ms. Merchant did. Through watching her fingers move over the keys, I learned that the rhythm of a piece lived not in the notes but in the spaces between them. That you could make a room hold its breath by delaying the expected note for half a second, and make them gallop with you by eliding it.

I learned that being good at something—deeply, passionately good—was more satisfying than having fun, or being liked, or being happy. That the pursuit of perfection made you a world unto yourself.

And when you were a world unto yourself, you didn't need the things other people needed. Food or sleep or friends. Love.

It was Ms. Merchant who got me the audition for Berklee College of Music, and a scholarship once they'd accepted me. It was Ms. Merchant's voice I heard in my ear years after I'd left Philadelphia and the little piano my parents had eventually installed in their living room for me when I was thirteen. Her voice that whispered to me the first time I auditioned to play alongside the Boston Symphony. Whispered *Slow down, Slow down, Slow down* as I strung out the notes in the final phrase, the scrim I played behind vibrating with the final chord.

When I'd called to tell my parents I'd gotten the job, they'd whooped and shrieked and told me how proud of me they were, and I'd hung up the phone numb. When I told Ms. Merchant, she said, "That is as it should be," and when I hung up I was so overwhelmed by her approval I sobbed.

———

IT ONLY TOOK about fifteen minutes to walk to Faron's from the McMastersons' but my memories of Ms. Merchant were so thick that it felt like I'd lived my whole life again when I got there. And all I wanted to do was play.

The second the garage door was open I went to the broken piano and fit my fingers to the keys. Nearly all of them stuck but I pressed them anyway, and it took a moment before it registered that I was ghost-playing Beethoven's Sonata No. 29, the piece I'd auditioned with all those years ago.

"I hope someday I get to hear what that would've sounded like," Faron said.

As soon as we were inside, Waffle galumphed over to me and I let her lick my knuckles and dance clumsily around my knees until she flopped back on the rug with her head on her paws.

"So, uh, how do we do this?" I asked, suddenly feeling intensely awkward about being painted.

"I'll sketch you for a bit first, if that's all right."

"Sure, yeah, okay."

I fumbled with my shoelaces that had somehow double knotted, and dumped my shoes by the door.

"Hey." Faron took my elbow and tipped my chin up. "If you aren't comfortable with this, we don't have to do it."

"No, I'm— It's okay. I just hate being stared at. It makes me self-conscious."

I imagine what they see when they look at me. I can't stand being in my own skin.

"Then let's not do this."

Faron said it like it was the obvious conclusion to draw, but it wasn't. He sat on the couch and I sat next to him, dumping my phone on the coffee table.

"No, seriously. I hate it usually because I feel like when people look at me they're judging me. But I don't feel like that with you. Mostly I just feel awkward. But awkward usually goes away, right?"

"Depends why you feel awkward."

He looked at me expectantly.

"Because I feel…" I searched for a way to say it that didn't sound pathetically self-loathing and failed to find one. "I feel ugly," I said simply. And watched Faron's eyes melt with an empathy so pure I felt it like a fist to the gut.

It was physical, yeah. Call me superficial, but when you've spent your whole life skinny, pale, covered in freckles, with bright orange hair, compliments were few and far between. Even the kindly meant comments were mostly of the confused, *I'm weirdly into you* variety, or the conflicting *You look like I could split you in half* one. And that's to say nothing of the unkindly meant ones.

I didn't know how to explain that it wasn't merely physical though. It was the way not feeling sexy made sex feel like a performance rather than any kind of desire—like I was watching myself fumble through a jazz piece where my job was to riff off whatever I was given. I'd never been very good at riffing.

It was the way my partners had always seemed to want something from me but I never knew what it was. In how I'd never wanted what they gave me. And the longer I felt that way, the more the feedback loop became a downward spiral where someone looking at my freckles fast-forwarded in my head to them imagining what it would be like to fuck someone covered in freckles like that, which became me failing to satisfy them and not enjoying myself, which started it all over again.

Before Faron could say anything or I could figure out a way to explain, my phone beeped on the table and lit up with a text.

Call me please.

It was Kaspar. I'd deleted a few more emails this week without reading them.

"Do you need to take care of that?" Faron asked when I made no move to pick up the phone.

"No, it's my ex."

"Does he bother you?"

Faron's shoulders were squared and he was sitting up tall, like he'd happily grab the phone and bother Kaspar right back. Warmth rushed through me at the idea that he felt protective of me.

"He probably just wants to get rid of all my stuff. He's still pretty mad at me."

Another beep and my phone lit up again.

It's Rimsky-Korsakov. Call me.

All the blood rushed to my head and my ears rang.

"Oh god," I said. "Oh no."

"What's wrong?"

"Our cat. That's our cat. Oh, shit."

The panic had sunk its teeth into me and all I could see was Rimsky's little black and white face contorted into a look of fear or pain. I'd called her Piano Face as a nickname because of her black markings. She'd always curled up next to me on the couch or in my lap when I played piano. She licked tears off my chin and liked to bat at my hair. She snoozed on the radiator in the cold weather and woke up to watch the snow.

I'd welcomed the feel of her fur and the movement of her breathing even when I couldn't stand to feel anything else.

I felt like I was going to puke and I grabbed for the phone.

Kaspar answered on the first ring.

"What's wrong with her, what's going on?" My voice was reed thin.

"So you leave without a trace after we were together for five years, ignore every one of my emails and calls when I don't even know if you're alive or dead, but I mention the cat and you'll call immediately. That fucking hurts, Jude."

I could hear the genuine hurt in his voice.

"Please, Kaspar, tell me what's wrong. Is Rimsky going to be okay?"

He sighed. "Yeah, she's okay. Look, I need to talk to you. About us. This is ridiculous, babe. I get that you needed some time, and I support you being with your family. But it's been months. It's time for you to come home."

I couldn't quite believe what I was hearing.

"Are you telling me there's nothing wrong with Rimsky?"

"Rimsky's fine. You just wouldn't answer my—"

My voice shook as anger roared through me. "Are you telling me that you fabricated something being wrong with your cat to get me to call you?"

"Our cat."

I was speechless with fury but shaky with relief that Rimsky was okay.

"I– I– Don't fucking text me again, Kaspar, I could fucking kill you!"

I hung up and threw my phone across the room. Waffle lifted her head, but when he saw it wasn't a toy I'd thrown, she lost interest.

I was dragging in deep, ragged breaths, trying to tamp down the bloodlust, when I realized I was so furious that I was crying.

Faron took me by the shoulders and pulled me close. I cried even harder when his arms were around me. He stroked up and down my back and I said, "I really miss my cat," through my tears.

Then I started laughing at how ridiculous it was that Kaspar had used a threat to the cat as bait to get me to call him and then tried to woo me back. Fucking Kaspar.

"Welp," I said, pushing out of Faron's arms. "That was my partner of five years, go me."

I ducked into the bathroom to blow my nose. My skin was

blotchy, my hair was a mess, and my eyes were bloodshot, the rims of my eyelids pink and slightly swollen from crying. I looked even more like an alien than usual. Excellent. Just how I wanted to be immortalized.

Faron was pouring tea when I came out of the bathroom and I could feel his eyes on me as I sat at the counter.

"Using a cat to get me to talk to him basically makes him an automatic villain, right?" I said, trying to break the tension.

He didn't say anything, but slid his hand up my forearm and squeezed gently. The more time I spent with Faron the more it became clear that touch was a language he spoke eloquently. We drank the tea in silence.

My anger at Kaspar had just spiked, but in the queasy aftermath, I knew it wasn't only Kaspar I had left.

"I can't go back there," I said.

It sank into me with a finality that I hadn't felt before. All those months, in my childhood bedroom at my parents' house, I'd been marking time. First, the time until everyone stopped treating me like I might off myself at any moment if they so much as left me alone with access to a kitchen knife or a belt. Then, the time until I felt ready to slide back into the life I'd left behind in Boston. Not Kaspar, but my friends, and my music.

In my mind, my life there was on pause, suspended until I reinhabited it. When I heard Antonio hired Claire as the guest pianist for the show after I left, I said of course. Of course, when the player can't play they hire someone else.

But winter had been bad. Really bad, and by the time I'd emerged, checked my email or my phone, they'd begun prepping for the summer season and Antonio was taking Claire to Tanglewood in my place.

It would be her instead of me, going forward, I knew it. Why wouldn't it be? She was talented, driven, and conveniently devoid of my less savory mood disorders. Sure, we all had opinions on each other's abilities. Once you got to a certain level, the comparisons came down to the microsecond or the pound per square inch of pressure. But those of us at the top were all clustered so close together that it was just politics. There was no reason Antonio would put up with me when he could have Claire.

"Boston. There's nothing there for me anymore." My voice sounded detached. No lover, job, no friends—not after what Kaspar would have said to them. "Nothing besides that damned cat, and she's not even mine. Kaspar got her before we met."

"What will you do?" Faron asked.

I met his gaze and swallowed hard.

"I have no idea."

———

FARON HAD me sit on the couch and choose some music while he gathered his sketching materials. I felt too raw to put on anything I'd played, so I found a station of torch songs and Great American Songbook standards.

He pulled the armchair closer to the couch and settled in it, looking at me.

"I'm just going to sketch you as you are. You don't need to do anything, you don't need to stay still. Just try and relax, okay?"

I nodded, though I felt anything but relaxed.

The irregular scritch of his pencil against the sketchbook was all I could hear. It slashed the music to ribbons. I started to fidget.

"What's wrong?" His voice was low and hypnotic.

I shook my head, but he'd stopped sketching.

"I...I can hear the sound of your pencil and it's not in rhythm with the music and so it's all I can think about."

"Do you want to turn up the music?"

I would be able to hear the ghost of the sound even if the music was louder. There was a texture to it. A presence. I shook my head.

"One sec."

Faron rummaged around on the table next to the bed and came back with headphones. He plugged them into the computer and slid them over my head where they blocked out everything but the music. He snapped in front of me and I didn't hear it. I nodded at him and he gave me a warm smile and went right back to sketching.

Somehow, with the headphones on, even being looked at was easier. As if the inability to hear anything he might say excused me from engaging entirely. After a few minutes, I sank into a world of unrequited love, romantic tragedy, and raspy-voiced yearning. Ella Fitzgerald sang "Prelude to a Kiss," and I let myself watch Faron as he watched me.

I wanted to know what happened in the slide of his eyes on me to his fingers moving the pencil over the page. How did he find his way in? How did he choose which line began it all? Which of my shapes sparked it off?

I took off the headphones.

"How do you decide where to start?"

His eyes refocused on me in a different way than they'd been as he drew and his brow furrowed slightly.

"I'm not sure," he said softly. "I just do."

"I wish I could see you drawing."

He looked at me for a moment, then stood and moved behind me on the couch, leaning me forward. He settled in, one leg against the back of the couch, the other with a foot on the floor, and drew me back against his chest.

"This okay?"

I nodded. His smell was all around me.

He flipped to a fresh page in the sketchbook and held it in front of me. I let my head settle back against his shoulder so I wasn't blocking his view, and felt his lips at my hair. I took a shuddery breath and forced myself to relax against his body.

He began to draw. His hand moved quickly, and with light strokes my feet emerged, and the arm of the couch, then the shapes of the kitchen beyond. The first line he'd drawn had shaped the inside slope of my left foot and I touched it, pencil smudging slightly under my finger.

"Sorry," I said, and Faron kissed my hair.

"Take your socks off?"

He turned the page and I pulled my socks off and he began to draw again. This time, he drew my feet in detail. I watched the sketch unfold as surely as a piece of music unfurled before me as I played. The articulation of bony toes, the tributaries of tendon and blood vessel, the subtle shadows of instep. It all began as the lines that differentiated my foot from not-my-foot. As simple as that. Object and non-object; line and space. Sound and silence.

I'd never been so aware of my feet as seeing them through Faron's eyes. I turned my head just enough to see his chin.

"More?"

His breath caught and he slid his hand along the outside of my thigh. He put the sketchbook on my knee and his hand came to rest on my stomach. My heart started pounding and unexpected arousal crept over me, setting my skin to a tingling awareness. I clutched at his thighs where they cradled mine, the muscle beneath his thin linen pants firm and tight.

His touch was slow and sure, like he was sketching, learning the planes of my stomach and the ridges of my jeans with his fingertips. He brought his fingers to the hem of my shirt and paused there. I pressed into his touch and he slid his hand under my shirt. I gasped as his warm hand slid over the sensitive skin of my stomach. It felt like no one had ever touched me there before.

I'd tangled his foot with both of mine without noticing it but now I felt his bare foot slide against mine.

"Hold this," Faron murmured into my hair, and handed me the sketchbook. I held it so he could draw with his right hand as his left continued to explore my torso. He sketched our feet, his elegant and high-arched, and mine, bony and slender; his dark, mine pale. And all the while, his fingers sketched other shapes against my skin. He dipped into my navel and ran along my ribs, sending shivers down my spine. When he skimmed a fingertip over my nipple I gasped and tensed against him.

He traced my nipple until it was a hard peak, then squeezed it, and my hips jerked, making the sketchbook jump in my hand. Faron's breath went rough and he nuzzled into my hair.

My heart was pounding and I knew he could feel it. I squirmed to try and take my shirt off, but I couldn't quite get it. Faron stripped it off me and ran sure fingers along my ribs. Then he traced the blue veins visible beneath my skin from my heart to where they disappeared under my waistband.

With my oversized shirt out of the way, the bulge of my erection in my jeans was obvious.

I drew my knee up, resting it against the back of the couch. He slid a hand up the inside of my thigh so slowly I held my breath, but he didn't touch my hard cock and I shuddered with arousal.

"Jude," Faron breathed, and I let the sketchbook fall between us as I went for the button on my jeans. I felt like I was made of pounding heart, flushed skin, raging need, and it felt like nothing I'd ever experienced. It didn't even feel like sex; it felt like desire. It felt like what I knew sex was supposed to feel like but rarely had for me.

Faron lifted my hips and I shimmied the jeans down and kicked them off. I had a moment of regretting it when I realized my pale, skinny legs were now on full display, but Faron's groan at the sight of my bared skin was so sincere and gratifying that it eclipsed my self-consciousness. When I settled back against him, I slid my ass back, nestled it between his legs and felt the hardness there. Thank god. He clutched me to him and shuddered as his erection slid against me.

I spread my legs again, one knee against the back of the couch and the other slung over his knee. He was fully clothed and all I wore were clinging briefs that were wet with my arousal and straining around my hardness. Faron cupped my cock and balls through my underwear and I jerked in his hands, my body hot and out of control. I kept my hands on his thighs, but I ground back against him and forward into his hand, trying to get more pressure, more friction.

With a shuddery breath, Faron reached between my legs, and I tensed, waiting for his touch. But he pulled the sketchbook back and held it up for me. My every nerve ending was alight with the need for release, but I realized that I wanted to see what he would do more than I wanted to come.

I propped the sketchbook against my right thigh and Faron picked up the pencil. With his right hand, he drew the triangle of my crooked knee, and the curve of my bare foot where it rested on the couch. With his left hand, he roamed my body, setting my skin on fire. He played with my nipples and stroked my stomach. He traced the crook of my knee and where my thigh met my groin. He trailed fingers up and down the inside of my thigh until my whole leg was shaking with tension. Finally, he drew a fingertip along the rigid length of my cock and I gasped.

My erection jerked and I thought I might come. The tip of my cock pressed out the top of my underwear, straining red against my stomach, and I felt Faron's arousal as he stiffened further against my ass. His self-control was unreal. I could feel the faint trembles in his thighs, his stomach, his chest, but he kept still.

When I threw my head back on his shoulder, I could feel his hot breath against my ear and my throat and I wanted desperately to kiss him. But I didn't want to be the one to choose. I wanted to see what he'd do more even than I wanted to kiss him.

He shaded in shadow at the crook of my knee with his right hand and with his left, he circled the flushed, weeping tip of my cock. I cried out, so exquisitely sensitive that my head pounded. My thighs were visibly trembling and the sketchbook was shaking.

"Lift up," he murmured, and stripped my underwear off. I

pulled one foot out and left it around my other leg. My erection raged, and Faron made a rumbling sound of appreciation in his throat. He touched me so slowly that I thought I might scream, because each swipe of his thumb over the head of my dick, each rasp of his hand on my inner thigh, each pinch of his fingers at my nipples had me lightheaded.

He was playing me like an instrument, and I sang like one.

He took in a huge breath and propped the sketchbook up on my thigh again.

"I can't," I gasped. My fingers couldn't do anything but clutch at his legs.

"Yeah you can," he murmured, kissing my ear, and I gripped the sketchbook in my shaking hand.

My eyes were glued to my crotch. Finally, his hand closed around my erection and I nearly screamed. His hand was so big and it felt like he held my whole life in it. He stroked me slowly, up and down, as my hips tried to punch up, my ass clenching. But he took his hand away and began to draw. I felt like I might cry from desperation.

"Please, please, please," I chanted, and Faron rumbled at me. He began to flex his hips ever so slightly, dragging his erection against my ass. Everything between us was hot as fire and slow as sap and I was trembling so hard it felt like I was caught at the edge of orgasm in my whole body.

The pencil was jerky in Faron's hand, his finesse gone. He drew my cock as he touched it, one hand teasing, the other rendering the effect, and I watched the scene unfold almost as if the erection didn't belong to me.

In front of me, another man was being fondled, another man was being watched so closely he could be drawn, another man was shaking and gasping, his ruddy erection leaking precome into the hand that worked it. In front of me, another man was being made a spectacle of, brought to the edge of orgasm over and over and then soothed back from it. Another man was crying out in desperate, unhinged need.

I made a sound like a keening animal, and Faron's control snapped. He dropped the sketchbook on the floor, hooked his hands under my thighs, and dragged me tight into his body. He took my balls in one hand and my cock in the other, and with firm strokes and squeezes, he wrenched from my body an orgasm so huge it seemed to balloon around me.

My stomach clenched and my asshole clenched and my thighs went rigid and a gasp seized my lungs until I felt like I might black out. The pleasure tore through me in a hot surge of white light that left me shaking and writhing, and I shot hard in Faron's hand, screaming out my release.

Faron groaned deep in his chest and I felt him come against my ass, the wet heat exploding from him as he crushed me to his chest.

We were both shaking in the aftermath, and I kept getting little frissons of aftershocks that jerked through me. I must have forgotten what it felt like to come like that—no. I'd never come like that.

Finally, I couldn't take the feeling of exposure anymore. I didn't know if I wanted Faron's arms around me, or my clothes back on, or to leave. I covered my face, as if that might make me feel less vulnerable, and Faron made the choice for me. He eased onto his side and pulled me close, chest to chest.

"Jude," he murmured, and kissed the back of my hand where it was over my eyes. I felt like I was drowning. He said my name again, and ran a calming hand up and down my spine. I moved my hand reluctantly and looked at him for the first time. He was so stunning it took my breath away, and I realized exactly what I needed. I kissed him with everything I had. Kissed him deeply and sank my tongue into his mouth until we both had to break apart for air. That was a little bit better.

Nose to nose, we both smiled at each other, and that was even better.

After a minute, Faron winced and looked down.

"Take a shower with me?" he asked.

When we'd begun dating, I had showered with Kaspar a few times, but it had always felt vaguely uncomfortable, as if it was an invitation for him to scrutinize me without even the haze of sex to render me desirable. In the context of utility, no doubt I looked even less appealing.

I hesitated. I didn't want this to end, but I didn't want to sour it with my own cringing self-disgust.

Faron leaned in and kissed the bridge of my nose, then my eyebrows.

"You're so sexy," he murmured. "Beautiful." A kiss to my cheek. "Watching you made me so hard." A kiss to my other cheek. "I came all over myself."

My face was hot and I nodded that yes I'd shower with him even as I was shaking my head that I wasn't sexy. My signals were beyond scrambled and my tongue tripped over telling him that he was the sexy one as I let him maneuver us to the bathroom.

When Faron began to strip, I realized that I still hadn't seen him naked. His body was a work of art. Smooth, dark skin traced with black ink, sculpted muscles, broad shoulders, and a flat belly. He saw me looking at him and met my gaze with a half-smile. When he slid his pants off, he revealed the gorgeous, round ass I'd peeked at when he was in jeans, and a cock that managed to look elegant even soft and sticky with come. It was like in addition to his movements being graceful, even his body was immune to looking awkward. I wrapped my arms around myself self-consciously as Faron tied his hair up.

When we were under the hot spray, I let the water soak me. We ran soapy hands over each other's bodies reverently and I did my best to concentrate on him instead of on myself. On the exquisite musculature of his back and shoulders. On how smooth the skin under his ear felt against my lips. On the way his hands felt as they stroked me.

He washed my hair, tipping my head back so soap wouldn't get in my eyes, and I felt something inside me break open a little.

I kissed his mouth and traced the lines of the tattoos on his arms, making a mental note to ask him about them.

"I want to ask something, but I'm not quite sure how..." I trailed off trying to gather my thoughts.

"Just ask," he said, eyes half closed in relaxation. I put my palm against his and twined our fingers together.

"I, well. You're so fucking beautiful. And when you took your shirt off, I wanted to say how your body is gorgeous. How your skin is gorgeous. The texture, the color. But I wasn't sure...I wondered, um." My heart was pounding.

"You wondered if that wasn't okay to say because I'm black and you're white and black skin is either villainized or fetishized."

"Uh, yes. Exactly." I cringed, and he shut the water off and handed me a towel.

When I looked up, he was watching me. He didn't look upset, just serious.

"It's complicated," he said. "If you were black and you complimented my skin, I would take it like any other compliment. But yeah, since you're white, I would definitely have thought about it differently. I've been with white guys who got off on the contrast between our skin tones specifically, and that didn't feel great. So it really depends on how someone means it. And on the context of other things they say, and other ways they act in the world."

I nodded, and held out the towel to him, liking the idea that it had dried both of us. "I've been with guys who thought it was hot that I was so much skinnier than them because they associated it with me being weak. Like they could break me open by fucking me. And that didn't feel great because of the association. But if someone thought I was hot but not with that association...just because…then." I shook my head, not sure how to finish my thought, and suddenly sure that it was an ignorant comparison.

"It feels different. You can tell," Faron murmured. I nodded.

Faron took my chin in his hand and looked at me.

"Race is going to come up, Jude. It's going to come up a lot, probably. The best thing is to talk about it."

"Okay."

He hung up the towel and walked out of the bathroom completely comfortable in his nakedness. I watched him shamelessly as I untangled my own clothes. He put on clean sweatpants and a loose white tank top and grinned when he caught me blatantly staring.

"I want to paint you even more now than I did before," he said. "Only now I really want to paint you naked."

"Oh god." I felt my ears heat up and a zing of arousal go through me at the idea of him looking at me.

He caught me in his arms as I was turning my shirt inside-out. "Your cock looks like sherbet," he murmured in my ear. "Peach and pink." My breath caught. "And that orange hair." He slid a hand down to my crotch and cupped me gently. "The way you blush." His other hand found its way to the nape of my neck and I went boneless against him. "Since we were talking about skin color. You're all the colors of a sunset. And I'm gonna paint the fuck out of you."

Then we were kissing again, my shirt forgotten on the floor.

CHAPTER SIX

I FLOATED home after my evening with Faron and fell asleep with visions of sugar plums dancing in my head. But I woke with a jolt of reality to find that my dreams had shaken loose what had happened before he blew my mind.

Kaspar. Boston. The final nail in the coffin of my career there.

I pulled the covers slowly over my head and tried to go back to sleep. This time, my dreams were a disturbing superimposition of Kaspar and Faron. Faron was sketching me and Kaspar was doing sit-ups, then Kaspar took Faron's pencil and began using it as a conducting baton. Then Faron and Kaspar were kissing, the wand drawing lazy shapes in the air between them. Then it was only Faron and me and I was trying to tell him something but all that came out of my mouth were notes that floated toward the ceiling and popped like bubbles.

When I finally dragged myself out of bed, it was afternoon and I wandered around the apartment idly. I felt floaty and light-headed so I made myself eat a Pop-Tart.

I chatted with Maggie while my tea steeped.

Jude: *What if, hypothetically, my crush had blossomed into a full-*

on Thing at the same moment as my ex tried to tempt me back to him by lying about the cat?

I wandered away from the computer to peek outside. There weren't many windows in this apartment, which suited me okay, but it made it hard to feel any sense of time passing, or remember what month it was.

My computer dinged almost immediately.

Maggie: *i assume by "hypothetically" you mean that's exactly what happened?*

Jude: *Yeah.*

Maggie: *start with the cat.*

I told her about Kaspar's texts and what he'd said when I called and she interjected with many all-caps swear words and angry emojis, which was satisfying.

Maggie: *you know this about ghosty—he wants you with him bc he likes to play the martyr and he likes that yr more fucked up than him*

Maggie: *so he gets to feel all great about himself for being such a good person and for being comparatively together.*

Jude: *Yeah.*

I knew she was right. Hell, I was the one who'd told her exactly that in the hospital. But knowing it was probably true didn't erase five years of its effects.

The first year or so that Kaspar and I were together had felt good. The idea that someone who I actually thought was interesting and attractive would want something serious with me? It was a fantasy.

He was a musician, so he understood the time and dedication that it took, and didn't get upset if I had to practice, since he was practicing too. He liked to go out, and he'd wheedle me into coming with him, so all of a sudden I had a whole new group of friends. They thought I was funny and smart and they wanted me around.

And he wanted me around. He wanted me to go shopping with him and cook dinner. He wanted my opinion on what he was wearing and whether his adagio was too lugubrious. Most of all, he wanted me.

In bed, on the couch, in the hallway, he just wanted me. It was heady to have someone so handsome attracted to me. With his shiny, perfectly cut dark hair and his strong profile, he looked exactly like the picture of an elegant violinist. It was why his picture was often on our brochures even though he was third chair. He was handsome and sophisticated, and he wanted me.

I floated through that first year like it was a Mozart piano sonata. I felt...okay. For the first time since I was fourteen, I felt okay for long enough that I thought maybe—maybe, maybe, maybe—it was over. I knew what depression was. I knew what my medications did. I knew it wasn't something that was ever really over. Of course I knew. I'd seen more doctors and therapists than there were keys on a piano over the years. Yeah, I knew.

But the way I felt overshadowed what I knew. My hope was more intoxicating than any facts I'd been told. My desperation to be better, to be fixed, to be transformed was deeper and burned brighter than any acceptance I'd gained or kindness I had found for myself.

I knew and I didn't know. I hoped and I didn't admit to hoping. I prayed.

Soon, though, every day when I was okay shimmered with a threat just out of view. I'd stop in the middle of doing something and check in: did I still feel okay? I did. I would reassure myself, *See! You are still okay!* But once I began to look down and check that the ground was still flat, every step felt like the one that might suddenly slope downhill. And even when it didn't, the edge felt like it was growing nearer and each day became more and more vertiginous.

Because in a cycle, the ground is flat until it's not.

Maggie: *get to the part where you're in love with faron!*

Jude: *I didn't say I was in love with him.*

Still, my heart gave a little zing.

Maggie: *yeah yeah tell*

Jude: *He's amazing.*

Jude: *I'm terrified.*

Jude: *Well. It probably won't come to anything anyway.*

Maggie: *why terrified?*

Jude: *Bc eventually people either start to hate me or I start to not be able to stand them and the idea of Faron hating me is awful.*

Maggie: *that's trash. ghost didn't start to hate you, he was so insecure that the second you couldn't give him 100% attention he punished you for it. you "couldnt stand" him meaning sometimes you were in a place where you couldnt bear being touched or talking. dont be a dick to yourself.*

Jude: *I know, but doesn't it amount to the same thing, really? Just by being me I hurt him and then he acted terrible and it all went to shit. So why wouldn't the same thing happen with F.*

Maggie: *nooooo it does NOT amount to the same thing. ghost wasnt a good fit for you bc he couldnt hang. he needed stuff you couldnt give and he couldnt give what you needed, period.*

I stared at her message for a long time. She got angry at me a lot because she said I believed that being depressed meant I didn't deserve what people without depression did. The world isn't set up for people with mental health issues, she said. We learned that we were wrong or broken because we were different, but that didn't mean it was true

When she said it, I believed her. I believed it about everyone, except me. When it came to myself I couldn't shrug a kind of utilitarian fatalism. Maybe the narratives of normality and history were all working against me. But when I lay in bed at night, all I could do was tally the day over and over, and if the column I titled *I hurt someone* had more Xs in it than it would have had if I were quote unquote normal, I condemned myself.

After all, pain is pain, right?

That was the kind of math that had landed me in the hospital last year. Because what is there to do when the *I hurt someone* column wasn't a column anymore, but a cluster of Xs so dense that it looked like a black page?

What can ever balance the scales if you're a black hole of misery that sucks in every scrap of light and turns it to your own material? You can't climb out of a black hole if you are the hole. There's nothing to do in that equation except throw the paper away. If X persistently equals X, you have to get rid of X and the tally will be reset.

So I'd erased X. And I'd managed to fail at even that, the simplest equation.

I only realized I was crying when I tasted salt.

I wasn't in that place anymore. My meds had been adjusted; I'd removed myself from a situation. That was good. Those had been the right things to do.

Retell the story—that's how a counselor in the hospital had put it. Do whatever you have to do to step outside the narrative you've told about yourself, your life, your brain, and see it in another way. So instead of erasing X, I'd erased the rest of the variables. Kaspar. Boston. The symphony. My friends. I'd excised everything to try and stop the darkness from metastasizing.

It was good. It had been the right thing to do. The problem was that with everything else shorn away, I didn't have anything left. Nothing to hide behind or distract myself with. Just a bed and a couch and some plates and forks. And none of it was even mine.

I wiped my eyes and tried to pick apart what I was trying to say to Maggie.

Jude: *When he looks at me...I feel like maybe he sees me. Maybe he could care about me as I am. And that feels too important to risk fucking up.*

Maggie: **heart emoji**

Maggie: *if he really cares about you as you are then thats worth a lot. maybe its not soul mate love. doesnt mean its not valuable.*

Jude: *I wish I were young like you and could embrace such openness.*

Maggie: *ok old man*

Maggie: *not saying you go all poly princess with faron cuz we all know yr way too obsessive. just saying a relationship can be important and not be marriage*

Jude: *Obsessive?!*

Maggie: *yr obviously baiting me. you know yr obsessive af. own it boo*

Jude: *I should never have told you about that drummer I was obsessed with.*

Maggie: *psshhh deflection w/e*

Maggie: *just saying: practice figuring out how to have a relationship that doesn't make you want to kill yrself slash murder everyone for like one millionth the number of hours you used to practice piano and maybe you'd be good at it.*

Jude: *As ever I bow to the wisdom of your piano-related advice.*

Maggie: *you just love to bow period*

The stage an ocean of dark around me, blinded by a spotlight. My fingers buzzing with the music, my calf tight from the pedal as I took my bow. The applause. The applause that was only hand hitting hand but meant that I had accomplished something.

Jude: *Guilty.*

———

I WENT to Faron's again after my Thursday lesson, armed with more hours of watching videos of fixing pianos than I cared to admit. I smiled at him when he opened the door and immediately glued my gaze to the ground. I'd been thinking about him nonstop since Tuesday and to be suddenly faced with the object of my daydreaming made me feel guilty and awkward.

Faron kept his distance. He let me navigate around him and

nodded as I told him I was ready to start on the piano. I was relieved, and then I was disappointed.

We wheeled the piano into his apartment and I piled the tools and materials next to it. Since there was no bench, I brought one of the kitchen stools over.

I might have watched videos and read tutorials until my eyes burned, but the damage was still overwhelming. Stuck keys, bent pins, a warped soundboard bridge, two broken hammers.

"I don't know where to start," I said.

Faron came over and looked at the piano for a while.

"Does it matter?" he said finally.

I wasn't sure.

He drifted away to work on designs for clients at Small Change the next day and I stared at the piano. I googled *how to restore a piano* on my phone even though I'd already googled that a dozen times. Then I stared more.

I felt a hand on my shoulder and looked up into Faron's beautiful eyes.

"What's wrong?"

I shook my head.

"Want me to leave you to it?"

I managed a shrug.

"Want me to kiss you?"

I shook my head, even though I did want him to kiss me, desperately. Because I knew I couldn't do anything else right now and I didn't want to lead him on. That had always made Kaspar really mad.

"Jude." I looked back at him. "What are you worried about?"

"I don't want to mess it up."

"The piano is unplayable right now. If you break it or mess up trying to fix it, it's no harm done. It'll be no worse off. So there's no pressure."

He didn't say the next part, but I knew it was there: *But if you succeed, it will live again.*

I really, really wanted it to live again.

I nodded and he gave me an intense look and went back to his sketches. This time he sat with his back to me, and it didn't feel like a rejection, it felt like he was giving me privacy. My heart lurched with gratitude, and a trickle of shame that I needed the privacy slid in too.

I looked back at the piano and took a deep breath. I'd been wrong before. I did know what I had to do; I was just scared to do it.

If I really wanted to see how deep the damage went, if I really wanted to give it a fighting chance to make music again, I had to disassemble it and check every key and pin, every hammer and string.

I had to tear it apart.

Three hours later, I was surrounded by the pieces of the piano like I stood at the epicenter of a bomb that had detonated. At first I'd tried to take pictures of every step and label every screw, but the deeper I got the faster I went, and I stopped paying attention to anything except the feel of wood and metal under my fingers, the wrench and tumble of dislocation.

The piano was where the music lived. It was the locus of every ambition I'd ever had. I had always viewed it as something almost mystical or animal. Something I had to approach with respect and fear. The piano mastered me, rewarded me, punished me. My successes and my failures played out on it. It was my joy and my sorrow, my torment and my absolution.

It was my god. And I had dismantled it with a screwdriver and a whim. God was dead, and I had killed it.

A sound tore from me that I thought was a laugh until it became a sob. I dropped into a crouch and tried to cover my mouth. Tried to make myself smaller in the hopes that Faron wouldn't see, even as I knew it was impossible.

I crouched in the debris of everything I'd ever worshipped and I sobbed out my broken heart.

———

"WAS IT TRUE, WHAT CHRISTOPHER SAID?" Faron asked a while later, once I'd gotten myself together with the application of half a roll of toilet paper and some fairly embarrassing scrambling with the computer to put on "Flower Duet" because it always calmed me down.

"Hm? About what?"

"Do you really hate eating? Because I'm hungry and I'm gonna cook dinner. Do you want to join me?"

My heart started to pound.

"You should go ahead and cook," I tried to deflect.

"I will. But I do want to know, if you'll tell me."

I sighed.

"Food just…disgusts me. Anything slimy or like…tough." I shuddered. "Meat grosses me out a lot. Cheese. Eggs. Stuff with sauces or fillings."

I shrugged and bit my lip. I didn't like to think about it. Or about the awkwardness of trying not to eat in front of people so they wouldn't notice their hollandaise sauce making me gag.

"Has it always?"

I nodded.

"When I was little I wouldn't eat anything except saltines, applesauce, and animal crackers. But a lot of kids are picky, I guess? Ugh, then when I was older, my mom would ask me what she could do to make her cooking better. I tried to explain that it wasn't because she was a bad cook, but…"

I shook my head. I'd never had an answer that could satisfy her. I could look at the brightly colored vegetables and appreciate them, but the second a cooked carrot gave against my teeth in a fibrous mush, or a broccoli floret bombed my mouth with its tiny green balls, I would gag. Flank steak, roast chicken, meatloaf… even cold cuts on white bread repulsed me. I couldn't stand meat at all.

Thanksgiving had been the worst, with its worship of turkey, and its globs of wet bread and gravy. Christmas was a lurid pink ham and a casserole of canned green beans mixed with soup that began to haunt my nightmares the second the calendar flipped to December. At least at Christmas, my parents had usually thrown parties, so no one was watching my plate.

When I'd moved in with Kaspar he'd been appalled at my eating habits and had thought I just didn't want to gain weight, but that was never it. He'd tried to get me to drink protein drinks, so I wouldn't be so skinny, but I'd hated them. They tasted like chalk and made my mouth feel disgusting.

Mostly I just tried to avoid eating with people altogether, so I didn't have to think about it.

"I know it's not that fun to eat with me," I said. "I have a pretty limited diet."

Faron raised an amused eyebrow. "I think I'll survive. Is there anything you actually like?"

I rolled my eyes at myself. "Pop-Tarts. Brown sugar cinnamon Pop-Tarts. I've always really liked them and I have no idea why. Christopher even made me homemade ones once. It was really sweet and I think they were probably a lot of trouble. No clue, since I don't bake. I didn't have the heart to tell him I like the ones in the box much better."

"What else?"

"Some cereals. Toast. Macaroni and cheese. From a box. Um, some fruit is okay. Well, apples, really. Plain noodles. Tater tots sometimes. Birthday cake."

Faron smiled. "Well, you're in luck."

He rummaged through the cabinets and put three things in front of me on the counter: a box of macaroni and cheese, a box of Cheerios, and a package of spaghetti.

The mac and cheese was an organic brand that promised its packet contained "real aged cheddar!" so I passed it over. And I didn't want to twirl noodles around a fork right now. It seemed too close to the unscrewing I'd been doing all evening on the piano. I tapped the Cheerios.

"Thanks," I said.

I ate dry cereal out of the box while Faron made himself broccoli and rice and beans, and he didn't seem to care in the slightest.

CHAPTER SEVEN

APPARENTLY THE KEY to getting gigs giving lessons was to get hired by one family with a lot of connections, because over the next week, three of the McMastersons' friends called to inquire about lessons for their children. By Friday evening, I was drowning in scales, dissonance, and the particular sweat that comes from attempting not to scream while listening to music being torn note from note at the sweaty hands of prepubescents.

My walk home took me a few blocks from Melt so I decided to pop in and say hi to Christopher. He'd texted me a couple times over the last week asking if I wanted to hang out and I'd kind of blown him off.

"Hey!" he said when I came in, and motioned me back.

"That's my replacement, I presume?" I nodded at the woman behind the counter.

"Yeah, Roshani. She's great. Thank god I fired you." He grinned at me, the same happy, easy grin he'd had since he was a kid. I patted his arm and smiled back.

"I'm proud of you," I said. "For all of this. I should have said that before."

Christopher's smile turned shy and pleased and he ducked his head. "Thanks, bro."

"Yo, Chris!" Roshani called from the counter, and Christopher disappeared for a minute.

"So, listen," he said when he came back. "If you're free tomorrow, you should come out to Marcus and Selene's. Ginger's closing the shop and everyone's going. They're gonna have food and we're gonna lounge around all day."

Marcus tattooed at Small Change with Ginger, and he and his partner Selene lived in a converted barn outside the city.

"Faron's coming," Christopher said, and I shot him a glare even as my heart raced at the sound of Faron's name. "Aw, come on. I don't get to know anything?"

"Faron's great. You already know that," I said.

"Wow."

"Shut up," I muttered.

"You're blushing, bro."

I rolled my eyes. "Faron's great, and he could have anyone, so he's sure as hell not going to pick me."

"But I thought you guys were— I thought you already...were."

"Did he say that?"

"Faron? Of course not. That guy's like the soul of integrity. But, uh...Ginger obviously tried to get it out of him and every time she did he got this very private, half-smiley look on his face. Ginger said it was a 'You have mentioned the name of my beloved, which pleases me, but I shall reveal nothing, because it also pleases me to hold the information close to me like a soft, soft blanket' look."

"Ginger certainly has a repertoire of specific descriptions."

Christopher sighed. "Okay, fine, none of my biz, I get it." He raked his hair back, shoved his hands in his pockets, and looked at his shoes.

I instantly felt guilty. Christopher had poured his heart out to me when he was falling in love with Ginger.

"I…I like him a lot, okay? We'll just…we'll see."

Christopher's grin was sunshine and joy.

"Okay," he agreed. "So, tomorrow?"

"Tomorrow."

MARCUS AND SELENE lived in Broomall, about ten miles west of the city. Christopher drove with the windows down and was in a great mood.

"Hey, bro," he said apropos of nothing. "For whatever it's worth, I really hope stuff with Faron works out. I think he's awesome."

"Thanks," I said. Then, even though hope was terrifying, I forced myself to add, "I hope so too."

Marcus and Selene's barn was set back from a side road, on a winding dirt drive. Its wooden exterior was painted a deep peacock blue that glowed against the green trees and blue sky. There was a smaller wooden structure next to the barn that looked like a stable.

Inside, the walls went up forever, to a vaulted ceiling, and the wooden floorboards gleamed. The open front area was a living room with mismatched couches and chairs clustered around wagon wheel tables, suggesting this was the provenance of the one in Ginger's apartment. This was separated from the kitchen by a long, wood countertop lined with barstools. The kitchen had hanging baskets of vegetables and fruits and fresh herbs lining the sills of the two large windows. A large, six-burner gas stove dominated the far wall of the kitchen.

Out back, Marcus, Faron, and a woman who must have been Selene were putting the finishing touches on the food that was spread over the picnic table. There were finger foods like deviled eggs and stuffed mushrooms and pigs in a blanket. There was a kale salad and a fruit salad. Plates were piled with ingredients and condiments for sandwiches, and three kinds of homemade bread were sliced and ready. There were pitchers of lemonade with fresh thyme and lavender, iced tea, white wine, and a tin washtub full of ice and beer. It looked rustic and effortless and beautiful, and I found myself imagining what it might be like to live in such a place.

Kaspar, Boston-born and raised, had always said he'd wither and die if forced to live outside a city. But I liked the quiet.

Faron was wearing gray cotton leggings and a purple tunic that left his gorgeous arms bare. He was barefoot and his hair fell around his shoulders in a riot of glorious curls. As soon as he saw us, he smiled.

"Jude, right?" said Selene, coming around the table. She was absolutely stunning. She was short and fat and had dark brown skin, perfectly arching eyebrows over wide brown eyes, and the kind of cheekbones that would turn heads. Her hair was braided on the sides and in natural curls on top, and she wore a gauzy black dress and bright pink lipstick.

"Hi. Thanks for having me," I told Selene.

"Welcome." She opened her arms to ask if I wanted to hug, and somehow the clear option to say no made me comfortable to say yes.

Marcus slid his arm around Selene's shoulder and held out his hand to me. "Glad you joined us," he said with a smile. Then they turned to Christopher, who told them that Ginger was on her way, and I went to Faron.

He didn't say hello, just pulled me into a hug. Hugging Selene had been welcoming, friendly. Hugging Faron felt like coming home. He ran a hand up my back to stroke my neck and I shivered at his touch. His fingers combed through my hair and I flattened my palms to his back, wanting to stay this way forever.

"Hey," he said finally. "I was on grocery duty. I brought something for you."

He lifted the dome that covered one of the plates to reveal

familiar silver foil. He'd brought me brown sugar cinnamon Pop-Tarts.

I felt my eyes fill with tears. It was such a simple gesture, but it was one of the kindest things anyone had ever done for me.

I pressed my cheek to his collarbone and when I finally pulled away there was a wet spot darkening his shirt. I turned away quickly and slid my sunglasses on.

In the bright sun to the left of the barn was a large garden that looked like it was for vegetables. To our right was a stand of tall trees that provided some shade. Their leaves moved gently in the breeze. Past the picnic table where the food was set up was a fire pit circled by white stones and surrounded by logs to sit on. In front of the picnic table were folding chairs and two chaise longues arranged in a semicircle around a soft flannel blanket on the grass.

Selene was pointing out what all the different foods were when we heard a car pull up. Ginger came around the side of the barn holding a bottle of whiskey and grinning. Her dark brown hair was long and curly, and shaved on one side, and the breeze blew it around her face like something out of a music video. I watched my brother smile the smile that was only for her.

"Hey! Morgan and Phee couldn't make it but guess who I brought instead," she said, brandishing the whiskey.

"Whiskey isn't a person, no matter how much you want it to be, bud," said Marcus.

Ginger flipped him off, then mused, "I really do want to be friends with someone who's the personification of whiskey."

"I think I'm already dating her," Christopher mumbled, and Ginger grinned at him.

Around the corner came two men. One was about my height, and covered in tattoos. He had messy dark hair, sharp features, and cheap gas station sunglasses that sat crookedly on his face, like he'd sat on them. He was gesturing while saying something to his companion, who was a few inches taller and thickly built, with the kind of muscles that looked like he worked construction. He had chin-length brown hair and tanned skin and was listening intently to whatever the other man was saying, a hand hovering at his shoulder.

"Hey, Daniel! Rex," Marcus called.

Daniel was Ginger's like-a-brother best friend who had moved to Michigan the year before for a teaching job and fallen in love with Rex, who Ginger always called the lumberjack. I could see why. Daniel and Rex had moved back to Philly in August because Daniel had gotten a job teaching at Temple, and I knew Ginger was ecstatic to have him back.

"Jude, right?" Daniel asked me. I knew that he recognized me since Ginger had already told me she'd shown him a picture of me, hence his *Wuthering Heights* evaluation. "Christopher's brother. That's cool."

"Yup, I'm Jude."

"Hey." He gave an odd jerky wave, but his smile was sweet. Up close he had beautiful green eyes that seemed to dart everywhere, like he didn't want to miss anything. "This is Rex," he said. He turned like he was going to pull Rex over to me, only to find Rex was already there, so he bumped into his chest awkwardly. Rex steadied him with a hand on his shoulder.

"Nice to meet you, Jude," Rex said. His voice was low and much softer than I'd expected from such an imposing figure. His handshake was equal parts firm and gentle, and he looked away from me as soon as he'd spoken and I remembered Christopher telling me he was shy.

We got drinks and plates of food and sprawled out in the chairs and on the blanket. I put some bread and a scoop of fruit on my plate because maybe I'd be able to stomach them, and I grabbed a packet of Pop-Tarts and a glass of white wine.

Faron was lying on his side on the blanket and I sat next to him, hoping that was okay. I wasn't sure where we stood, exactly, and with a lot of people looking on, I was self-conscious. But I couldn't help the tug I felt to be near him.

As people ate, Marcus and Ginger regaled us with amusing shop gossip from Small Change. Faron didn't contribute, but seemed content to listen. When it became clear that they were heading down a rabbit hole of problematic customers, Christopher asked Daniel how the semester was going.

Daniel's head jerked up at his name, like he'd forgotten anyone could see him.

"Huh? Oh, yeah, I think it's okay so far. It's only been a few weeks, so." He shrugged. "One of my classes is an intro survey, and freshman are...uh..." He glanced at Rex. "They're learning a lot really fast. It's super different than high school so some of them aren't really sure how college works."

"Oh!" Ginger said. "How's your thingie? Did you turn it in?"

"Article. Uh, no." Daniel cringed. "I ended up having to totally change this one part of the lit review because— Doesn't matter. Anyway, I came here instead of finishing."

He was perched on the edge of the chaise longue Rex was sitting on, and he started to bounce his knee nervously.

"I'm gonna work on it when we get home." His knee bounced faster and faster and Rex put out a hand and stilled it. Daniel leaned toward Rex like a sapling growing toward the sun.

"You can finish it tomorrow," Rex said, almost too softly to hear.

"Yeah. Yup. Tomorrow," Daniel murmured, and then he was gazing at the treetops again.

"How're you settling in?" Selene asked Rex. "They moved into this spot in Fishtown that's an apartment over a warehouse space," she explained to me.

"Not too bad," Rex said slowly. "I'm gutting the first floor so I can fit it for a wood shop. It's slow going, but I want to do everything myself."

Daniel elbowed him. "It's not 'not too bad'; it's amazing. He's tearing out the...stuff and putting in...uh, all this other stuff. Anyway, point is it kicks ass now and it's gonna kick even more ass when he's done."

"Helping a lot then, are you?" Ginger said.

Daniel muttered something incoherent and they both grinned.

"How's work going, Selene?" Ginger asked, bumping Selene's leg with her shoulder. Selene and Marcus shared a speaking look and clasped hands.

"Well, actually," she said. "We have some news. We decided we're finally ready to become foster parents."

Everyone broke into excited chatter that made me think this was something that had long been in the works. Marcus was grinning hugely and Selene was practically glowing with contentment.

"We're going to start by fostering one or two kids. Since this will be so new, we want to try and learn all we can first. But then, if everything works out, I'll take some time off from the foundation and we'll see about moving forward with everything." Selene turned to me and explained, "Marcus and I want to try and create a space for kids in the system who are queer or questioning to connect with each other, get resources, ask questions."

"I'm hoping maybe some trans and questioning kids will feel comfortable talking with another trans person about how they're feeling," Marcus added. "Selene's family's foundation gives a lot of money to create resources for youth of color, and they're going to help us out with this project too."

"That's really amazing," I said, and they beamed at me.

Everyone was talking about one another's projects and accomplishments and I closed my eyes against the sun and lay back, trying to feel its warmth. I was overwhelmed by their joy for each other, and their generosity. My friends had always been mostly other musicians, and even when we celebrated one another's accomplishments, our pride was always tinged with envy because we were in competition for the same gigs, judged against one another.

Even with Kaspar, I always shared my accomplishments with a carefully offhanded air—he could be happy for me for a few minutes, but any such good news inevitably came back to haunt me later.

Something cast a shadow on my face and I opened my eyes to see Faron leaning over me. Conversation had died down and people were looking at me.

"What?" I said.

"I just asked how you spend your time these days," Selene said. "I remember Christopher told us you were a pianist, right?"

"Shit, I'm sorry," I said. "I zoned." There was a buzzing in my head and I could feel the frown dragging the corners of my mouth down. "I was a pianist. I'm afraid I don't really do much of anything now."

I grasped for something else to say. Selene was so kind to ask, and had been generously explaining things to me since I'd arrived, and I'd given a dud of an answer. But everywhere I reached was just emptiness.

"That's not true," Faron said softly, chiming into the conversation for the first time. "You've been giving piano lessons to four different kids, and you found a broken piano that you're completely restoring."

"Whoa, you can do that?" Ginger asked, as Christopher said, "That's amazing, bro," and the others chimed in with questions. They seemed genuinely interested. Rex leaned forward, his gaze intent, and asked me a bunch of questions about how pianos were put together. I was amazed to find that I could answer a lot of them.

"I'd love to hear about that when you're done," Rex said after he'd exhausted my knowledge. "Or, I don't know. If you ever want help..." He shrugged and looked away self-consciously.

Daniel leaned against his shoulder. "Fixing stuff is Rex's all-time favorite thing to do," he assured me.

"Not my all-time favorite," Rex said so softly I almost missed it, and kissed Daniel's jaw as Daniel's expression turned embarrassed and pleased.

I lay back down, flicking my hair out so it wouldn't tickle my neck, and shut my eyes again. I had started to zone out again when I felt a gentle tug on my hair. Faron. He spread my hair out on the blanket and began running his fingers through it absently, untangling a knot here, twisting a strand there. It was so intimate, so…possessive that it sent a shiver up my spine. I imagined myself sinking into the ground, tethered to the surface only by the strands of my hair that Faron held on to like balloon strings.

I must have drifted off because the sound of my phone jerked me to awareness. It almost never rang, so I was shocked to see Antonio's name on the screen. I scrambled to my knees, my instinct when my conductor called being to answer the phone immediately. But then I remembered that Antonio wasn't my conductor anymore and I froze. Surely he couldn't have anything good to tell me.

Years and years of habit won out and I swiped to answer the phone and headed toward the trees to talk.

"Jude, Jude, it's so good to hear your voice," Antonio said, his Italian accent and light voice so painfully familiar.

"You too," I told him, surprised to find that it was true. Antonio might have been demanding as hell and intimidating to boot, but we'd gotten along well. He'd always shown concern for me when I wasn't doing well, but had never seemed to doubt that I was still able to do my job. I appreciated that.

I took the opportunity of being away from the others to light a cigarette so it wouldn't bother them.

I asked him how Tanglewood and the rest of the summer was going and he told me briefly. Never one to chat, though, his reason for calling quickly became clear.

"Kaspar tells me that you have decided to leave us?" he asked.

"I...well, you have Claire now..."

"Claire is very talented. She's my second choice. But you have always been my first choice, Jude. Kaspar told me you were not well but would be returning when you were better. Now he tells me you won't be returning?"

Fury and shame warred in my gut. I hadn't even realized I still had a chance to go back, and now Kaspar had tried to take it away from me. Of course, Kaspar hadn't been the one to tell me I had no chance. I'd learned Claire was stepping in for me and I'd assumed after months of not practicing I'd signed my own death warrant with the symphony. But clearly Kaspar had been busy behind the scenes after our most recent phone call.

"Antonio, I'm so sorry. I'm not sure what to say. I think Kaspar might have given you the wrong impression. And I'm sorry I haven't been in touch. It's been...I've been a little overwhelmed. I didn't think coming back was on the table."

"Jude. My friend. You were the pianist I most wanted to work with when I took over this group. When you play, you play as I hear. This is not the only way to play, yes, but it is the way I want it. You would be welcome here if you wished to return. If you are...taking care of yourself?"

The real question was clear. Was I going to ruin everything again the way I'd ruined it last year?

"I just don't know," I said. "I'm so sorry. I wish I had a better answer for you. What's my timeline here?"

"The season is set, of course."

"I know." My voice was barely a whisper. I'd looked at the website and heard the soaring strings and the racing brass. The sweet low chords of the piano underlying it.

"Perhaps it's best to revisit in the winter, yes? You could come for the summer program to ease in for next season? Let's talk in the new year and see how you feel."

"Okay. Thank you. And Antonio? Kaspar doesn't speak for

me, all right? He doesn't know anything about what I want or what I'll do."

I hung up the phone and slid it back into my pocket with a shaking hand.

I could go back. If I wanted to, I could go back to my life.

CHAPTER EIGHT

OVER THE NEXT WEEK, it felt like all I did was give lessons and sand the edges of piano keys. Nearly every key had swollen and at some point a sticky substance had been spilled, leaving a tacky residue that needed to be sanded off. I'd been wearing Faron's noise-canceling headphones because the sound of the sandpaper against wood was like rubbing something against my eardrums.

As I finished sanding the last one, I decided I was done with the piano for the day and collapsed onto the couch.

"Hey, come here," Faron said softly. "The light's perfect right now."

He gestured me toward his bed and I swallowed hard. The white cotton was worn soft and I could smell Faron all around me.

Standing next to his easel, dressed in gray and purple, he looked like something out of a fantasy photo shoot.

"You look like a model," I said.

"You're the model."

Suddenly it seemed imperative that he know how attracted I was to him. He hadn't kissed me when I came in the door today and I felt ungrounded without that acknowledgment that there was something between us. Whatever it was felt fluid and natural and undemanding. And I didn't know what to do with that.

"Because you're gorgeous, I mean," I said awkwardly.

Faron turned back to me, his expression soft and serious. "Thank you."

"You're welcome. Okay. I just wanted to make sure you knew that." I winced.

Faron knelt in front of the bed and looked at me closely. "You know that I think you're beautiful, right? Exquisitely, uniquely beautiful."

I looked away from him and bit my lip. *You look like an alien. Firecrotch. You've got more freckles than skin.* I shook my head.

Faron caught my chin and his eyes were intense. "You'll see."

I wanted him to kiss me. Wanted him to slide his fingers into my hair and kiss me on his bed. But he didn't. He went back to setting up his paints.

"Will you put on some classical stuff you like? I want to paint you while I listen to your music."

I pulled his laptop over, running through what I'd play. I put on Beethoven sonatas, and the first notes of Sonata Pathétique ripped through the apartment and settled in my stomach.

"Okay, how do you want me?" I asked.

"Just however you want right now. I want to play around with the colors."

I thought of what he'd said about my skin, that when I was flushed and turned on, I was the colors of a sunset. Arousal crept over me and I sat cross-legged on the bed.

"Do you like orchestral music?" I asked him.

"I'm not that familiar with it. I know it from movies and doctors' offices and fancy restaurants. And I went to the *Nutcracker* once as a kid. My mom mostly played classic blues records and sixties and seventies folk records at home. My dad played R&B and disco. He's a big guy. Used to play football. And he'd put on Grace Jones and Sylvester records and boogie around the house." Faron smiled.

"He sounds fun."

"Sometimes he is. I was terrified of him when I was little though."

"Why?"

"He was in his late forties when we were born, and with his other kids nearly grown, all he did was work. He was an engineer. He got home late and left early, and on the weekends he locked himself in his room and worked and we weren't supposed to disturb him. He and his friend were the only black people of their generation who worked there, so for a while they'd been the only ones. They were used to having to do more and better to get by there. He was always nervous he was going to lose his job, so he made sure he never gave them even a hint of a reason to take it away from him."

"Did he tell you that?"

"He didn't have to."

"What about your mom?"

"She taught third grade, on and off. She'd taken a break when my brothers and sister were young, and then gone back to it. When we were born, she took a couple years off when we were babies, but went back to teaching and had the older kids watch us. My mom's very...private. She doesn't like to talk about anything personal but she does like to ask all her children about the details of their lives."

"That sounds very mom-like."

"Yes. How was it, living with your parents again after all this time?"

"Awful. Humiliating." I shook my head, feeling guilty for saying that. "I'm an asshole because I know how incredibly lucky I am that my parents were willing to let me stay when I had nowhere else to go. They were kind and supportive, and–and–and it was horrible."

"How do they deal with your depression and anxiety?"

He asked it so casually, as if it were a fact that had been established between us, and a rush of gratitude washed through me. It was the way Maggie talked about it too. The way she referred to my depression the way she might say "acid reflux" or "high blood pressure." Just something I had that should be taken into account but didn't define me.

"I know they deal with it pretty well compared to some," I said. "I've known people whose parents screamed at them and hit them if they cried, or dragged them out of bed and pushed them out the door to get them moving. I've known people whose parents kept them so drugged to the gills as teenagers that they didn't even know who they were anymore. So, I'm aware that I'm pretty lucky."

"Okay."

"But…" I chewed on my lip.

"But?"

"But that's part of the problem. My parents are lovely people. They're incredibly kind to me. They love me so much. And I can't be…I can't *be* around them. I can't be myself, I can't be what they want. When I'm near them, all I can think about is how I've made their lives ten million times harder than they would've been otherwise."

My stomach felt hollow and I curled around it.

"When Christopher and I were little they told us over and over again that all they wanted was for us to be happy and they'd support us no matter what. All they wanted was for me to be happy. And I wasn't. I never have been. It hurts them so much. I know it does. Sometimes they can hardly look at me. My mother physically winces sometimes at whatever she sees when she looks at me. I'm like this black hole that sucks all the happiness and joy out of their lives."

The sheets were fisted in my hands and I hadn't really meant to say any of that.

Faron knelt on the floor in front of me and untangled the sheets. He kissed my palms and put them on his shoulders. I could feel how red my ears must have been.

"People learn to live with great sadness and regret," he said. He slid my socks off. "They lose people. They get hurt. They hurt others and feel guilt. They want things they can't have." He took the hem of my shirt in hand and slowly pulled it off me. "They watch atrocities occur in the world and can do nothing to stop them. They experience atrocities and go on living."

He undid my jeans and worked them off my legs. I swallowed hard at the feeling of being so exposed.

"They experience all this suffering, and they still find ways to be happy. In tiny moments in between the suffering. In celebration of still being alive. Or in resistance to that suffering."

He slid his fingers beneath the elastic of my underwear and paused. I nodded. He stripped it off me and then sat back on his heels, not touching me.

"I'm sure your family has suffered along with your suffering. I'm sure they've grieved for your pain. But you haven't sucked the happiness and joy from them. You don't have the power to do that. They control their own lives. They have the power to feel things that aren't about you. To feel things in spite of you."

I took a shaky breath as his words sank in.

"You're not all-powerful, Jude. You don't control everyone."

Shame flooded me, and gratitude. I knew he was right. It was a constant difficulty. Depression and anxiety were self-abnegating and self-centering at the same time. It was so easy to believe that because my feelings were huge, they exerted a force beyond me. It was so easy to forget that even though I was always being forced to think about myself, not everyone else did.

"I don't want to," I breathed. "I've never wanted to control anyone. I don't want to make choices for them. I just want them to do what they want. I want them to act as if I weren't even there."

"You don't," he said. "You don't control people. But you are here."

Sometimes I wish I weren't.

But not now. Now, I didn't want to be anywhere else in the world. I nodded, half miserable and half fascinated.

Faron paused, eyes on me like he was reading every single glance and swallow.

"You want people to do what they want," he said slowly, and I shivered. "Me included?" I nodded. "Is that... Do you want that in bed?"

My heart began to hammer and I blinked rapidly. He put a knee on the mattress beside me and pressed me down on my back. Every inch of my skin lit up so quickly I felt lightheaded. I was completely naked and he was fully clothed. I was in his bed. My breath got shallow.

"Jude," he murmured, leaning in to my neck and taking a deep breath. He traced the lines of my face. I let him, relaxing into the bed as he did what he pleased.

"You don't want to choose," he said. "Choosing feels hard because it could always be a mistake. And if it's a mistake and you chose it, then it's your fault. You don't want it to be your fault. You already feel guilty enough. You don't want to feel any more."

I cried out. A sound that felt torn from my chest. An animal call of recognition, of pleading. How had he known? How had he seen it when even I couldn't have put it quite that way?

I was nodding and trying to get him to kiss me, but he pulled away and I felt it like an actual wrench in my chest.

"Jude," he said, low. "You're going to be my model. That means I choose. I'll tell you how to move and what I want you to do. Okay?"

A shiver of lust shot through me. I nodded again and said okay, though no sound came out.

Faron told me where to put my arms and legs and how to position my hands and I did exactly as he said. Peace flowed through me at the knowledge that I was doing it right. That I was giving him what he needed. That I wasn't ruining his painting by making the wrong choice.

He had me lying on my side, facing him, top knee up, and bottom arm under the pillow so it cradled my head. When he came close and swept a lock of hair in front of my shoulder, I shuddered even though he barely touched me. I looked down to see my cock fully erect and pink against the white sheets.

"Perfect," he murmured. My dick pulsed and my heart thudded and my stomach lurched.

In the background the Sonata Pastoral rose and fell.

"What are we listening to?"

I told him about Beethoven as he began to paint. Just as when he'd been sketching me, his gaze flicked constantly between me and the canvas as if we were connected. It was like a musician looking between the music and the conductor when they were learning a new piece.

"Are there any black classical composers?" Faron asked. "Not contemporary, but composing at the same time as the famous composers?"

"There were, yeah. Chevalier de Saint-Georges was probably the first to achieve fame. That was mid- to late eighteenth century. People called him 'le Mozart noir,' but actually Mozart was the one who was inspired by his violin techniques. He was the son of a plantation owner and a woman who was a slave in Guadeloupe, and then came to France when he was young. He taught violin to Marie Antoinette. He composed a few operas and symphonies, and a lot of violin concertos. I don't know how many off the top of my head, but he was very prolific. Um, George Bridgetower was also a violinist. He was…maybe Polish? His father was from Barbados, I think, and took him to London to perform for the aristocracy. He performed with Beethoven and they were apparently good friends until they had some falling out over a woman. The music for some of his compositions is still around, though I don't think there are many recordings. There's an opera about him that debuted a few years ago."

I worried I was rambling, but Faron nodded encouragingly.

"Samuel Coleridge-Taylor—no relation—is interesting. He died really young, like in his thirties, maybe. He started out studying composition by white English teachers and writing pieces that were total fin de siècle romanticism. But when he started to get some notoriety, he traveled more and got more political. His father was from Sierra Leone and he became really interested in learning about African musical traditions because of his father. He was really inspired by Du Bois, and Frederick Douglass, and Paul Laurence Dunbar. Dunbar gave him a push to incorporate African musical influences into his compositions. This is a little later, like late nineteenth and early twentieth century, right at the height of modernism. So you have someone like Dvořák and Grieg incorporating Hungarian and Norwegian folk themes into their compositions, as opposed to erasing specific cultural traditions. Coleridge-Taylor did the same. He set some of Dunbar's poetry to music."

I knew I was forgetting people.

"Oh, and Florence Price. She was American, so it was a really different context. She was the first well-known black female symphony composer. She won a Wanamaker award for one of her symphonies—Wanamaker like the department store, you know? Now it's the Macy's in Center City? The organ's still there."

Faron nodded, smiling faintly.

"Once she won the award, the Chicago orchestra performed her winning symphony, which made her the first black female composer to have her work performed by a major orchestra. I'm sure I'm forgetting people…"

"It's okay," Faron said. "Maybe you can tell me all that again while we listen some time."

"Yeah, okay, sure," I said, then bit my tongue because I sounded like an eager fucking puppy dog.

"Jude," he said softly. "Lay your right hand on the bed in front of you."

I did as he said.

"Spread your legs more."

I let my knee fall open even farther. I'd relaxed as I was telling him about music, but now I felt like I was on high alert again, my skin pricking with the awareness of being watched and the low buzz of arousal creeping over me again.

"You look perfect," he said, and the word zinged up my spine and hardened my cock.

I watched him as he painted. His broad shoulders and tight muscles. His bleached curls held back with a fabric headband. Every movement looked like a dance. I'd never known anyone who moved as gracefully as he did—certainly not actual dancers, who looked as if they weren't built for mundane movements like walking or sitting.

"Jude," he said. Every time he murmured my name it was like an incantation. Like a command. "I want you to touch yourself. Anywhere you want."

I lifted my hand, but didn't know where to move it. Usually I didn't like touching myself at all. I felt repulsed by the feel of my own skin. But I'd do it if Faron wanted to see… I just wanted him to tell me where.

"Touch your nipples," he specified when he saw my hesitation. "I want to see you make them hard."

I traced the skin around my nipples until they pebbled, pink nubs against my marble pale skin. I squeezed my eyes shut so I didn't have to look at myself.

"Jude, open your eyes. Look at me. Keep looking at me. Squeeze your nipples."

I gasped at my own touch, pressure zinging over my skin. I kept pinching one and then the other, slowly, since he didn't tell me to stop. After a few minutes I winced, the skin gone swollen and over-sensitive. It hurt, but I wouldn't stop until Faron told me to.

Sometimes I'd played until my wrists and the tendons in my fingers felt like they were on fire and my back ached and my calf cramped before I'd been told to stop.

"Jude, stroke the insides of your thighs for me."

The *for me* really got to me, as if all of this—every touch—was for Faron's benefit and I was just an incidental instrument of his desire. It was what I wanted. I'd a million times rather do things for him than for myself.

I ran my fingers up and down the insides of my legs until the skin was sensitized and my thigh muscles were trembling. I kept my eyes on Faron, but I was hard against my stomach and every time I took a breath, I smelled Faron's intoxicating scent and imagined that the sheets I was lying on had touched every part of his body.

"Jude, touch your belly for me."

I touched myself, skin jumping beneath my fingers, and wanted to close my eyes but forced myself to keep looking. I could feel my heartbeat in my stomach and it was getting faster and faster.

I felt floaty and light but also anchored on the bed. It was a strange, dislocating feeling. I felt as if I would disappear entirely if Faron looked away from me.

"You're so hard," he murmured, and I groaned, arousal and shame chasing one another higher and higher.

My heart was pounding and my breathing was shallow. My body was his. I would do anything he wanted.

"Jude, stroke your dick for me. Three times."

I was panting as I wrapped my hand around my erection. At the first stroke, I arched into my own hand, so desperate for the contact that it shot pleasure through every nerve ending. I cried out, shocked at how one touch could feel like coming.

"Two more."

I stroked myself up and down, up and down, and felt my balls draw up tight.

"Now your inner thighs again, Jude."

Trembling, I went back to stroking my thighs. One glance at my crotch showed my swollen erection, straining and wet-tipped, and I shuddered.

Faron painted for what seemed like forever and might have only been a minute or two, but I was so electrified that every breath felt like an eon.

"Give yourself two strokes for me, Jude," he murmured, eyes on mine.

I was so turned on I thought I might actually be able to come from two tight, fast strokes, and I considered it. I'd never felt so sensitive, so exposed, so desperate. And so cared for. No. No way could I bring all that to an end.

"You know I don't want you to come yet, Jude."

"Okay." My voice was thick and scratchy.

I touched myself so softly it was more agony than pleasure, and it sent my hips straining forward against my will, seeking friction. My breathing was a mess.

When I let my cock go, it slapped against my belly wetly and I cried out.

"Now I want you to stay very still and keep your hand on the bed."

I whimpered, but pressed my palm to the sheets. After what felt like hours of touching myself—of being touched—I was vibrating with need, and the sudden lack of contact had my skin searching for any sensations. I took a deep breath and even the rise of my shoulder, which pulled the skin of my chest, sent my body into a feedback loop of arousal, and my cock jumped and oozed a bead of precome. I could feel it sliding down my length, like the ghost of a touch, and it nearly brought me off the bed.

My head was spinning and the more I tried to control my

breathing, the shallower it became. My heart started to beat even faster and the fear descended on me that Faron might never touch me. That I might lie here, trapped within my own skin forever.

I heard myself whimper and then I heard myself say, "Faron," so softly it almost wasn't a word.

"You're perfect just like that, Jude," he said, and when his eyes met mine, so present, and so aware of me, I felt my balls tighten even further, and I moaned. "You have no idea what you're doing to me, do you?" he said softly. "Spread out on my bed, naked. Completely at my mercy. Wanting to do anything I want simply because I want it. Desperate for my command. Feeling the pleasure I want you to feel. So turned on I bet I could make you come just by talking about it."

"Oh god," I groaned. It was probably true.

"Jude, touch the tip of your dick. I can see from here how you're dripping for me. Spread that slickness around. And don't come."

It felt like moving through molasses. The instant my finger touched my tip I shuddered all over. I ran my finger through the precome and circled my tip so slowly I almost wasn't moving at all. I held my breath until Faron said I could stop.

"Jude. Do you like to be fucked?"

I moaned and gasped and almost choked.

"I...I...sometimes...I..."

My head was a wreck and I couldn't even make words.

"Jude, do you think you'd like me to fuck you?" he specified.

"Yes, fuck, yes, please, fuck."

"Roll onto your back."

I moved slowly, every muscle tense.

Faron put down his paintbrush and approached the bed. His erection pressed against his loose pants and I could see a wet spot where he was leaking for me. I groaned at the thought of him hard and painting me, in perfect control while I almost lost it in his bed.

He reached into the bedside table and brought out a tube of lube.

"Give me your fingers."

I held out my fingers and he squeezed lube onto them.

"Slick yourself up for me."

His eyes burned into mine and the other command was clear: *Don't come.*

As I slid two fingers inside myself I watched him strip. He dropped his clothes on the floor in a pile and his hard cock sprang out, heavy and gorgeous. I groaned at the thought of it inside me and slid my fingers deeper.

Faron rolled on a condom and knelt between my legs.

"Let me see," he said. And the command to expose my hole to him, said in such a soft, gentle voice, did things to me I'd never imagined.

I held myself open and he bent forward slowly and kissed the inside of my thigh. I nearly screamed.

He leaned over me, slicked his fingers, and slid them in alongside mine. It was slick fullness and the almost filthy feeling of our fingers sliding together.

"Do you like doing what I tell you, Jude?" he asked, lips a breath from mine.

"Yeeeeeessss," I moaned, heart pounding.

He pulled his fingers out and pulled my wrist away, then he teased my hole with the head of his dick. I groaned at the feeling of him, poised just on the edge of being inside me. Opening me up. Owning me.

"I want to put this—" He nudged the tip against my hole. "Inside you, Jude." I whimpered and tried to move my hips to get him to breach me. "I want to move inside you until you come screaming on my dick."

I writhed on the bed, so desperate I couldn't do anything but nod.

"Tell me you want it, Jude. Tell me you want me to fuck you open and make you scream."

"Yesyesyesyesyes."

Faron slid inside me so slowly I felt like I was being torn apart. I squirmed and thrashed because he felt overwhelming and the pressure was so intense, but also it felt like finally, finally, every touch was coalescing into the inevitable fullness that was taking over my whole body.

When he was fully inside me, my muscles spasmed and then relaxed and I blinked owlishly up at him.

"Perfect," he murmured, eyelashes fluttering. He leaned in close and smelled my hair, then the skin of my neck. He licked delicately at my lips, like he wanted to see if they tasted different than my tongue. He was savoring me with every single sense.

He held my hips still as he slid in and out of me, so that all I felt was that amazing friction and fullness. We both watched as my cock bobbed between us with every thrust, ruddy and swollen and streaming.

Then Faron took my ass in his hands and changed the angle and he buried himself inside me in a powerful thrust that dragged the tip of his cock over my prostate and I screamed, the pleasure boiling through my belly and groin and thighs and spreading through my ass like something dark and sweet that I was instantly addicted to.

After that moment I lost control of my body in space, and all I knew were Faron's hands on my skin and Faron's cock inside me. He was sweating and I was shaking, and as he started to groan, I felt something happen to me. I felt like I was shaking apart, relaxing instead of tensing as I had been. And as my muscles let go, gave out, I felt a tidal wave of pleasure pulse through me, from my balls to my ass to my gut. I screamed out my pleasure but it went on and on until I was shaking and weak, the last of my come dribbling out of my cock with another thrust and another.

I shook and shuddered as Faron thrust again and again, my pleasure centers confused into feeling like I was coming all over again, a long pulse of pleasure deep inside me that left me wrecked.

Then Faron buried himself deep in my ass and groaned like his heart was breaking. I felt him swell and then thrust wildly as he came. He buried his face in my neck and his hair tickled my face. Finally his hips stuttered and stilled, and he collapsed on top of me, breathing wetly against my neck.

I couldn't stop shaking and he wrapped his arms around me tightly.

"Jude," he murmured against my jaw. "Jude." He kissed me and I clung to him. He kissed me deeply at first, and then eased off into lazy, appreciative kisses. I hissed as he pulled out of me and he stroked my hole gently with his thumb to soothe me.

He pulled away to throw the condom in the trash, and the second he wasn't touching me anymore, darkness crashed over me. I squeezed my eyes shut tight and tried to calm back down again, but the sudden sadness was so overwhelming it almost felt separate from me. I rolled onto my side with my back to Faron.

"Hey, what's wrong?" His hand slid up my spine and curled over my shoulder. I shook my head and he pulled at my shoulder, trying to see my face.

"That was the best sex I've ever had," I said.

Faron pressed a kiss to my shoulder and lay down behind me, so I could feel his warmth and solidity all along my back. It helped a little.

"I'm honored," he said. I didn't know how the hell he could manage to sound so damned sincere all the time.

"I mean, by a factor of like…fuck, I don't know how factors work, but just by a lot, okay."

"Okay." He kissed my neck.

"I've never really…I haven't…I, ugh."

Faron slid his arm around me and hugged me tight to his chest.

"You asked if I liked to get fucked?" He kissed the back of my neck. "I have sometimes. A little. Or, I do like it, but it hasn't gone well." I felt him tense against me. "I have trouble sometimes. I…" I could feel the flush at my neck and my ears. "My medication. Sometimes I can't…g-get hard." I shook my head like I could banish the memories.

This kiss was to the skin behind my ear and I could feel how gentle Faron was being. How he wanted to soothe me. He spoke so eloquently with his body that he didn't need to say anything.

"Kaspar, my ex? He wouldn't, uh. He hated it when I didn't get hard because he felt like I wasn't into it. Wasn't into him. Even when I said I wanted it anyway, he didn't want to fuck me. Or he wanted me to take a pill, but…"

I shook my head. I'd hated the drawn-out, almost numb pleasure Viagra provided, and I'd worried about taking anything, convinced the slightest change to my chemical cocktail would send me spiraling.

"I tried to adjust my medication. Tried to figure out a lower dosage that wouldn't have that side effect, but—"

Faron made a sound and squeezed me to him, burying his face in my hair.

"It never worked. Not really. Sometimes it was no problem and sometimes I just…couldn't. But I still wanted to be intimate with him. It still felt good. But he…yeah, you get the idea."

"He was selfish and insecure," Faron said, voice tighter than I'd ever heard it. "And had a very uncreative idea of what sex can be."

I huffed out a laugh, because that was true. For all that Kaspar was a truly gifted violinist, his subtlety and creativity began and ended with his instrument.

Faron twined his fingers with mine and rested our hands on my chest.

"I guess I just wanted to tell you that in case it happens while we're—I mean, if we keep—you know."

"If you tell me that you want me, I'll believe you," he said. "There's a lot more to sex than dicks."

"Yeah." I scooted my butt back until I felt his crotch. "Incidentally, yours is pretty great."

Faron chuckled and readjusted his hips so his cock was nestled against my ass.

"Thanks, I'm fond of yours too," he murmured, and cuddled me closer. "Will you stay with me?"

The sun had set at some point, but I hadn't noticed. It couldn't be that late, but I was exhausted to my core.

"Yeah, please," I said. I wrapped his arm even tighter around my chest and tried to relax, concentrating on Faron's smell, and the heat of his body. His lips in my hair, and the expansion of his chest as he breathed.

It was the first time in almost a year that I'd fallen asleep with someone. And if I were honest with myself, the other people I'd shared a bed with? Not one of them had felt anything like this.

CHAPTER NINE

EVER SINCE MY conversation with Antonio, every free moment found me thinking about one of two things: Faron, and the decision that I would have to make about Boston. Faron had crawled inside me somehow. Curled up in a hollow spot next to my heart and made it beat for every little thing about him.

I'd been enamored before. Felt that hyperawareness of when someone enters a room, or when their eyes are on me. Been charmed by the way they said this word or how they ate that for lunch every day. I'd even been in love.

My feelings for Faron were nothing like any of that. In a way, it felt childish. An oddly uncomplicated joy buzzed in my stomach whenever I knew I was about to see him. When I was in his arms, I felt like the whole world disappeared. And yet he was the first person to make me think that maybe the world was a thing I might like to engage with.

But how long would he be interested in someone who had run away from his life? Who had turned heel on the one thing he was good at?

So I'd bought two tickets to the Philadelphia Orchestra, partly because I wanted to take Faron as a thank you for the piano, and partly because I couldn't stay away any longer.

I was early when I got to Faron's and he'd just gotten out of the shower. When he kissed me, his skin was hot from the water, and I considered telling him the performance had been canceled so we'd have no choice but to stay home, in bed.

"I wasn't sure how dressed up you'd be," he said, examining my gray trousers and black button-down at arm's length.

I'd thought about wearing a suit, but all my suits were for performance, and the idea of sitting in the audience dressed to be onstage...it felt unbearable.

"I don't really have many clothes right now," I muttered, a little embarrassed. "Some people dress up—suits, gowns. But some don't, especially younger people. You really don't have to dress up if you don't want to."

Since he looked like a model or a fashion designer in jeans and a T-shirt.

He gave me a sharp look. "I'm not even about to be the black guy at the symphony who didn't dress up."

"Sorry," I said. I hadn't thought of it like that. "You'll look amazing no matter what you wear."

He kissed my cheek and started flipping through clothes on the dressing rack. I wandered over to look at the easel, where the painting of me sat.

"Can I?"

He waved me on, distracted.

He'd painted me lying on my side, as I had been that day. My pale, freckled skin was like marble flecked with gold, glowing as if lit from within. My hair was fire. My eyes were fire. My mouth and my nipples and my firm cock were a glossy pink that looked almost obscene. I lay in a tangle of white sheets, but there was no bed, the sheets looking instead like a cloud or a crumpled piece of paper. And behind me was a blue so dark it was nearly black. I was on a soft raft, adrift in the maw of the cosmos. Gold lines cut through the blue-black, like an art deco frame, or a cage. My expression was caught halfway between fear and ecstasy.

"Holy shit," I exhaled. "Holy shit, Faron."

His smile was private and pleased.

"See," he said. "Look at how beautiful you are."

I wanted to hear all about the painting, but his words stopped me in my tracks. And then I got a look at him and I found myself saying "Holy shit" all over again.

He was wearing a longish plum cotton shirt with an asymmetrical hem, slim-cut, tailored black trousers that hit just above his ankles, white wing-tips, and a dark purple jacket that at first glance simply looked like a very well-fitting blazer, but when I looked closer was seamed with copper zippers so that the sleeves could zip off and it could be cropped.

"Jesus Christ," I muttered. "I need to go change." Not that I had anything to change into. "You look amazing."

Faron kissed me softly. "Thank you."

"Seriously, I…I feel really…I can't go with you like this. I look —" I shook my head and simply gestured to the world's most boring outfit that I was wearing. The truth of the matter was that I'd never cared much about clothes. I cared how they felt against my skin and that they didn't announce quite how skinny I was, and that was pretty much it. Kaspar had dragged me shopping, claiming that he didn't want to be seen with me in the same jeans and fraying sweaters, but I'd hated the scrutiny that came with it, and he'd been annoyed that I didn't like the things he picked out for me.

"Jude," Faron murmured, in that deep, soft voice that made goose bumps rise on my arms and reminded me of the commands that could come after he said my name that way. "I told you. You're beautiful." He kissed my cheek. "You don't express yourself through your fashion choices. That's fine."

I pressed my forehead against his shoulder and his hand immediately went to my hair.

"But, babe, your hair."

I pulled back and looked at him, my brain stuck on the fact that he'd just called me babe. I'd never heard him use anything but everyone's full names when he spoke to or about them.

"Can I please fix your hair?"

Dazed, I reached a hand up to my ponytail. It felt like it always did. I shrugged my assent.

He sat me down on the arm of the couch and grabbed something from the bathroom. I drifted at the feeling of his fingers in my hair.

"Is it always a mess?" I asked.

"Usually." I could hear the fond smile in his voice. "You run your hands through it when it's up, so it gets all bumpy and then you yank on pieces." He dropped a kiss on the top of my head. "It makes you look like a little boy."

"I'm old," I sighed.

"Okay."

"Older than you."

"That is a true fact."

When I'd found out that Faron was only twenty-seven, nine years younger than me, I'd immediately added it to the reasons-he-will-never-want-you list. He didn't seem to care in the slightest.

I sighed and forced myself to concentrate on the tugs and twists on my hair. When he finished, Faron steered me to the bathroom mirror.

I stared at myself. A French braid ran through the middle of my hair, leading back into a messy bun. But stylishly messy, not the kind of messy I apparently rocked all the time. It looked... awesome. I looked almost the way Faron had painted me. Ethereal.

"Wow."

Faron slid his arms around my chest from behind and kissed my neck. In the mirror, with only our shoulders and heads on display, we almost looked like we could go together. With my hair like this, my pale skin and freckles took on an air of drama that they didn't usually have.

Faron opened a small tin from the medicine cabinet and ran a gentle finger over my lips, leaving them soft and pink. I'd been chewing on my lower lip a lot lately, if the chappedness was anything to go by. He slid the tin into his pocket.

"Thank you," I said. He turned me to him and kissed me, our lips sliding together easily. "Sorry if my lips were gross."

His thumb stopped my mouth and he shook his head sternly.

"Not gross. I just thought it must hurt."

I shrugged. If it did, it was a pain so slight and inconsequential that it didn't even register.

———

THE LOBBY of the Kimmel Center was vast and echoey. Faron and I got glasses of wine in clear plastic cups and stood off to the side, people-watching. It was all so familiar.

"Since it's Friday night, there's an end-of-the-week buzz, and a lot of the men go right from work to dinner to here, so they're wearing suits they wore to work." I pointed at a group of older men. "Then you can tell the people who have subscription tickets because the men are always dressed to the nines, and the women wear dresses like that." I nodded toward a woman in her forties with a glamorous spangled silver gown cut low in the back. "It's not as fancy as in New York, but that group definitely wants to be seen. They all know each other and they always want gossip about behind-the-scenes stuff."

"What about...them?" Faron pointed to a cluster of men and women in their twenties, near the bar.

"Those are music students, for sure. They're wearing performance clothes because they're probably the fanciest things they have. All black, opaque tights, passable but comfortable shoes."

"Him?"

He indicated a large man, comfortably sporting an impeccable tuxedo, with a white scarf thrown around his neck and aggressively fashionable glasses.

"Opera singer."

Faron pointed to more people, clearly engaged in the game, and teased me when all I could find to say about one man was a dismissive "critic."

But I missed the next person he pointed to because someone familiar was coming toward me in the crowd. Shit.

Thomas Groen was a contemporary composer out of New York. He was brilliant and prolific, and seemed to have his fingers in every musical pie out there. He'd done the orchestration for rock albums, arranged Christmas carols for the Met's holiday ball, composed chamber music that had been performed all over the world, and had, I was pretty sure, debuted multiple operas in the last few years. I'd met him when the Boston Symphony Orchestra did a showcase of contemporary composers two years ago. I'd been hired for it and he'd come to conduct it himself. It'd had a lovely piano piece, and we'd hit it off.

"Jude Lucen? It is you. Hello!" He shook my hand enthusiastically, then kissed my cheek, seeming genuinely pleased to see me.

"Faron Locklear, Thomas Groen," I said. "Faron is an amazing painter and tattoo artist. Thomas is a composer. I was lucky enough to play one of his pieces a few years ago."

"I heard you left Boston," Thomas said. "Are you here now?" He said it casually, but I could spot gossipy speculation from fifty paces. The world of classical music was small. Someone leaving an orchestra position meant that position needed to be filled, and people kept an ear to the ground for themselves and their friends at all times. This gossip seemed a little below Thomas's pay grade though.

"My family's here," I said vaguely. "I'm...not sure what I'll be doing in the future. What are you doing slumming in Philly?" I asked before he could respond. He was a New York baby with all the ride or die snobbery that went with it.

He winked conspiratorially. "My opera is premiering here. Well, pre-premiering." He said it as if I didn't know exactly how it all worked.

"That's great, man. Congratulations." I was surprised to find that I didn't actually care enough to ask Thomas about the opera and I hoped I didn't sound as unenthusiastic as I felt.

Faron's hand skimmed my lower back and I leaned into him.

"We should go find our seats," I said. "It was nice to see you, Thomas. Good luck with the premiere."

As we went upstairs, I tried to remember what I'd liked about Thomas when I met him before, and all I could really pinpoint was the way he talked about the music. But then, I suppose that was all we'd really talked about.

"I remembered liking him more," I said.

Faron cupped the back of my neck and I shivered. "He seemed like a weasel."

I turned to him, surprised. It was the first unkind thing I'd ever heard him say.

"Really?"

"He wasn't interested in you, he only wanted to hear gossip about why you left Boston. He didn't ask anything about how you are. He only wanted to talk about his own work. He practically glared when you didn't ask him about his opera. And he didn't even make eye contact with me."

"Shit. I guess he is a weasel." And anyone who didn't want to make extended eye contact with Faron clearly had no taste whatsoever.

We took our seats and I was grateful we'd had the distraction of Thomas, because I hadn't gotten a chance to freak out yet. Which made me realize that Faron had been keeping me distracted in the lobby, asking me about person after person when he was usually perfectly content to stand quietly and watch.

Jesus, he was way too good for me.

"Oh, look," I said, pointing in the program. "The violin and flute soloists are twins. That's cute. Uh. I don't know why I said that. I mean, I pointed it out because you're a twin. But I don't know why I thought you might have some kind of mystical connection to the very concept of twinness or anything. And it's not cute. I...uh."

"Are you okay?" Faron asked, brow furrowed.

I nodded quickly, but I wasn't sure. The lights began to dim and Faron took my hand. It didn't feel like holding hands; it felt like he was keeping a part of me safe.

I was immediately grateful for it because when the musicians filed onstage I felt my heart start to race. It was such a dislocation, to be sitting here looking at the stage when so often I had been onstage looking at the house. Of course I'd attended hundreds of performances over the years too, but it was different to attend a performance while I was regularly performing. It felt like an extension of my job. I felt like an insider. Now I just felt lost.

The soloists walked onstage in unison, smiling broadly. They were thin, white women with curly brown hair pulled back into elaborate updos. Their sequined dresses were the same, but one was blue and the other was black. I wondered if they had been asked to dress alike as part of the twin gimmick. My eye snagged on something that it took me a minute to process. They lifted their instruments, and began to play one of Mozart's duets for flute and violin, originally written for two flutes.

"They're gonna switch instruments," I whispered to Faron.

"How do you know?"

I tapped my lips and winked, and he looked puzzled for a moment, then leaned in and kissed me. That hadn't been what I meant, but it was incredibly sweet.

The twins cut off playing with exaggerated, shocked looks at each other. Then, as I'd predicted, they switched instruments, gave nods any mime would be proud of, and played it again, this time with their proper instruments.

Faron turned to me, eyes wide.

"The one who started out playing the flute was wearing lipstick," I whispered, tapping my mouth again. He was giving me an unfamiliar look and his eyes danced.

I'm not much for pandering, but the audience was clearly charmed by the twins, and once the gimmick was over and the piece began, they played with complete professionalism, and clear skill. Hey, it's a tough business. I wasn't going to judge what people did to get a foot in the door.

I was fine until it was almost over. I closed my eyes and moved my ear from section to section, letting the strings be dominant, then brass, woodwinds, then percussion. The melodies settled into my skin and made my fingers twitch.

It was like the music was swirling around inside me with no way to get out. Would it just fade away if I didn't give it an exit? Or would it turn to lead inside me and press me farther down into the dark?

I missed it. I missed it so fucking much.

But how could I go back to Boston? How could I play with all the people Kaspar played with? Just the thought of his smarmy face made my stomach clench. Even if I told him not to speak to me, he'd still be there. Thinking he knew what was best for me. Worming his way inside my head like he had so many times before.

I know you think you're pissed at me, Jude. But honestly, you're not being fair. I love you! I take care of you! Do you seriously think there are many other people out there who would put up with all this? So just take a minute and think about whether you're really mad at me. Because I think maybe you're mad at yourself.

You don't want to talk to me but you don't want me to leave—I guess I can't do anything right, huh?

Look, can you try and be a little bit more up when we go to my parents'? I'd rather not get asked why I'm dating a zombie for the hundredth time. You know how my mother is.

Fix your face, Jude. Just smile at people when they're talking to you, it's not that difficult.

Honey, do you really think it's a good idea to accept that tour? It's a month long! What if you have your usual issues and I'm not there to take care of you? You don't want to embarrass yourself again if you can avoid it.

Well since you never want to fuck me, what do you expect, Jude?!

"Jude." Faron was squeezing my hand so hard my knuckles ground together and I realized that tears were streaming down my face and my breathing was all messed up. It felt like the ceiling of the concert hall was pressing down on top of me.

I scrambled out of my seat and climbed over Faron's legs and made a break for it, painfully aware of stern eyes following me up the aisle. I burst out of the doors and was halfway to the bathroom when Faron caught up with me.

I wanted to disappear. I wanted a black hole to open around me and tear me to nothingness. And I really, really didn't want the ushers to see me.

"Sorry," I said into Faron's chest. "Sorry, I'm sorry, I'm so sorry."

Faron rubbed my back, but didn't say anything, and I pulled away enough to see his face. He looked worried. I'd done that. I'd ruined his night out and made him worry about the pathetic little freak who couldn't even keep his shit together for a couple of hours out. He would never want to be with me now.

I could feel the last of my energy draining out of me. Sometimes my battery lasted all day, sometimes only an hour, but it always happened this way: I was there until I wasn't, with no warning in between.

"What do you need?" Faron asked finally.

I couldn't say anything, just pressed my face to his shoulder and hoped the energy would come back enough to answer him. Eventually.

"Baby?" His voice shook and I squeezed my eyes shut as tight as I could, like maybe I could will the words to come out, but there was nothing there. Maybe we would just stand here until the doors opened and the crowd flowed out around us. The thought of that filled me with panic and I pressed even closer to Faron.

Probably any minute he'd decide I was too much trouble, too pathetic, too disgusting. It made sense to try and absorb as much of the muscle memory of him as I could.

Then we were moving toward the front doors, Faron's arm around my waist. On Broad Street, he hailed a cab and ushered me inside. I stared out the window as we turned east. Then we were back at Faron's, and Waffle was barking hello and I was in bed. Faron left and then came back and then got in bed next to me. He must've taken my shoes off and undressed me to my underwear and T-shirt, but I had no memory of it.

"Is it okay for me to be in bed with you?" he asked, and tears leaked out of my eyes at the thought that he might not feel welcome in his own bed. That I had made him feel unwelcome with me.

Is it one of the nights you're going to banish me from my own bed, or am I allowed?

I reached for him and he slid closer to me. I did want him here, I just didn't want to have to say anything to keep him. I couldn't say anything.

"If you want me here, I'm here," he said. "If not, I'll just be on the couch, but I'm not going anywhere. Okay?"

Okay okay okay okay please please please.

I yearned toward him, trying to speak with my body the way

he did. Trying to communicate how much I wanted him at the molecular level, without expending energy I just didn't have.

"Okay," he said softly after a minute, and my heart started jamming against my chest at the thought he might be getting up. But he just settled against his pillow and took a book off the bedside table. He arranged himself so that he wasn't touching me, and began to read.

Thank you thank you thank you thank you thank god.

I fell asleep with tears on my cheeks and woke up when Faron turned out the bedside lamp. When I stirred, he froze.

"Sorry," I murmured in the darkness.

I leaned closer to him and he opened his arms for me. I curled up at his side.

"Don't be sorry," he said. "Don't ever be sorry for who you are."

CHAPTER TEN

THE NEXT MORNING, I woke feeling drained and fuzzy. My eyelashes were gummed together and I probably had the worst breath in history. Faron didn't wake up when I rolled out of bed and went to take a shower.

I had a text from Christopher from the night before: *Dude, remember Derrick Kayson? I told you he came in here last year and freaked when he realized I was your brother? I think he might for real have a boyfriend now...he came in this afternoon all cozy with this guy. Idk but I hope so!*

Then he'd sent a heart eyes emoji.

Derrick Kayson was the first guy I'd ever been with. I'd tuned out most things at school. I'd barely been getting by, and any energy I had went to piano. Besides, it was easier not to listen when the things people said to you were garbage.

But Derrick's desperation and fear had cut through. He was twice my size, and he'd made varsity football as a freshman. He was handsome and confident and people at school adored him. He had everything going for him, which meant he felt like he had everything to lose.

We'd been lab partners junior year and he'd looked at me like he was starving. Touched me like I would disappear at any moment. And I? I'd wanted to feel something. Anything.

I wrote back: *Derrick Kayson was actually a pretty sweet guy if you can get over the whole football thing. And the whole ashamed that he wanted to fuck me thing. Secrets suck. I hope he's happy now.*

When I got out of the shower, Faron was still asleep and I padded over to the bed to look at him. The morning sun fell over him like a benediction. Like an acknowledgment that he deserved the spotlight. Against the soft white sheets, his shoulders looked so strong and his skin looked luminous. His bleached curls were a halo around his face, and his arm was still outflung, like even in sleep he was making space for me.

I slid back under the sheets and curled into the place he'd left me.

He jerked awake immediately.

"Oh, shit, sorry." My wet hair on his bare arm must've been shocking. Once he realized what it was, though, he grabbed me and pulled me down next to him, arms locked tight around me and chin on my shoulder. I breathed in the smell of him and he held me closer. I could feel his morning wood against my ass so I pressed my hips backward and felt him harden even more.

I turned and slid down Faron's body, pushing the sheets and his boxer briefs aside, and took his gorgeous erection in my mouth. This, at least, was something I could do.

He was saying something but I wasn't listening, until I felt a jerk on my hair and he was rolling away from me and I realized what he'd been saying was "Stop."

"I— What's wrong?" I asked, on my hands and knees.

"You don't have to...service me," he said. His erection was gone and he looked really upset. Shame washed over me. He didn't want me. I was making a fool of myself.

"I wasn't. I just thought..." I shrugged and turned away to sit at the edge of the bed.

Faron sat beside me.

"You thought you owed me something because you feel bad about last night."

That...wasn't exactly wrong. It always made Kaspar forgive me for fucking stuff up. After he had come down my throat, he'd put his hand on my head and smile like everything was fine again.

"Please don't," Faron said, voice tight. "It's insulting."

"I just wanted to make you feel good." As I said it I realized it was true too. I was desperate to make Faron feel good because he made me feel better than I ever had. But part of that desperation was rooted in fear. In trying to prevent him from being mad at me. Disgusted by me. I cringed. "I'm sorry."

I felt like utter trash.

He sighed and took my hand in his. "Thank you for wanting to make me feel good. I would love that, another time. Let's talk now."

I nodded but couldn't meet his eyes. No matter how understanding he'd been last night, how much he'd seemed to care, in the harsh light of day, there was no way that I wasn't looking like a pretty bad bet right now.

"What happened last night?"

"It just happens sometimes. I can't...I just run out of energy and I can't talk any more. I thought I had told you."

"You did. I meant what happened in the concert."

I flopped onto my back on the bed and threw my arm over my eyes.

"Antonio, my conductor in Boston, called. At Marcus and Selene's. He said if I wanted to come back, he would hire me. I had thought...I was sure I was done. There, anyway. You don't run away and miss performances and get to come back. But now?"

I took a deep breath and blew it out.

"Last night, I was imagining what it's like. The heat of the stage lights. The moment when the conductor raises his hands and everything falls silent just before the first note."

I opened my eyes to find Faron's intent on me.

"I miss playing so fucking much," I choked out. "It's everything to me. The music...I love it so much. And it isn't easy to get hired. It's competitive and cliquey. But...Boston..." I shook my head. "And Kaspar's there. All my friends there are his friends. I just started thinking about what it was like and I... I..." I felt completely hopeless. "I guess I freaked." I threw my arm back over my eyes.

I felt Faron soften. Felt the energy between us change. He sat next to me and put a slow hand to my stomach. When I didn't pull away, he started stroking me. Not to arouse, but to soothe. He stroked my stomach and along my ribs, then he took my hand.

"Will you tell me about Kaspar?"

I didn't even like to hear his name come out of Faron's mouth.

"What do you want to know?"

"I want to know what he did to make you think that you don't deserve anything good."

His voice was gentle but my eyes flew open. He was looking straight at me and he still had hold of my hand.

I opened my mouth and nothing came out. But this wasn't me not being able to speak. This was me not being able to say these things out loud.

I motioned for him to pass me the sketchbook on the bedside table. I wrote some of the things Kaspar had said that'd been running through my head last night. I wrote lightly in pencil so I could erase them. I didn't want those words in Faron's sketchbook. I passed him the book and turned my back so I didn't have to see him react.

"This is not okay," he said finally.

"I know."

"This is not okay, Jude," he said, voice strained and furious.

I scrambled out of bed, shame boiling through my stomach. I couldn't believe I'd told him.

"I know that!" I yelled. "Don't you think I already feel like an idiot for letting him talk to me that way? Don't you think I know how pathetic it is that I was so desperate for someone to love me that I stayed with him? I already know!"

Faron was on his feet but I held out a hand to keep him away.

"I know that he's an asshole and I know that he was manipulating me!"

"But you clearly believe him."

"Or what? Or else I would have left?"

"Yes!"

"I did! I tried to leave! And I fucked that up too."

Faron's eyes went wide and I slammed my mouth shut so hard my teeth clacked together. I shook my head.

"That's not— I didn't mean. I mean, I did, but not..." I turned away, cursing myself.

Faron turned me around to face him and his eyes were blazing. I wished he would hit me. I wished he would do something.

He picked up each of my hands and looked at my wrists. He pulled my shirt this way and that, then knelt to do the same with the sweats I'd borrowed from him, searching for scars he wouldn't find.

His movements were jerky, afraid. For the first time, his grace was gone, his eyes wild. And seeing him like that shocked me out of my anger.

"Sweetheart," I said. I put a hand on his shoulder and pushed his hair back with the other. It was tumbling around his face. "I didn't— I took pills. I'm okay now. I'm sorry. I guess I thought you knew. I thought my brother would've told Ginger and Ginger would've...shit."

Faron pressed his face to my belly and wrapped his arms around me tight. I stroked his hair, hoping it might calm him down like it did me.

It was the first moment I considered that maybe Faron might need me. Just a little.

"I'm sorry," I murmured. Then I said it again, and this time I wasn't saying it to him. I was saying it to Christopher and my mom and my dad. Hell, even to Kaspar, who found me. I was saying it to them here and now because I'd never said it to them in real life. Not because I didn't mean it, but because apologizing would have meant acknowledging that it had happened at all. And I hadn't been able to bear seeing their faces.

Christopher knew because he's the one Kaspar had called. If for nothing else, I was grateful to Kaspar for that. But Christopher never said he had told our parents. They must have known, even if I hadn't come right out and said it. They knew about the hospital. They knew I'd left Boston like it was on fire. They knew I'd had to rejigger my meds all over again. But I'd never said it.

Faron stood up and ran his fingers over my face, but he looked shaken and his movements were still jerky. He went to the kitchen and put on the kettle and I took the rather awkward opportunity to rummage in the pocket of last night's pants for my medication. When Faron clunked a mug loudly onto the counter I looked up. He raised his hands.

"I'm not trying to be mad," he said. "But I guess I am."

I nodded and slid onto one of the stools.

"My meds were all messed up," I said. "I was in a really bad place and we were in the middle of performances and I was stressed about time so I didn't go to my doctor. It just...it got worse and worse and it got away from me. And I'm doing a lot better now."

It was an almost absurd way to summarize a year-long process of sinking that happened so slowly the ooze was up to my waist before I knew I was mired in it. But there was no narrative to these things, no logic or explanation. No code or symbology. I wished there were. The formlessness was its own kind of death.

He looked at me for a while then said, "That's part of what scares you about going back to playing in Boston."

I nodded.

"The schedule is hard for me. I do better when I have a little consistency. When I'm performing at night, I sleep half the day; when I do accompaniment I have to get up earlier; if I'm traveling for a performance, all bets are off. I take my meds in the morning so they don't mess up my sleep, but when our schedule's not consistent it's hard. Traveling's...really hard. When I'm with people, living out of hotel rooms, no privacy, no real chance to recharge away from everyone before going back to it the next day. When I'm by myself it's...so easy to lose the thread. To just hide."

"But you love the music."

"I love it so much." I smiled at him sadly. "I don't mean to sound all tragic about it. It just feels a little bit like torture that the thing I love to do is all caught up in a bunch of shit that makes me feel awful. At least it is since Kaspar."

Faron sighed and reached a hand across the counter, palm up. I slid my hand into his and watched as he brought my knuckles to his lips so slowly I almost convinced myself we'd stay that way forever.

"I know what you mean," he said, lips against my hand.

"Yeah?"

He poured the tea and we took our cups to the couch and Waffle immediately put her paws on Faron's leg. Usually Faron didn't let her on the couch, but he just sighed and Waffle shambled up and collapsed on Faron's legs, tail thumping against the back of the couch like a mallet.

"You know Marcus and I, we've known each other for a long time. I apprenticed at the shop he was tattooing at in New York."

"I didn't know."

"Yeah, since I was eighteen or so. I was doing tattooing as a night job and going to art school during the day. My parents hadn't been keen on art school because they said I could never make a living at painting. They wanted me to go to a four-year school, get a degree in something practical. Have a normal job. But I got a scholarship and I went and I loved it. All I wanted to do was paint."

I nodded. I knew the feeling.

"My mentor at school was connected and he always invited gallery owners and agents to the senior showcase. He talked me up to one of the gallery owners who he thought would be into my stuff. The guy loved my work and asked to see more. Before I knew it, I had three pieces in a gallery in Manhattan. It was utterly unreal."

"Holy shit, that's incredible."

"Yeah. I was done with school so I had more time to paint, and I had enough money coming in from tattooing to pay rent, so when I sold those paintings I could use the money to buy more supplies. It was perfect. I thought if I could keep doing that, keep getting a couple paintings in at this gallery or that one, I'd be flying."

He began stroking Waffle's fur absently and Waffle snuffled happily.

"My parents weren't particularly impressed with the tattooing. But I was making enough to support myself and not getting in any trouble, so they didn't give me too much shit for it. That was when Sabien had re-upped with the army, too, so they were busy worrying about him."

There was a catch in his voice whenever he said his brother's name.

"But when I got two more paintings in a show, they were... they cared. They were impressed. They'd never been that impressed by me. They loved me, I know that. But Sabien and I were so much younger. They had their own lives, their other kids were adults. Sabien was always a handful. Me? They mostly let me alone. I'd always taken care of myself."

Faron bit his lip and when he looked at me, he looked raw.

"I wanted that. For them to be proud of me. At the opening of the show, this agent approached me. Said he knew Baynard—my teacher. I called Baynard and he confirmed it. Said I should sign with him. I didn't know anything about it, really. But I asked around. Some people told cautionary tales, but everyone said this guy was legit."

"And you wanted your parents to be even more impressed," I said, tangling my feet with his. He nodded.

"When I told them I got an agent, they were over the moon. Francis Alouette. Even his name sounded fancy. It meant something to them, that mark of professionalism. Validity. Made them think maybe I wasn't just living this silly fantasy where I would be the next Kehinde Wiley. Francis listened to what I wanted to do with my work. The things that mattered to me. And he was black—he knew the difficulties of navigating a pretty white world. At first, he was great. He made me feel comfortable. He facilitated connections with gallery owners, got me spots in shows I couldn't have gotten myself, helped me apply for grants."

"That's amazing," I said, even though clearly the story didn't end well.

"I think that's why it was so hard to see where things went off the rails. Because I trusted him. I thought he was my friend."

My stomach clenched at the thought of anyone betraying Faron's friendship.

"Over the next year or so, I started selling more paintings, and getting more spots, and then this gallery owner—the one who'd first shown my stuff when I was finishing school. He gave me a solo show. It's a big deal. I was over the moon. Francis got art critics from the Times and New York Mag to come. He sent a car to pick my parents up in Brooklyn and bring them to the gallery."

He had a faraway look on his face remembering it, then shook his head.

"It went really well, and after that things just...changed.

Francis was fielding all these calls about my work, but he wasn't keeping me in the loop. He accepted a commission on my behalf for a lot of money without even discussing it with me. I'd never done a commission before, but he said he assumed I'd want to because of the money. He booked another solo show and another off the back of that one, and I had to paint so fast to meet the deadlines for the shows that I hardly had time to tattoo, so I was canceling work shifts, which screwed over my coworkers."

"Oh no," I murmured. If there was anything Faron hated, it was behaving in ways he considered unethical or dishonorable.

"I talked to him really seriously though. Told him he couldn't keep doing shit without telling me. Couldn't book shows so close together. He apologized, agreed he'd slow things down, talk everything through with me first. It seemed like he understood. And he kept his word, for a while."

Faron's hand tightened on Waffle's fur.

"But then one night, I went to the opening of a show for a painter I admired. Had admired for a long time. And when I went to go introduce myself, Derrell wouldn't even shake my hand. I was…shocked. But I think I knew before he even said anything that it had to do with Francis."

Faron wiped his palms on his shirt and winced.

"It makes me sick even thinking about it," he said. "Derrell finally took me aside when it became clear I really didn't know what his beef was. Explained that the last solo show I'd had. The one that Francis had seemed to scrounge up out of nowhere. It was supposed to have been his. Francis had somehow convinced the owner of this gallery I was a better bet."

Faron looked sick and furious.

"I still don't know what he said and I don't care. I was mortified. Furious. Totally gutted. Derrell was an artist I'd admired for years. And he was a brother. I…I couldn't believe that Francis had stolen this from him. Had screwed over another black artist on my behalf. I…fuck, I cried. Derrell told me and I cried and I begged him to believe that I would never have let that happen if I'd known. Jesus."

He pushed back his hair with a shaking hand.

"Derrell told me he believed me, but he gave me this pitying look. Said that success in this business was a snake pit. He said Francis might've fucked him over—messed with me. But Francis wasn't an outlier. That was the way the business went. If you wanted to succeed you had to take and take and take everything, or someone would take it from you. There was no room for ethics or good intentions. It was money and politics all the way down."

Faron shrugged and I could see the same disillusionment in his face that I'd seen so many musicians go through when they realized the orchestra could be as cutthroat and backstabbing as any boardroom coup or political race.

"I don't know anymore if that's true," he went on. "But at the time, it sure as hell felt true. The next day, I met Francis for a drink, ready to ask him his side of things. Hoping he had something—anything—to say that would make me understand. And before I could ask him, he pulled out his phone and showed me an invitation to show a piece in the Pretext exhibition. The show he'd stolen from Derrell had been because he knew folks from this one would see it. It hadn't been a horrible mistake, or even careless greed. It had been a calculated move that he thought I'd thank him for."

"Jesus, he didn't know you at all."

"Yeah. I fired him. Didn't even stick around to see his expression. Just said 'We're done now' and peaced the hell out."

"Good. Fuck him."

He nodded, but bit his lip. "My parents said I was a fool to fire him. To throw away everything I'd worked for."

"Oh no."

"When I told them I was leaving, that I was coming to Philly? Oh man, they thought I had blown it. 'Who gets a chance to make money at painting and throws it away?' my mom said. I didn't tell them the details. I was too...ashamed."

He shook his head, expression bitter.

"I haven't been to see them since I left. I was the twin they didn't have to worry about and they thought I'd gone and screwed it all up."

Waffle had been wriggling ever closer to the edge of the couch in her sleep, and now she awoke on the precipice, legs flailing and tail wagging, before falling to the ground.

Faron and I both burst into laughter as Waffle slunk away.

"Do you regret leaving?" I asked when our laughter turned to giggles. "Leaving the art world, I mean."

He was quiet for a while, then shook his head.

"No. I had to leave that version of it or I would've hated myself. It was easy to get caught up in everything that wasn't the painting because the idea that I could make a living was so wild. The process of turning painting into a profession ended up making me feel less connected to the art. When I had Francis in my ear, telling me who he was going to compare me to for this press release, or asking me what three words summed up my work for an interview, I started thinking about my own work that way. As I was painting. I started rejecting ideas because they didn't fit with the concept of a show I already had in mind, or changing a piece to make it fit. "

He got up and walked to his easel and I followed him.

"I'm not saying I believe there's no way to have integrity and also be successful. I'm sure there is. But it made me feel...unworthy, I guess."

"Of the attention?"

"No. Of the art."

I slid my arm around his waist as we stood in front of the painting of me. Again, I was struck by his talent. Hell, he'd have to be a genius to make me think a painting of myself was beautiful.

"But now I'm painting again," he said softly. "And I love it again. Truth, I don't know what will happen in the future. But it's not for Francis and it's not for anyone to see. Yet. And I feel worthy of doing it again, because I'm doing it out of love."

His arm tightened around my shoulders.

"Amateur," I said. "From amare. For the love of the thing."

"Yeah, that too."

CHAPTER ELEVEN

THE PIANO WAS STARTING to come together and Faron had begun painting like a man possessed. One morning I woke to find he'd already been at it for hours and he said that ever since he'd told me the story about Francis he'd been thinking about everything differently. He seemed to be right on the edge of piecing the puzzle together, but I was no closer to figuring things out.

My piano lessons had taken on an air of looming threat, and no matter how grateful I was to have something to pay the bills, I trudged to each one like I was going to a dental appointment.

Christopher had taken a very Christopher approach when I'd filled him in. He'd grabbed a piece of paper and had me list all the pros and cons of going back to Boston, then rank them. Unfortunately, deciding not to go back to Boston still meant I had no idea what to do instead.

Maggie had great ideas for dramatic career changes that were still music-adjacent when I chatted her to ask.

Jude: *You're the younger generation that will save us. Tell me all the jobs that you can think of that have to do with music/piano.*

Maggie: *hmm ok. music lessons, conductor, orchestra teacher at a high school (cringe please dont do this it screams desperation and regret), ooh accompanist for those fancy shows like maybe in vegas where the gorgeous ladies end up singing while lying on yr piano? please! please do that and invite me to meet the singers plzzzz*

Maggie: *jingle composer for like cereal and batteries and shit, OOOOH COMPOSER FOR FILM SCORES!!!*

Maggie: *ummm house band for shows like the voice or that late night white dude my dad watches. music therapist, studio musician, playing on gaygay cruises, playing piano at fancy department stores/hotels/restaurants. church organist? (is the organ the same as the piano?) omg, if so: playing the organ at movie theaters with silent movies at halloween, or anytime they show silent movies.*

Maggie: *i feel like google must have some kind of thing you could do, like compose the music for their doodles or w/e? they'd probably pay you like 20k for a 30 second doodle song.*

Maggie: *to sum up, clear best choices are: letting ladies lie on yr piano, composing film scores, playing organ with movies at halloween.*

I had to hand it to her, it was a pretty great list. I'd played on a film score with a few other musicians once for the extra cash. It had been pretty fun. They'd projected the movie onto the screen and we'd timed our playing to the action on screen. Composing would be something else entirely, of course, and that wasn't really in my lane.

There's a myth about musicians, that all of us secretly write music and are just waiting for our big break to take our place among the ranks of the greats. Some do, of course. But most of the musicians I'd met whose goal was to perform played because we loved to interpret music, not because we wanted to write our own.

Maybe Vegas was the way to go after all.

———

KIRA MCMASTERSON WALKED me out after my lesson with Nate, so that she could have a word. "What would you think about adding a third lesson a week for Nate?" she asked. "He seems to be improving and we thought maybe if he continued to improve, by the time he's in high school he could really do something with his music."

Kira clasped her hands together nervously. Clearly this was something she and Bart had discussed.

I sighed. I took no pleasure in breaking it to someone that their kid wasn't going to be a musical genius. It galled, though, that a parent could be so oblivious to the reality of what their own child wanted.

"Kira, have you asked Nate how he feels about adding a third lesson a week?"

"No. I thought I'd ask you first."

"Okay. Listen, I think that studying an instrument is always valuable. It's great for coordination, for rhythm, for discipline, for mental exercise. So, if Nate wants to add a third lesson, I'd be happy to do that. But let me be honest with you. Nate doesn't enjoy the piano. He's not going to want to practice more. He's not going to want to continue with it."

"Has he been rude to you?" Kira asked, immediately on guard.

"No, nothing like that. He just doesn't like it. He doesn't love the music. He'd rather be doing other things."

Her jaw was set with the kind of stubbornness that meant she didn't want to integrate this new information into what she'd already decided was true.

"Why do you want him to play?" I asked.

She had the grace to look sheepish. "My parents never had the money for lessons when I was younger, so I never learned how to play. I want Nate to have better than I did."

I looked at her with new eyes and now I could view her brittleness through a different lens.

"I totally understand that. Look, talk to Nate. Tell him there's no pressure. Maybe he'd like it more if he didn't think he was working toward some nebulous goal. Let me know."

She nodded and closed the door without further comment. For a moment, I felt satisfied that I'd been honest and that I'd gotten a new perspective on someone. Then I realized I might have just talked myself out of a quarter of my income. *Great work, Jude.*

I wandered aimlessly for a while and ended up near Small Change. It was busy in that way it always seemed to be busy, with people waiting and people tattooing. I liked the idea that busyness meant something when you couldn't rush.

Lindsey, the shop manager, waved to me while she was helping a customer. Her teenage daughter Tara was sitting on a stool behind the desk thumbing her phone intently and didn't seem to notice anything that was going on around her.

The second I walked past her, she said, "Hey, Jude," without looking up.

"Hey," I said. "How are you?"

"The world keeps on turning," she said flatly, eyes still on her phone. "At least, that's what they tell us."

"I see."

She looked up at me suddenly and grinned. Then she went back to her phone and I felt very, very old.

"Hey, bro," Ginger said. She was sketching a skull and flowers and a pomegranate from some photographs at her station. "Is it still cool if I call you bro? I figure I'll check in about it every six months or so."

Secretly I was starting to like that she called me bro because it was an acknowledgment that we were both something more and something less than simply friends.

"It's fine."

"Great. What're you up to?"

"Oh, just slashing my already meager weekly earnings by twenty-five percent. All in a day's work."

"Uh oh. Who'd you piss off with an inconvenient truth?"

"You know me too well." She winked. "One of my students'

moms. I didn't piss her off, but I told her that her kid doesn't actually like the piano, thereby crushing her dream of his virtuosity, and told her to ask him if he even still wants lessons. He'll take the out in a hot second because he hates it."

"You did the right thing, though, obviously."

"Yeah. Sadly, thousands of years of human history have demonstrated that doing the right thing does not pay the rent. Alas."

She looked up from her drawing. Ginger made me very aware of myself. She seemed to notice the things I did to seem natural and recognize them for the choices they were. It was unsettling but refreshing. And it made me think that if I ever spent more time with her, maybe we really would be friends.

"You hate giving piano lessons anyway. Sounds like a calculated move."

She was probably right about that.

"Yeah. Well, I don't know what the fuck I'm doing with my life, so."

"I heard. Christopher said he went with a pros and cons list. It's a little bit charming."

Christopher had never lacked for good intentions or charm, it was true.

But Ginger continued, "It's a little bit charming that he thinks the problem is choosing yes or no about something instead of feeling like there are infinity other paths you could pick instead. Or that there's no choice."

"Uh. Yeah. My friend Maggie suggested playing in Vegas with women who sing while lying on top of my piano."

"Yeah, that seems super feasible. I hear you can live for years by creeping from hotel to hotel and never having to actually set foot outside. So there's that. Also...buffets are kinda great. Like, when else do you get to eat mashed potatoes, cereal, lo mein, a bunch of bacon, and slices of Swiss cheese for dinner?"

"I feel confident Christopher would make you that for dinner any time you wanted."

"Holy shit. Holy shit, you're right." She grabbed her phone and sent a text, then grinned up at me. "Thanks for the best future dinner ever."

I laughed.

"Okay, listen I'm gonna say something and you probably won't want to but I think you should anyway."

"You are truly a gifted salesperson."

"I think you should come hang out with me and Daniel tonight. Faron's working, so you can't be with him anyway," she added, and I felt my ears heat. "He's said nothing, I know nothing, except obviously I know everything. Point is, Daniel's the best, I'm basically great, and you clearly need a night."

"A night."

"You know, a night. A night where you drink with people you don't know very well but who share a certain intimacy with you and in the sudden change of social scenery you unburden yourself and realize all sorts of possibilities for your life and solutions to your problems that had previously dwelt in the murky darkness of uncertainty, and then you're best friends forever."

"Ah, a night. Well, I can't drink much with my medication, but I guess I could hang out for a bit..."

"Great. We'll do the drinking, you do the unburdening. Meet us at Tattooed Mom at like nine?"

"Fine."

"Jude. Seriously, come."

"Okay. Okay, I'll see you there."

When she smiled it felt like she was telling me I'd made a really good decision. It made me feel warm all over.

Faron had been with a client in the back room, and he came out and did a double take when he saw me. Then his eyes got soft and a slow smile spread over his lips and I realized why Ginger said she knew everything.

"Hi, Jude," he said. And somehow hearing him say my name still hit me just as hard in the gut as it always had, even though we'd been spending a lot of time together.

"Hi."

He finished up with his client and then tugged me into the back room. He ran his knuckles over my face and then hugged me tight. There was a need in his hug that I didn't usually feel.

"You okay?" I asked. He nodded against my hair. "You sure? You seem...not okay."

He kissed me softly. "I'm okay, just a little frustrated."

"What's up?"

"I got an email from Sabien this morning. He was quizzing me on how Mom and Dad were. I wrote back and said I thought they were fine and I talked to Mom the other day. That he should ask Mo, since she saw them the most often. But he hasn't written back. It always takes him forever."

"That sucks. Do you think there's a problem, or is that just how he talks?" I rubbed his back and rubbed his scalp with my fingers.

"You're gonna make me all frizzy," he murmured, but he finally seemed relaxed.

"Okay," I murmured.

"It's how he talks. I know I have to wait until he writes back. It's just frustrating."

"Sorry you have to work tonight when you're frustrated."

"It'll be good to have something to focus on. Do you want to go hang out at my place even though I won't be there?"

I'd confessed to Faron that even though I was intensely glad to have my own space that wasn't my childhood bedroom, now that I'd seen how homey his place felt, being at Christopher's old apartment, with its bare walls and no light, was kind of a bummer.

"Actually I just got roped into going out with Ginger and Daniel."

Faron chuckled. "Good."

I shrugged.

"I like Daniel. I can see you guys as friends."

"Yeah? Okay."

"Hey. Don't drink on an empty stomach."

A warm feeling flushed up from my belly the way it did anytime Faron said these caring, slightly bossy things to me. At first I'd tried to tell myself I didn't like it. I didn't like it because when other people had tried to tell me what to do it had always seemed patronizing or untrusting. But somehow when Faron said them, I did like it. I liked it a lot. I liked the way I liked when he said my name in that low, soft voice and then told me where to touch myself.

It felt like we were a team.

I nodded and wrapped my arms around him again. How was it possible that I was already anticipating missing him tonight?

———

THE SECOND I stepped inside Tattooed Mom I could see why Ginger liked it. Not to my taste, but definitely to hers. It was dark and the walls were even more packed with stuff than the walls at Small Change, from velvet Divine posters to signed flyers for bands I'd never heard of. Dioramas with huge plastic dinosaurs and altars to toys I vaguely remembered from the eighties occupied every window and the bulbs in many of the lights were red, casting the whole place in hellish light.

A hand snaked out and grabbed my sleeve as I walked past, and I turned to find Ginger and Daniel in a circular booth in an alcove I hadn't even noticed.

"Jude!" Ginger crowed, and Daniel waved. They already had cocktails and there was a litter of candy wrappers on the table, along with some broken crayons, scraps of construction paper, and several plastic rings with spiders on them.

I slid in and found the little booth was actually pretty insulated from the din of the bar around us.

"Ugh, you smell good," Ginger said as I sat down, and it took me a moment to remember she liked the smell of smoke.

"Thanks for inviting me," I said.

"So, Daniel and I are not gonna be polite because we're way past that in our friendship," Ginger said, and Daniel nodded. "Which means even though we don't know you that well, you should just go ahead and skip it, okay?"

"Lovely. Invitation accepted."

"Okay how much can you drink without fucking up your medication?"

"It depends. Too much just makes me feel...worse for a day or two sometimes. Two or three?"

"Well who wants to feel worse? Okay, should we cut you off at three, or keep our mouths shut?"

Ginger often sounded flippant, but if I ignored her tone, she always seemed to mean what she said.

"Cut me off. Thanks."

They both nodded and Ginger yelled, "Turner!"

A tall white woman with light brown hair held back with a bandanna appeared. "You know I love it when you scream my name."

"I know." Ginger smiled angelically. "This is my friend, Jude." She cupped a hand around her mouth like she was telling a secret, but spoke at full volume. "Christopher's brother."

"Oh, yeah, I totally see it. Hey, Jude. I'm Turner."

I took a page out of Daniel's book and waved.

"What can I get you?" she asked me. I ordered a gin and soda, and Daniel and Ginger ordered something called a pickletini which I already knew would make me vomit if I so much as tasted it.

"Can we order food too?"

"On it," Turner said, and tapped a waiter before going back behind the bar.

"Jude, important q. Daniel and I are about to order all their tots—like tater tot nachos kinda. Do you want in?"

"That's a hard no," I said. But then I remembered Faron telling me not to drink on an empty stomach and I ran through what I'd eaten so far, and asked, "Do they have plain tater tots?"

"Sure, they can just leave the stuff off."

Daniel and Ginger commenced an elaborately ritualized order and I asked for plain tater tots, baked in the oven instead of fried. The waiter wrinkled her nose at the idea.

"It'll take longer that way," she said. "And they're not that good plain."

"That's fine."

When the food came and Daniel and Ginger both reached for the same cheese-drenched tater tot at the same time, their fingers bumping like some swoony first-date couple's in a tub of popcorn, they both grinned.

"Thank fucking god you moved back," Ginger said. "How's Rex doing with being here?"

"He's okay so far," Daniel said thoughtfully. "He moved around a ton as a kid. So at first I was worried he'd feel like coming here cuz of my job was like his mom dragging him around all over again. But." He shrugged and got a tender look in his eyes.

"He feels like it's home because you're with him," Ginger supplied.

Daniel ducked his head and stuffed another tater tot in his mouth, but finally he nodded.

"He got in touch with Christopher's friends last week. I think he's gonna build in that bar for them. He said to say thanks to Christopher for him."

"Oh, perfect. I'll tell him. Those guys are decent. I mean, you know, they're bros opening a bar together so it's not like I'd wanna hang out with them. But they won't dick him over or anything."

"Do you want to hear something outrageous?" Daniel asked, eyes wide.

Ginger and I both nodded.

"He can build stairs. Stairs. Like okay, obviously, stairs get built, sure. But Rex can build them. In our place. Like, hey, want a staircase that goes from the floor to the ceiling for no reason? Rex could construct you one."

"Well now I obviously want one," Ginger grumbled. "What's he building stairs to?"

"I don't know, maybe nothing, but the point is that he can! Is this not...am I the only one who thinks that's amazing?"

"Well Jude's rebuilding a piano, so."

Daniel's eyes got even bigger. "Right, right. Amazing." He shook his head. "How is it...going? Hell, I don't even know what to ask about that. Do you have pictures?"

I dug out my phone and found a picture Faron had taken of me standing in a nimbus of piano pieces from when I first took it apart.

"Hooooly shit," Daniel said. "All that stuff's inside every piano?!"

I found myself charmed by Daniel. The combination of obvious intelligence and the willingness to admit complete ignorance about topics outside his purview wasn't one I'd come across much.

"Right? From the outside they just look like wooden boxes with keyboards stuck in the front," Ginger agreed.

I laughed. "They'd be a lot cheaper if that were true."

"How much are they? Like, the fancy, shiny ones that you'd play onstage?" Ginger asked.

"Give or take, probably somewhere between a hundred and fifty and two hundred thousand dollars."

Daniel almost sprayed his mouthful of pickletini and clapped a hand over his mouth. Ginger passed him a napkin.

We ordered another round and Ginger asked Daniel to tell her the plots of all the books he was teaching in one sentence, which seemed to be a longstanding game between them.

"So, Jude might smack me," Ginger said to Daniel. "But in the true spirit of jettisoning politeness, which is mostly just social sanctioning to avoid talking about the really important-slash-interesting shit, Jude needs our help."

Maybe it was the gin, or maybe it was how nice it felt to be out with people who actually made me feel welcome, but I didn't want to smack her. I just waved her on, and from the look on Daniel's face resistance would've been futile anyway.

"Do you want me to summarize?" Ginger asked me.

Daniel rolled his eyes and looked at me. "When I was in grad school teaching composition classes, one of the first assignments was to learn how to summarize a book or an article. Ginger wanted to do all the assignments along with the students."

"Until I realized a lot of them were boring," she interjected.

"Right. Until she stopped wanting to, which was at approximately assignment number three. But I gave her an A-minus on her summary and that set her on a course of believing she's an excellent summarizer ever since."

"I'm demonstrably an excellent summarizer, unless you think an A-minus isn't excellent."

But she winked at me, clearly giving me permission to summarize my own plight. Curious to see how she would explain it, given that I hadn't told her any details, I told her to go ahead.

"Kay, so. Jude was playing piano with the orchestra in Boston. He was dating this dude Kaspar, who also plays in the orchestra. Christopher clearly does not have the full story on this Kaspar guy, but I'd bet big money he's a first-rate creep."

I nodded.

"Jude just learned that maybe he could have his job back if he returned to Boston. He doesn't know if he wants to. Also he's totally sprung on our bud Faron, but I'm not supposed to know that. Except it's completely obvious and everyone knows it and Faron's crazy about him too but neither of them talk about it because it's all very soul mates serious connection next-level spiritual love shit going down."

I felt my neck and ears start to flush.

"Anyway, the q is: should he stay or should he go? And since he should obviously stay, what should he do with his life?" She turned to me, pickletini in hand. "How'd I do, bro?"

"Um. Pretty well."

"C-minus for non-objectivity in the summary," Daniel said sternly. "But A-plus for engaging gloss on the material."

Ginger blew him a kiss.

"Also, not to pull focus, but why doesn't Christopher seem to get that Kaspar is terrible?" Ginger asked.

I sighed. "I was with Kaspar for a long time. Five years or so. Christopher just thinks of him as my partner. And...when I ended up in the hospital last year, Kaspar's the one who told Christopher, and then kept calling him to ask about me because I didn't call him when I came back to Philly."

"Well, yeah. But why didn't you tell Christopher he sucked?"

Daniel tried to kick her under the table.

"That was me," I said.

"Shit, sorry."

I looked at them, prepared to dismiss the question, and saw such compassion it almost choked me up. Ginger wasn't asking to shame me. She was asking because she was worried that Christopher had failed me. Daniel wasn't trying to kick her because it was awkward. He was trying to remind her that these were the things we did for love and hate and fear. I felt, all of a sudden, that we truly were friends.

"Honestly?" I asked, testing the waters. Both of them nodded without hesitation. "I was embarrassed as hell about how I let

Kaspar treat me. How bad he made me feel for having depression and anxiety. Embarrassed that I stayed with him for so long. And I didn't want Christopher to think I was pathetic. So I just never told him."

They both nodded immediately, like this made complete sense.

"Okay, so you can totally tell us about Kaspar or not. But I assume he's a big part of why you don't wanna go back to Boston?" Ginger said.

I told them about Kaspar in broad strokes. Ginger looked murderous and Daniel looked upset and both reactions warmed me from the inside.

"I guess I'm just trying to figure out what the hell I'm good for if I don't play?" I admitted.

Daniel said, "Is playing in Boston your only option? I mean, I'm sure it's super competitive. But, like, with academia, there's always a shuffling going on, you know? Someone takes a new job for x reason, and that frees up y position that another person takes, which frees up their position, et cetera."

I nodded. "Yeah, that's exactly how it works. It's just, okay, the thing with the piano is that it isn't actually a part of the orchestra. Often the orchestra plays pieces that feature a piano, and then they engage someone to play it. That's either a super big deal soloist who will draw a crowd and get donors excited. Or it's someone who's less of a big deal, like me, but costs less for the orchestra. Or, pianists also play celesta and harpsichord, which are sometimes needed, but still we don't play in every piece, so… it's not a salaried position, like a violinist."

"Oh, it's like being a featured artist at a tattoo shop but not having a permanent seat there," Ginger said.

"Uh. Yes?" Daniel nodded. "And because Antonio, the conductor, liked my playing, he'd always hire me if he could. And I played for the opera orchestra sometimes, or for rehearsals. And then sometimes I was the pianist who was hired by other orchestras to be their draw. Anyway, point is that to turn down a sure thing—even a probably-sure-part-time thing and try for something else is..."

It just wasn't done. People played under conductors they loathed, next to people who'd divorced them, and at events organized by their nemeses, because that's how the business worked.

"But if you're not doing it at all right now, and you wanna be..." Daniel said.

"Have you talked to the people at the Philly orchestra?" Ginger asked.

"No."

I'd daydreamed about it, of course. The Philly orchestra's featured pianist falling ill and suddenly needing a replacement. But the truth was that I hadn't done anything. I hadn't made a single move to see what my options were here. At first, I just hadn't thought I'd be here long. Then I hadn't had the energy.

Now, though? Now I was too scared to find out there *weren't* any options for me. Because that would mean I'd have to leave Faron or I'd have to give up music. And even thinking about those options made my stomach scream.

"I don't know. Fuck, I don't know. Maybe things would be as bad here as they were in Boston if I start playing again."

"Nah," said Daniel. "You're just putting the bad feeling on the music instead of where it belongs."

"But it's not just Kaspar that was the problem. It's me."

Ginger shook her head.

"You are how you are," she said, eyes intent. "You're not the problem. You're the whole thing. The good and the bad. You're not one element of your own life. You're all of it."

"Am I?"

"Duh."

"Eloquent."

"Well, okay, fine, you want to hear what I think?" She was brandishing the pickletini dramatically.

"I do," Daniel said with a smirk. "She always gets an A-plus for truth-telling," he told me.

"That's right. A-plus, motherfuckers." She beamed. "Okay, here's what I think. You don't know whether stuff in Boston would've been fine without everything that Kaspar made terrible. You can't separate them because you can't know for sure. But playing is still what you want, right?" I nodded. "And you don't want him, right?"

I shook my head emphatically.

"And you want Faron."

She said this as a statement, but I nodded anyway.

"So…first things first, you need to find out whether there's a chance you could play anywhere in Philly. Or even New York— the train's super fast. Especially if you don't play in every show, that would mean you have more down time if you have to commute for a bit. But most importantly, if you can play here, you just do it. You try it! That's the only way you'll see if it's the schedule or the lifestyle or whatever that's the problem. And if it is, you quit. And then you figure out what to do next."

"But I couldn't just quit!"

"Um, obviously you can. You just did it last year."

"I was in the hospital!"

"Yeah! I know! But you did it! Which proves it can be done!"

"Why are you guys yelling?" Daniel asked.

"I don't know!" we both yelled, and Ginger dissolved into laughter.

"It's one thing to quit because you're literally strapped to a bed in a hospital, okay?" I said. "It's another to take a highly coveted engagement with the intention of maybe quitting. It's just…it's irresponsible."

Ginger glared at me. "That's stupid. You think it's more important to feel self-satisfied that you have responsible intentions, secretly, in your own head, than it is to be happy and get to do the thing you love in a way that doesn't completely tank your mental health?"

"Well. When you put it like that."

"If it's really that competitive," Daniel said, "then if you do end up having to leave, there will be tons of people vying to take your place. You won't be, like, silencing the symphony or anything."

"That's true."

I finished the rest of my drink and turned that over in my mind. Could it possibly work out? Could I possibly have a chance to play here?

"I guess I can ask around…" I said.

"Ask your people in Boston," Ginger said. "Y'all've gotta basically all know each other, right? If it's anything like the tattooing world. Like, 'shake the orchestra phone tree and see what falls out' style, ya know?"

I did know. My mind was whirring with possibilities now. Ginger was right that New York wasn't that far away. And there were a hell of a lot more opportunities there than here for classical music.

"Also," said Daniel, "you don't need to solve the problem forever, right? Just for now?"

"What do you mean?"

He shrugged. "Well, I took a job at this school in the middle of nowhere in Michigan and I met the love of my life. And I only had the job for a year. Now I'm here. Something doesn't have to be forever to be the most important thing you do."

CHAPTER TWELVE

OVER THE NEXT TWO WEEKS, I put out tentative feelers. I emailed a few people I'd been friendly with in the BSO to ask if they had orchestra contacts in Philly or New York. My stomach was in a knot as I did it, imagining the things Kaspar might have told them about me.

Antonio was my last email. I couldn't bring myself to call him because he got so excited about the music and about my playing that I couldn't think. I wrote that I hadn't made any decision yet and was just trying to see what all my options were.

I felt...tentatively hopeful. My head had been such a tangle of details, but hearing Ginger and Daniel ask clear, simple questions cut through the knot. Maybe there was still a chance that I could do what I loved and not go back to Boston.

I'd been working on the piano whenever Faron wasn't at Small Change. He preferred to work days so he could get up early and paint in the mornings when he liked the light. Then, in the evenings, while I sanded keys and stripped varnish, he sketched, or read with Waffle curled up at his feet.

Sometimes he painted quick sketches on small things he found around the house—the backs of junk mail envelopes, a flattened cereal box in the recycling bag, the extra lid of a mason jar. He'd leave them where he painted them, forgotten as soon as he was done, and I would take them before he threw them away. I loved the way the paint made ordinary things into art.

I loved that Faron made ordinary things feel special in general. All he had to do was walk into the room and I got this sense that everything was going to be better.

Talking about the simplest things with him felt new because he didn't come at them the same way I did. He had firm principles, yet still came at each scenario with such attention to particularity. It was a combination of intelligence and empathy and generosity that I admired more with each day we spent together.

And often, we didn't talk at all. There was such a peace to sharing space with him with the burden of speech removed.

I'd never had that. The sense that just by existing as myself, I was participating positively in someone else's life.

When I'd lived with Kaspar, I had stayed away from him if I didn't want to interact. If I didn't have the energy to talk, then I didn't walk into the kitchen when he was getting coffee; if I didn't want to have sex, then I didn't touch him. I learned not to make any promises with my presence that I wouldn't be able to deliver on. It was easier that way.

But Faron and I seemed to move around each other with awareness but no obligation. I'd tried testing the waters—kissing Faron on the cheek as I walked by the couch when he was reading. He'd smiled and run a hand through my hair, but when I continued on to the kitchen, he made no comment. I'd sat on the couch next to him another time, and put on headphones to listen to music, and he didn't try to talk to me, just rearranged himself on the couch so I could put my legs over his if I chose.

It was like learning a new language of proximity. A language that finally felt like my native tongue.

Sex with Faron was another new language. Because for all that he expected nothing from me, I could tell that he desired me.

He watched me with the same attention as when he was painting me—as if every movement and detail mattered. And in bed, that attention electrified me.

He would watch me for hours, ramping up my awareness so slowly that my skin felt hypersensitive by the time he so much as touched me. He caressed, licked, kissed every inch of me. Laid me bare to him until every beat of my heart and pulse of my cock belonged to him.

Where I'd sometimes had trouble getting hard with Kaspar even if I wanted sex, now my arousal built so slowly and steadily that there was plenty of time for my body to catch up to my desire.

And every time I came, screaming or gasping or moaning, I felt a rush of connection with Faron that left me craving the next time, and the next. Every time he came, the pleasure so clear on his face, I felt a satisfaction that seemed like a miracle: that I had something to offer him that was actually me.

Just me.

And sometimes those feelings would even last longer than the few minutes it took for my mind to reclaim my body. Sometimes I could make myself believe it until I drifted off to sleep, where it would entwine with my dreams.

––––––

ONE MORNING, Faron didn't feel like painting before work so we took Waffle for a long walk instead. We walked in silence and I could smell the promise of rain in the morning air. The Sleeping Beauty Waltz played in my head and Faron walked close enough that our arms brushed sometimes. Every time it happened it filled me with a quiet joy that fizzed up and died back down, like wavelets foaming over wet sand.

We dropped Waffle back at Faron's and I walked with him to

work. With time to spare before he started at Small Change for the day, we detoured to Melt for coffee.

But where Christopher usually greeted us with a grin that was part happy hello and part knowing eyebrow raise at seeing us together, today there was concern on his face when the bell above his door tinkled our arrival.

I saw why when the man at the counter turned around.

Kaspar.

His face was just the same as it had always been, but in this context it was as strange as a hallucination.

A jolt of adrenaline weakened my knees and made my heart pound in my chest and in my ears. I wanted to run but was frozen. I wanted to disappear but he was a step away from me.

"Jude. Thank god! I'm so glad you're okay."

His face, his voice, both were sincere and familiar. He hugged me as I stood there. He smelled a little sour, like sweat and airplane.

"What are you doing here," I managed.

"Hello, I'm Kaspar Zalewski," he said, extending a hand to Faron.

"I know who you are," Faron said evenly, and he let the hand hang in the air between them.

Kaspar's nostrils flared and he gave a familiar sniff of affront. "Jude, where can we go and talk?"

"What do you want to talk about?" I asked warily.

Kaspar looked around the way he always did when he wanted me to be aware that people could hear us and he didn't want to cause a scene.

He leaned in. "I'm worried about you. I want to talk about you coming home."

Someone I'd emailed must have told Kaspar I was looking for work in Philly.

"I don't want to talk."

My voice sounded thin and unsure.

"Honey, you never want to talk, but you know communication is important."

I felt a chill, then the sensation of insects crawling up my spine.

Christopher came out from behind the counter and ushered us all into the back of the shop to where his small office was. I let myself be led.

"You okay, bro? You want me to ask him to leave?"

I wanted to say yes. I wanted to watch Christopher kick Kaspar out of Melt. But it wouldn't actually end this. Kaspar would still try to contact me. He'd still live in the back of my mind. Maybe we really should talk. Maybe I could finally end this forever.

"It's okay," I said.

"Okay. I'm right out front."

Faron, Kaspar, and I walked in.

"I'd like to speak with Jude alone, please," Kaspar said.

I grabbed Faron's arm before I was aware I'd done it and forced myself to let go. I couldn't very well ask for him to stay and listen to Kaspar's attempts to win me back.

"I'm not going anywhere," Faron said softly, and I felt his hand on my back like a tether to my life here.

Kaspar turned to me.

"I want him to stay," I said.

Kaspar smiled tightly and threw his hands up. "Whatever you want, Jude. That's how it usually goes anyway. Right?" His statement was to me, but the question was directed at Faron and my chest felt hot. My stomach was empty. I was empty. Faron said nothing.

"What do you want?" I asked again.

"Look, I understand that you needed time away. Time with your family. Christopher's a great guy; it's good you had your brother to support you. And I even understand why you did…

what you did. I know...I know things were hard for you then. I do."

His eyes were big and sympathetic and he was talking to me like there was no one else in the world.

"I think I can even forgive you for it."

His gaze fell to the floor, the perfect pose of sad confusion.

"I know I wasn't always the best partner. So I guess you deserved to be the selfish one for a while."

My mouth was so dry I couldn't make a sound. When did I swallow a desert? When did it creep into my throat and fill my mouth?

As I stayed silent, Kaspar's mouth opened and closed. Then his eyes narrowed and I saw the glint of cruelty. Kaspar's cruelty was blanket-warm and blade-merciless because it was usually true.

"You know he left with no explanation, right?" Kaspar said to Faron. "I took him to the hospital. He was almost dead. When I went there to check on him he wouldn't see me. And then he ran away in the middle of the night and never spoke to me again. I had to call his brother to find out if he was alive or dead!"

Kaspar was shaking with something that might have been anger or maybe betrayal but I couldn't quite tell because I was floating on the ceiling and the air between us was so thick and oily it was hard to see.

"I took care of you for five years and you didn't even have the common decency to answer a fucking phone call!" Kaspar was yelling.

"I need you to lower your voice," someone named Faron was saying, and there was a vague sensation of something brushing my shoulder, like maybe a branch or a clump of leaves.

"I see you have someone else to take care of you now, hmm?" Kaspar said primly. "Well, a piece of free advice from me to you. This one's a black hole. He'll suck you in with how much he needs you and how brilliant he is, and you'll give him everything you have, do anything you can to help, but it won't matter. Because nothing can help. Nothing will ever be enough. And then when he's sucked everything he can from you, he'll just take off in the middle of the night. After five fucking years! Who fucking does that, Jude!?"

There was a thick drip of paint in the corner of the wall that Christopher had let dry. It looked like the office was crying. Or bleeding.

"You need to leave now," the man said.

Brush of leaves.

Five fucking years. Five years fucking. Fucking five years. Fucking fucking fucking years.

"So that's it, huh? That it, Jude? You tell Antonio—Antonio, who worships you, god knows why—oh, wait, I know why: because he wants to fuck you! You tell Antonio that you want to play with the Philly orchestra instead? Good fucking luck with that, Jude. You think anyone besides Antonio would hire you? When you're unstable and you haven't played in months? Ha, not likely. Jude. Jude, would you at least fucking look at me when I'm talking to you?"

"Get out. Now."

"Just tell me one thing, Jude, hmm? You really think this hot model guy's gonna stick around even half as long as I did? Huh? Because if so, you're stupid as well as fucking crazy."

There's a snarl and shiny black hair and then, "Christopher! Get this guy the fuck out of my sight before I kill him," and then quiet.

Leaves on my shoulder, leaves brushing up against my neck in the fog. A leaf fluttering against my cheek and I try to brush it away but my hand gets caught.

"Jude?"

Jude Jude Jude Judejudejudejujujujujud.

Something pinches me hard and I slam back into myself with a lurch.

I was sitting on the floor of Christopher's office and Faron was crouching next to me. Did he pinch me?

"Ow."

"Fuck," he breathed. Then, "I'm sorry. I thought..." He shook his head. "Let's go home, okay?"

Faron stood and held a hand down to me like a rope dropped over the side of a well. All you had to do was climb out, right? The rope was right there. Just one hand over the other and hold on and trust that the person on the other end in the sunshine can pull you up, right? Trust that they want whatever they pull out of the well, because it's all Little Timmies in the well, right, and they fell in by accident, except Timmy never fell in the well, Lassie did.

"Jude?"

"Where'd he go."

"Christopher threw him out. He won't be back. He won't contact you again."

The rope was right there.

"Let's go back to my place. Please."

All along the shabby baseboards the floor was dusty, and the long fluorescent light bulb leaning in the corner looked precarious, like it might fall at any moment and smash into a million pieces.

"I'm gonna go home," I said, and pushed to my feet. The rope disappeared.

"Come back to my house."

"No, I have to go home."

"Please, Jude. You can't be alone right now."

You can't. You shouldn't. You can't. You can't do it. You'll fail. You'll fuck it up. You can't do anything. Why would anyone want you. No one wants you. You ruin everything. You. Ruin. Everything.

"Yes I can."

Faron looked sad and desperate and I felt nothing because I was shrunk down to the size of a marble, rattling around inside this hollow meat suit, and you'll never find me.

"Baby, please. Let me take you back to my place. I won't bug you, we can just…"

I closed Jude's eyes.

"Why?" Jude said.

"Because I'm fucking scared!" Faron said. Broken voice, broken face, broken, broken broken.

You ruin everything.

CHAPTER THIRTEEN

IT WAS a familiar relief to be in bed. I didn't need to do anything. I didn't need to shower if I wasn't leaving the house. I told the parents of my students that I was sick. They told me to feel better soon.

I let movies play all day long, slipping in and out of bits of the stories in between sleeping and staring at the screen without absorbing anything. I thought about watching all the action movies that used classical pieces in their climactic explosion montages, but I didn't do it because it was too much work.

I smoked in the house, not caring about opening a window or the smell permeating the couch and bedclothes.

I didn't answer Faron's calls because I didn't have anything to say. I didn't answer Christopher's because I didn't have to. Maggie chatted me and sometimes I answered.

Finally Christopher texted, *Faron's really worried about you. He wants to come see you.*

Tell him I'm fine.

But you're not right?

I'm ok, really. Just lying low for a bit.

As long as you're really ok...

Yep, I am, I wrote, because that's what you wrote.

They couldn't do anything for me, so there was no use in worrying them. This would pass, or it wouldn't. No amount of talking or hugging would change anything, and I didn't have the energy to participate in any. Faron showing up wouldn't snap me out of it and I'd just feel worse to see him feel like a failure.

For all that Kaspar was a fuck, he was also right about that. I was a black hole. And black holes reduced everything to nothing. Caring couldn't exist in a black hole, or love. So it was pointless to throw them in.

I slept for days after that, my body logy and my mind like molasses. Maggie had a fight with her dad. Salieri had a fight with Mozart. Hilary Swank had a fight with Clint Eastwood. In the world, cops shot unarmed black men and nothing happened to them. CEOs chose money over the environment. Animals were rescued and people weren't. I slept some more.

———

ONE MORNING I woke up and I didn't go back to bed right after peeing, so that was different. I put on music instead of a movie. I thought about my piano, still in pieces.

———

THE NEXT DAY, I finally made myself think about it. The way I saw it, I had two choices. I could ease backward out of Faron's life like I'd never been there and hope he got the hint. Or I could tell him it was over. I wanted to do the former; I knew he deserved the latter. I went back to bed.

———

THE KNOCKING JOLTED ME AWAKE. I ignored it.

"Jude, please let me in."

Christopher. He'd leave if I just didn't say anything. Christopher was great like that. He always left me alone.

"Jude?"

He'd sit outside my door and talk to me. For years, he sat outside the door and talked. He never intruded. Even as a kid, he'd respected the closed door.

"Bro, I'm really worried that you're lying in there fucking dead. I still have the key and I'm coming in."

Shit.

I heard the key in the lock and the door opened.

"Jude?" His voice was softer now, and I could hear his panic.

"Yeah," I said. "Coming."

Before I could even get the covers off, though, Christopher came through the bedroom door.

"Oh thank god. Fuck! Don't do that to me."

He leaned against the doorframe and covered his face with his hand. He looked terrified.

You did that. Again.

"I'm okay," I said. My voice came out like sandpaper. "Sorry I scared you."

Christopher looked at me for a long time.

"You're not, are you? You're not okay. I mean, I knew you weren't. You obviously weren't. But I didn't want…"

He bit his lip and I sat up.

"Fuck, I was so scared of pissing you off that I just let you—"

He broke off and clamped a hand over his mouth, shaking his head. Then he crossed to the bed in two long strides.

"Anyway, I shouldn't have done that. I should've come over right after I kicked Kaspar out. I should've been here for you, even if you didn't want me here."

His voice was choked.

"I'm just so used to… I just never wanted to do anything to

make it worse. And I don't know what will. But I'm here now. Okay?"

My little brother. God, I'd hurt him so much.

I cringed at the thought of how much damage I'd done, but I didn't have the energy to convince him I was okay. And without the door between us, he could clearly see that I wasn't.

"Jude?"

He said it so softly, and it broke me.

"I'm sorry," I whispered. "I'm so, so sorry."

Tears welled up and spilled over and Christopher's eyes got wide. Then he kicked off his shoes and dropped onto the bed beside me.

"It's okay," he said. "It's gonna be okay. Let me help, please."

I was too tired to argue. I dropped my head onto his shoulder and felt my tears wet the flannel of his shirt. He put his arm around me and rubbed my back. Mortification burnt itself out after a few minutes, leaving me resigned. Christopher wasn't a little boy anymore. It did help a little, having him here. It made me feel a little less like I could disappear at any moment.

Christopher's hand stilled on my back, finally, and it felt like his fingers dug into my spine.

"Jude," he said, voice tight. "Jesus, you need to eat something."

I pulled away from him, my stomach lurching, and shook my head.

The Christopher who pulled me around to face him wasn't messing around.

"Bro. Fucking listen to me. I know you don't like to eat, but you're fucking wasting away in front of me. You look..." He bit his lip. "Bad. You look really bad. And this place smells like an ashtray. When was the last time you ate real food?"

I shrugged. I felt sick at even the thought of eating. I honestly didn't know how long it had been.

"Listen, please. I need you to eat or I'm taking you to the hospital. I'm not messing around."

My heart began to race at the thought of going to the hospital, and I nodded.

"I don't... I'm not trying to... It just makes me sick. I don't know why. Everything disgusts me."

Christopher was thinking hard, eyes narrowed.

"Is it worse when you're...down like this?"

I shrugged. "I don't even notice."

"Okay, I'm gonna go to the store and then I'm gonna come right back. You're gonna let me in, right?"

"You have a key."

"I mean if you throw that chain on, so help me god, Jude, I'll break the fucking door down," he snarled.

I almost laughed at that.

"I'll probably just stay right here," I admitted.

"Okay," he said, easing out of bed. "Okay. You need protein. No eggs at all, no matter what I do to them?"

My stomach lurched at the word and I shook my head.

"What about a drink? Like a smoothie."

"Maybe. But no protein powder." I could feel the way it coated my tongue with chalk.

"Okay. I'll figure it out. I'll be back."

He hesitated, then he bent down and kissed the top of my head. For some reason that made me cry all over again the second he was gone.

I drifted for a while. I lit a cigarette but got dizzy on the second drag so I put it out and buried my head in the pillow. Christopher was back so quickly I'd've bet money he ran through the grocery store like a bat out of hell.

"Do you wanna come in the kitchen?" he called.

I sighed and dragged myself out of bed. In the kitchen, he was pulling things out of the grocery bag. With something to do, his sunny smile was back in place.

"Okay, how about cashews?" He held up a bulk bag that confirmed he'd gone to Whole Foods.

"They taste like bandaids."

He paused and ate a cashew.

"I'll be damned. Walnuts?"

"They taste like dust."

He ate a walnut and smiled at me. "I like this game."

I smiled.

"Okay, you know what? Go sit on the couch and watch TV or something."

"You're the one who dragged me in here," I grumbled.

"Just go away from here and don't look."

Cabinet doors opened and closed, a blender that Christopher must've left here whirred, and after a few minutes, he handed me a metal cup with a lid and a built-in straw.

"What's in it?" I asked, moving to unscrew the lid.

Christopher batted my hand away. "Psh, why do you think I didn't let you look and put it in a covered cup? Just try it."

I took a sip and it was actually okay. It mostly tasted like blueberries, which were all right when I didn't have to feel them squish between my teeth.

"Stop thinking about what's in it!" he said, dropping onto the couch next to me.

"Can you just, uh, distract me while I drink it?"

He nodded. "Marcus and Selene just found out they got approved to be foster parents."

"I bet they'll be amazing at it," I said.

"Yeah, they're over the moon." He was fiddling with the seam of the couch cushion. "I was thinking...I don't know. Do you want kids?"

"No."

"Oh."

"Wait, do you?"

He shrugged, but he sucked his lower lip in like he had as a kid when his feelings had gotten hurt.

"Chris, do you want kids, for real?" I hadn't called him Chris since middle school when he'd decided that Chris was for little kids and he wanted to be Christopher, but it had just come out.

"Maybe, I don't know. I don't think…I don't know."

"Whoa. You do. You want them and you don't think Ginger does so you don't want to admit it."

"Shh."

"Shit. You really do."

He slumped deeper into the couch.

"Maybe. Yeah. Someday. I don't know. Shut up."

I finished the smoothie and put the cup down.

"You feel any better?" he asked, pointing to it.

"Yeah, actually. It wasn't too bad. Seriously, what was in that?"

"Fruit and a lot of protein. I'm not telling you, but I'll remember and I can make it again. And I'm gonna tell Faron so he can make it for you."

Everything in me cringed away from the sound of Faron's name. I couldn't ask Faron to be part of my fucked-up life anymore, so I'd just have to learn to make the smoothies myself.

"You'd make a really amazing father."

His head snapped up and there was something hopeful and delicate in his eyes.

"You think so?"

"I know so."

We sat in silence for a while, Christopher seeming lost in thought. Then he straightened.

"You gonna throw that up if I talk about Kaspar?"

My stomach lurched, but it was nerves, not nausea. I sighed. "Thanks for…whatever you said to get him to leave."

"I don't get it," he said. "Your face. When you saw him there, you looked sick. Horrified. And after, when Faron called me to get rid of him, you were…" His brow wrinkled. "Why didn't you tell me you were afraid of him? You let me think shit was fine with you guys. I just…I don't get it."

I curled my arms around my drawn-up knees. "I didn't want you to know."

"Why?"

"Because, Chris. I was fucking ashamed!" It came out so small.

"But, why?"

I closed my eyes.

"Because he treated me like shit and I let him. It's...embarrassing. Weak. Pathetic."

He lurched toward me and grabbed my wrist.

"Do *not* say that. *He's* the one who's pathetic. Don't ever think this is on you."

I shrugged because I knew if I opened my mouth I'd cry again.

"I just wish you'd said something. Let me kick his ass or something."

I snorted at his uncharacteristic machismo. "Yeah, cuz that wouldn't have made me feel way more pathetic, having my little brother fight my battles."

"Whatever, I'm bigger than you anyway," Christopher grumbled. And he sounded so much like he had as a kid that I smiled.

He grinned back at me, laughing at himself.

"Thing is," he said. "I spent so long wishing that I could understand how things were for you. Because I wanted to help. But I see now, really damn clearly, that I don't actually understand. And, Jude? I don't fucking want to. I don't think I could take it. I really don't. You're...really fucking strong. So much stronger than me. Maybe you don't see it, but I do."

He wasn't looking at me with pity. He wasn't looking at me like I was pathetic and couldn't handle my shit. He was looking at me with respect. Esteem. And such sadness.

"Okay so you don't need me to kick Kaspar's ass. But I'm still here. And you're here now. After so long away. And I...I want my brother back. I want to hang out. I want you to let me make you smoothies and for you to take me to a piano concert."

I smiled at the words piano concert.

"Do you know I've still only ever seen you play with the symphony that one time? Like, I went to your recitals and stuff as a kid, but, uh. They were boring. But I wanna see *you* play. You were fucking amazing when I saw you in Boston. You looked like...I don't even know. Some kind of magician. The whole audience was captivated by you. I wanna see that again. I want that for you."

He was leaning forward, sincerity alive in every word.

"Don't you want that? Don't you want your fucking life back?"

A tear streaked down my cheek, then another. But this wasn't a depths-of-despair leak. These were tears with a source. I did. I did want my fucking life back. But first I had to give Faron a chance to have his back too.

CHAPTER FOURTEEN

IT TOOK me a couple more days to get out of the house and head to Faron's, and I got there only to realize that I didn't know his work schedule for the week. He wasn't home and if he worked until his usual time, he wouldn't be home for three hours.

But maybe he wasn't even at work. Maybe he was just out with someone else. A friend. Or someone who could give him all the things I couldn't.

I sat down outside the garage door to figure out how long I would wait and what I should do and must've ended up sitting there for a while, because before I'd decided what to do, Faron turned the corner holding two Whole Foods bags and stopped short when he saw me.

I stood up and started to shake before he even got to me.

"I'm so glad to see you," he said, setting his bags on the ground. He stood stiffly, like he wanted to hug me but wasn't sure it would be welcome. I wasn't sure either. I'd never wanted to feel anything more than I wanted to feel his arms around me, but it would just make this harder.

He looked...rough. I'd never seen him anything less than basically glowing but now he looked worn out and pinched.

You did that. You ruin everything.

"Um, could I come in for a minute?"

Faron bit his lip, hard.

"Yeah, please come in."

It smelled the same. Cool and clean like a river stone. Waffle came running toward me and I dropped to my knees and threw my arms around her. She wriggled and broke free to lick my face, tail wagging hard. She was so full of joy just at seeing me that tears welled up in my eyes.

Faron put one hand on Waffle's head and held the other out to me. This time I took it and let him pull me up and into his arms. He held me so tight I felt like I didn't even need to depend on gravity, and I squeezed back just as tight, burying my face in his neck. I wished we could stay like this forever, but if I didn't do this soon, I'd lose my nerve.

I extricated myself from his arms and sat down on the couch. Faron followed me.

"I'm sorry you got dragged into that, with Kaspar the other day."

Faron snarled and squared his shoulders like he was ready to get rid of Kaspar all over again, and I held a hand out.

"But I didn't mean to do to you what I did to him. I didn't mean to...disappear."

Faron's face rearranged itself into the most neutral expression and it was like seeing the life drain out of him.

I took a deep breath and cut myself open.

"Because what he said was true. He did take me to the hospital and take care of me, and I did refuse to see him. I left Boston in the middle of the night and I even used his credit card to get a cab to the airport. I left and I came back here and I didn't answer his phone calls or his emails. I let Christopher be the one to tell him I was here. I... He was my partner for five years and I left him without so much as a goodbye. I... It was all true."

I was looking over Faron's shoulder because I couldn't quite bear to look at his face. The piano stood where I'd left it. With half the keys sanded and replaced, the other half lying on the drop cloth, it looked like a gaping mouth set in a grim, knowing line.

"Faron, I'm no good for you. I'm no good at this. Not now. I don't mean to be selfish but I am because it takes me so much energy to deal with my own shit sometimes that I don't have much left over to think about other people. I've done so many things I'm not— So many things I'm fucking ashamed of."

My heart tripped as light and fast as castanets behind the armor of my ribs. I felt almost lightheaded. It had been so long since I'd just been honest with someone.

"I care about you so much. I-I-I probably fucking love you, but I just ruin everything and hurt everyone and I can't do that to you—I won't. So, I should probably go, and…let you put the groceries away. Okay, I'm gonna—"

I started to stand up but Faron grabbed my arm and pulled me back down.

"Are you kidding me right now?" he asked, voice low and dangerous.

"I— What?"

"You seem to be in a truth-telling mood," he said. His hand was resting on my arm but it might as well have been his whole body weight because I couldn't have moved if I tried.

"I was trying, yeah."

"So your truth is that you love me and now I should go put away the groceries while you walk out of my life forever?"

His eyes on me were so intense I had to look away.

"I…it sounds really cold when you say it like that."

"You said it. And you *are* really cold, Jude. To yourself. You have no mercy. No generosity. No forgiveness for yourself at all. Do you?"

I shook my head. How could I have mercy for myself when I'd spent my whole life watching the hurt I caused? When I saw my mother's smile disappear as I didn't eat the food she cooked especially to try and get me to eat. When my father slapped me on the back and I flinched away from it and watched the sadness, the disappointment creep over his face. When I scrolled through my brother's dozens of unanswered texts checking in on me and heard the crack in his voice on my voicemail that spoke of the fear I'd caused him.

Thousands of tiny moments over two decades of watching the pain I'd inflicted on the people I loved, the people who loved me. Over and over, the very me-ness of me sliced into them like paper cuts but they never crumpled me up and threw me away. They kept me there with them, their blood slicking my edges and blooming ever closer to my heart.

And that was to say nothing of the big moments when I couldn't even look the hurt I'd caused in the face.

Faron's expression softened and he took my hands. "Tell me this truth, then. Do you want me? Truly. Do you want to be with me?"

A tear rolled down my cheek and I nodded.

"So this breaking up with me bit. Was that you being scared of making a mistake?"

He couldn't possibly gloss all of what I said as a mistake, though, and I started to tell him that, but he covered my mouth.

"Nod yes or no for me, Jude. Was you trying to leave me really you being scared of making a mistake?"

His voice wavered when he said "leave me," and I realized suddenly that that was what I had tried to do. I'd left Kaspar and Boston and everything else because they felt like poison. Now I was trying to leave Faron because he felt like the cleanest, most nourishing breath of fresh air.

What, then, would I stay for?

I nodded.

"You scared of hurting me?"

I nodded quickly, tears streaming down my cheeks.

"You scared I don't know what I'm getting into and when I figure it out I'll hate you?"

I nodded, crying harder behind his hand.

"You scared I'll get fed up with you once I realize this is who you are, and leave?"

A sob tore free and I nodded and nodded. Faron had to take his hand away so I could drag in more air. After being numb for the last I didn't know how many days, now the wave was cresting.

I cried and Faron let me and he didn't pull me into his arms and comfort me. He just squeezed my hand in his while I wiped tears and snot off my face with the other.

Waffle whined softly and plopped her shaggy face over the side of the couch.

"See," I said shakily. "You can't date me because I c-cry a lot and I'll sc-scare the dog."

Faron's smile was faint but it was there. He got a bandanna and handed it to me. It was worn soft and smelled like him. I wiped at my eyes and my nose and the smell of him just made the tears come again.

"I'm not a selfless person," Faron said. "The things you say about me make it sound sometimes like I'm..." He searched for a word in the air. "Like I'm above judgment, above emotion. I'm not. And it's important that you understand. I'm not perfect. I don't want you out of generosity. Or because I'm some kind of angel or savior. I want you because something inside you vibrates just so with something inside me."

His eyes on mine were intense.

"I've never felt this way about someone. With Sabien, I had an understanding. Other people I dated, I expected to feel an echo of that, and I didn't. But with you...I feel connected."

He slid a warm palm up my leg and I took a deep breath.

"But?" There had to be a but.

"I am concerned that your depression will be a problem if we have a relationship. Not because it's bad or you are. But because it has negative effects on you, and you affect me. We'll have to talk about it. We'll have other problems too, because relationships have problems."

I sighed. I did know that.

"It might sound like I'm oversimplifying," he said, a bit of an edge to his voice. "But to me, it is simple. Not your feelings or our problems. But it's simple to me that if you love something or someone you should fight for it. Fight for them. Until you can't fight anymore or until it does more harm than good."

He cupped my cheek, forced me to look at him. His voice was as even as ever, but his eyes burned.

"I think this thing between us is worth fighting for, Jude. I haven't been in many relationships. I don't... Like I said, I haven't often gotten much from them. I like spending time with the people I like. I enjoy sleeping with people I'm attracted to. But I like my own space, physically, mentally. I like to have room to stretch out into just the shape I want."

It was such a perfect description of what it felt like to spend time with Faron: like he was a glorious tree, branches reaching out and up, roots digging down, touchable, but immovable.

"There's something about you," he went on. "Something that makes me feel spacious. Like I can be alone, even while you're with me. Maybe you feel the same? When you go away in your head."

I nodded. Knowing Faron was there, across the apartment, but not interacting with him, made me feel peaceful and secure, but unpressured. "But, sometimes, I..." I swallowed hard. "Sometimes I do want to be close. Like, really close. I'm clingy."

That was the word Kaspar had always used.

"The spaciousness makes room for closeness." His eyelashes fluttered. "I like to watch you from across the room. Then from close up. Closer and closer. So when I finally make contact—" He pressed his palm to my heart and I gasped. "I'm ready to touch you everywhere."

I shuddered and Faron eye-fucked me for a moment before drawing back.

"Tell me what else you're worried about."

Worry tumbled over worry until I could hardly separate one out from the others. My pulse pounded hotly and no words came out.

"Try one. Even if it doesn't make sense."

"I'm worried that you'll think I'm bad."

My throat closed around the word.

"I might think things you do or say aren't great. But think you are bad? No."

He sounded so certain but I didn't know how or why. Suddenly I really needed to be close to him. I pulled on his hand and pressed myself close to his chest. He settled me against him and stroked my back slowly.

"I want to tell you this and you need to hear me. Okay?" I nodded against his chest. "Depression is a part of you. And I'm not foolish enough to think it isn't important. Everything about you is important. But you've spent so long feeling guilty for the ways it's affected you that you have a limited vision of yourself. You're painting the same picture over and over again. Same composition, same angle, slightly different color palette."

He was drawing something on my back, tracing lines only he could see.

"You feel like you've let people down. I understand. But you focus only on the ways you've failed to have relationships on other people's terms. By rules you didn't make. And if you do that? If you only judge yourself by whether you've mastered someone else's game? You'll fail every time."

He pulled me up to look at me and he looked fierce and sad.

"Because a lot of us? Those games are stacked against us. Hell, even if we play by every single rule and do everything right, there's no guarantee. So you have to stop. If we're going to have any chance together, we have to make different rules. Rules about what we expect from each other. What we need. What we won't tolerate. What we hope for."

The truth of it rocked through me. "And you...you'd want to do that. With me?"

Faron traced my lower lip with his thumb. "Yes."

I looked down and shook my head. My voice was a whisper. "Why?"

"Why do I want to be with you?"

My chest burned.

"I— No, I wasn't trying to get you to say nice things about me. I just..." I shrugged, helplessly embarrassed.

"Baby," Faron said, an ocean of tenderness in his voice. "Would it be so awful if you wanted me to say nice things about you?"

I shook my head, wanting it so much and not feeling like I had any right to ask for it.

"I want to say nice things about you. Wouldn't you say nice things about me if I wanted you to?"

"Yes, of course."

But you deserve them.

My heart was doing something strange. Racing then slowing then racing again. And my stomach was clenched. My shoulders were tight.

"I think I need some water." I stood up to go to the kitchen and the edges of my vision went black. Faron grabbed me before I fell and pushed me back to the couch. He came back with a glass of water and waited as I chugged it. I was suddenly so thirsty. "I feel like this was a bad context for you needing to take care of me by bringing me water. You know, what with me being concerned about being a burden and...stuff."

Faron sighed, half exasperated and half amused.

"It's a goddamn glass of water, Jude. I'd get one for my worst enemy. I'm not viewing it as emblematic of our entire future relationship."

"Okay, good." He was clearly kidding, but I wasn't. Not really. Because given the way I went over every detail of every thing, small moments really did echo in my head as emblematic.

As soon as I finished the water, Faron took my hands again.

"I love how you go so still when I touch you, as if you're paying attention to every single sensation."

"Thank you?"

"I'm telling you things I like about you. That make me want to be with you. Since you asked."

"Oh."

"Feel free to reciprocate." His eyes smiled and I was struck by the intensity of my appreciation for him. Not gratitude that he might want me, but appreciation for the person he was.

"Okay. When I'm around you, I get this feeling like you think anything could happen. Anything might be possible. It's inspiring. And really brave."

Faron leaned in and kissed my mouth, his lips soft and full. It felt like it had been forever since we'd last kissed and I put my arms around his neck.

When Faron ended the kiss, he looked a little dreamy and I smiled at him.

"More," I said.

I'd meant more kissing, but he said, "You make music all the time. Sometimes you hum or whistle, but even when you're just moving things around, you do it in rhythm like everything in your world is made of music."

I swallowed hard and tightened my arms around him, kissing him in thanks.

"Everything you do is like dancing," I said. "The way you walk, the way you tattoo. The way you, um...the way you fuck. You're so graceful sometimes I can't look away from you."

Faron's smile was slow and bright, and I could still feel it on his lips when he kissed me. I moaned when his tongue entered my mouth and played softly against mine.

"You're deeply compassionate. You even have empathy for a man who treated you unconscionably." He caught my chin and didn't let me look down at the mention of Kaspar. "It's not a weakness. Being able to see things from someone else's perspective is never a weakness."

I pressed him back against the arm of the couch and kissed him hard. He met me, kiss for kiss, and I could feel his cock hardening beneath me. He looked dazed when I broke the kiss. "I love how genuine you are. When you ask questions you really want to know the answer, and you take everything so seriously, like you believe other people are genuine too."

"Thank you," he breathed, but then he was kissing me again, mouth so hot and sweet I couldn't get enough.

"I want you," I gasped against his mouth. "I want to try. I want to be with you. Can we try?" He silenced my begging with his mouth and didn't even break the kiss to get us to the bed, just grabbed my ass and walked us over.

"Yes," he said, and kissed me in the bed that smelled like him. "Yes we'll try. Yes, I want you."

His *yes* was the most beautiful thing I'd ever heard.

We were naked in seconds flat and I needed him inside me, needed his body to deliver on what his words had promised.

"Please," I gasped. "Please, I need you."

I spread my legs, wanting to be taken, wanting to be filled, wanting Faron to be a part of me.

He kissed his way down my stomach and caressed the insides of my thighs. He was so gorgeous with his kiss-swollen mouth and his curls everywhere.

"I'm probably not...um..." I blushed furiously. "I had to up my meds and I don't think I'll...get hard. Is it...is that okay?"

Faron kissed the crease where my thigh met my groin and

looked up at me. "It's absolutely okay. If you say you want it, I trust you."

My chest tightened and tears of relief came to my eyes. I nodded. "I want you so much."

"I want you too, baby."

He licked the head of my soft cock gently. It felt so sweet, so perfect. Since I was soft he could fit all of me in his mouth and I moaned as he worked me, stroking the underside with his tongue.

Faron rubbed over my hole and I pressed my hips down, trying to get him inside.

"I want to taste you," he murmured, stroking my hole. "That okay?"

"Yes, please, yes, thank you, please."

I felt the soft huff of Faron's chuckle, then he flipped me onto my knees and elbows. My ass was sticking up and my legs were wide. I hid my face in the sheets but it didn't stop me feeling exposed.

"Mmmm," Faron murmured, and then he started to lick me open. Soft, wet swipes of his tongue, then quick flutters, then firm lips and the gorgeous, muscular slide inside. It was like being kissed, tenderly and deep, and it made me shake with need.

"Please," I said.

He kissed my hole and kissed all the way up my spine.

"Tell me how you want this, love."

"I— I want to see you?"

Faron kissed my shoulder and my neck, and turned me onto my back. He leaned over me to grab the lube and a condom and I bit my lip.

"And…"

"What?" he purred, and kissed me. "Anything. Tell me."

"Can we…?" I took the condom out of his hand and put it back on the bedside table. "I want to feel you. I want to feel you come."

A shudder rippled through Faron and he groaned and dropped his forehead to my shoulder.

"Yeah." His voice was rough and he took my face between both hands and kissed me.

He slicked his fingers and slid two inside me easily, still kissing me, then added a third and curled his fingertips over my prostate. Ripples of warmth ran through me and I wrapped my legs around him.

"Now, please, now."

Faron stroked himself with lube and opened me slowly on his dick. When he went slow like this it always had me clawing at the sheets and at his back, needing him to be completely inside me. He squeezed his eyes shut tight and his mouth fell open as he thrust in to the root.

He ran his left hand up my stomach and then down along the side of my ribs. I felt shaky and hot and everything was sensitive and throbbing. Then he stroked my cock and balls with his right hand, still slick with lube, and I moaned. I wasn't erect, but the friction as he stroked me was exquisite and my ass clamped down on him.

"Fuck me, please, please. I just want to feel you, okay?"

Faron groaned and kissed me again, then let loose. He thrust into me deep and hard and I grasped at his back so I didn't slide up the bed. His hips were like liquid, his movements smooth and fast. Then he slowed down for a while and we both shivered at the drag of his cock in my ass. I squeezed around him in pulses and he moaned brokenly.

I was doing this to him. My body. I was making him feel good, even though I wasn't going to get an erection. I'd never felt so close to anyone. Never felt so appreciated. So...revered.

It made my chest tighten and my eyes tear and I pulled him even closer with my legs.

I needed something. A word or a kiss or...I wasn't sure. I

heard a soft whimper I didn't mean to make and Faron's eyes shot open.

"How are you doing?" he asked, sliding all the way inside me and stilling. He stroked my cheek.

I nodded. "Do I...feel okay?"

It wasn't what I'd meant to ask.

"You feel amazing. You're so hot and tight and when you squeeze all around me. Fuck." He shuddered. He ran a finger over my mouth, then kissed me softly. "You're so beautiful."

I could feel myself flush and I smiled.

"You are," I told him, and squeezed my ass around him to watch his eyes flutter shut.

He jerked inside me and started thrusting again, slow and deep. He paused to add more lube and when he pushed back inside, he slid across my prostate and I shuddered as pleasure pulsed through me. He kept the angle and thrust harder and faster, groaning.

The slippery heat of him, the friction, the crush of his hard muscles, and the smell of his hair and his skin. It was everything I wanted.

"Fuck, baby, I'm gonna come," he said, and I moaned and nodded.

I squeezed around him as hard as I could and watched his face as he came with a broken cry. Wet heat filled me and as he thrust again and again I could feel the slick wetness of his come.

"Oh god," he moaned as I tightened around him one last time, trying to milk every drop from him.

I felt shaky and hot and when he pulled out I reached between my legs and felt his come seep out of my hole.

"Oh," I gasped, and looked up at him with wet fingers.

He crushed me to him and kissed me deeply, his fingers slipping against my hole too. He groaned into my mouth and pressed his fingers back inside me.

"I've never done that," I said.

"Me neither." He kissed my neck and I shivered at the feeling of his fingers playing in the come inside me. "How are you feeling?"

"Good," I whispered. "So good. Faron." His name escaped from my lips like something devout. I said it again. I felt so raw, so open, so connected. It was what I'd always wanted. "Thank you for believing me."

He looked at me searchingly and I felt a tear slip down toward my ear.

"I'm not sad," I said.

"I know," he said.

He watched me like he might watch me forever if I let him. I knew that I would.

He slid another finger in my ass and stroked my prostate softly and I gasped. I glanced down at my cock, which lay against my thigh. It was soft and flushed.

"I can't…" I gestured to my cock and Faron caught my hand and pressed a kiss to my fingertips, then pressed it to the bed.

"Does it feel good?"

He stroked over my prostate again. A shivery heat crackled inside me.

"Yes," I whispered.

He played with my ass, dropping kisses over my thighs and my belly. He kissed the tip of my dick and underneath my balls. I was so relaxed and at peace that I felt like I might float away. I reached my hand out to him, needing something to keep me here, and Faron laced his fingers with mine.

"Still feel good?" he asked, so soft it was like something out of a dream.

I nodded.

"You just tell me if you want me to stop. Okay?"

I nodded again and closed my eyes. He didn't expect anything of me. I didn't need to do anything. I just needed to be here. Here with Faron.

I whispered his name to remind myself that he was here. That he was mine. Tears leaked out of the corners of my closed eyes and he squeezed my hand.

He was moving so softly inside me and squeezing my hand so hard and his lips were on my stomach and his hair stroked my thighs and I was drifting, drifting on the warmth of being held.

Then an ocean opened up inside me and a deep, hot pulse of pleasure radiated through my pelvis. I gasped at the sensation and my eyes flew open and it was still happening, like I was liquifying from the inside out.

"Oh, oh, oh, oh."

The orgasm was deep and continuous and it washed through me from sternum to thighs and left me gasping.

I pushed at Faron's shoulder and he slid his fingers out and lay beside me.

"I-I— I don't…"

I curled in on myself as something broke open in my chest. I was crying but my tears felt clean and fresh and shocking.

"Oh, love. Come here."

I turned toward Faron and he wrapped his arms around me and held me as I wept.

"I don't know what happened," I mumbled into his chest.

"You mean having an orgasm without being hard?"

His voice was so gentle, like he knew that every sharp edge tore at me.

I shrugged and pressed even closer.

I knew that was possible, sure, but I'd never thought about it. Even when I'd gotten Kaspar to fuck me when I didn't have an erection, it hadn't felt anything like that.

"I just, I never… I felt…"

It was useless because I didn't have words.

Except…

I couldn't stop my trembling. I whispered it so softly against his neck that it was hardly audible.

"I felt so loved."

I could feel Faron hear it. His arms tightened around me convulsively and his breath caught. I started really crying, and the harder I cried, the closer he held me.

I cried because somehow I had landed somewhere I wanted to be and I realized perhaps it was the first time I'd wanted to be somewhere.

I cried because I finally knew what it felt like to love someone more than I hated myself.

I cried because the night I decided to kill myself, I wanted to use a knife. I wanted to watch the blood leave my body so I could see that it was really happening but all I could hear in my head was Ms. Merchant saying *Clean hands, clean hands* the day I showed up to my lesson wearing nail polish and I put the knife down just in case.

And I cried because I'd put the knife down and I was here and because Faron.

I was saying *I love you* and *I'm sorry* and I couldn't tell where one ended and the other began.

I was saying *I love you* over and over because if I stopped, I didn't know what would happen and I tried to make a promise that if I stopped and he didn't say anything I would still be okay.

Then I stopped. And he didn't say anything. And I was. I was okay.

Faron cleaned us up with my shirt because I couldn't let go of him, and then he pulled the covers up over us both as we lay on our sides, face to face. I was shaking and he tucked the covers tight around me. He slid closer to me and stroked my hair back from my face, but I was still trembling.

"Sorry," I said. My voice sounded shredded. "I'm not cold, I don't think. I just...can't stop."

He pulled me in and kissed me softly, twining his fingers in the hair at my nape. Little by little, I stopped shaking, until it was just a tremble in my hands and knees. I didn't know how long

Beautiful.
Now that's some real character growth.

he'd held me like that, just kissing and letting me calm down, but as I took a deep breath I felt okay. Tired, but okay.

Faron was gazing at me, playing with my hair.

"Can I sleep here with you?" I asked.

He nodded, but didn't look away. His mouth was soft and his eyes were bright and his fingers stilled in my hair.

"I love you, Jude Lucen," he said, even and low.

And *that* was the most beautiful thing I'd ever heard.

CHAPTER FIFTEEN

I WOKE up to find Faron clutching at me in the predawn dark. He was sweating and tears streaked down his face. He was saying my name like he was in a trance.

"What's wrong?" I asked over and over. "Are you okay?"

He was looking at my wrists, my neck, my chest.

"Sweetheart, stop," I said, trying to catch his hands.

He seemed to snap out of it, and let out a shuddery breath. Then he kissed my wrists and my neck and flopped back on the bed.

"Did you have a bad dream?"

He nodded haltingly.

"What happened?

He turned his head to look at me and all I saw there was anguish.

"I dreamt you were dead."

———

FARON FELL BACK ASLEEP after his nightmare, but I couldn't. I lay with his head on my shoulder, separating his curls as the sun rose and crept through the tall windows to spill along the concrete floor. It was Sunday. I hadn't answered any of my mom's calls since Kaspar came to Melt.

When Faron rolled over onto his back, I slid out of bed slowly. Waffle lifted her head from her dog bed and looked at me hopefully, with her mouth open. I pulled on my underwear and a sweatshirt of Faron's and crept toward the dog.

"Okay, okay," I whispered, and Waffle shambled up and trotted into the kitchen next to me. I tipped breakfast into her bowl and refilled her water and she immediately shoved her face in the food, scraping the bowl across the floor. I glanced back to make sure the noise hadn't woken Faron, but he was curled on his side, fast asleep. Fuck, he was so beautiful.

I forced myself not to sit at the edge of his bed and stare at him like a creep, and dug out my phone instead to text my mom.

I had a text from Christopher. He'd been texting me constantly since he'd come over the other day, but I didn't mind. There was an honesty to it now. As if before he'd been trying to hide that he was worriedly checking up on me, and now he was coming out and asking if I was still alive.

You eat? He'd written last night. Then, *I'm gonna make up a couple different smoothie recipes so you don't get sick of that one.*

I texted him back, *I know you're a food professional and you have a reputation to consider, but I've eaten the same ten foods for the last twenty years.*

But I added a smiley face and an apple emoji so he knew I appreciated it.

Then, with a glance at the bed, only Faron's curls and one arm visible in the tangle of bedclothes, I wrote: *Faron and I are together. For real, I think. Thanks for helping, bro. We'll hang soon, yeah?*

Then I started to text my mom, but even though Christopher and I had showed her how to use do not disturb on her phone, I still worried that she didn't do it and I might wake her. I got the feeling that she was afraid to turn it off now that I wasn't staying in my old room. I decided to email her instead. I dashed off a quick *I'm fine, just not feeling chatty* email and groaned at all the unread messages. I hadn't checked my email since Kaspar was here either.

I scrolled through the messages and ignored most of them, but there was one from Timothy. He was the percussionist for the BSO and had been one of the people I was fondest of in Boston, but he'd been Kaspar's friend first. In the last year I was in Boston, I hadn't seen much of him outside of performances, and I hadn't been in contact with him at all since I came back to Philly.

I'd assumed that like so many of the other musicians I'd thought were my friends as well as Kaspar's, he'd taken Kaspar's side when I left.

The email was a few days old.

HEY JUDE,

I know we haven't talked in a while but I hope you're doing okay. I hope we can get back in touch and have a longer convo but I wanted to email you because Kaspar told me he had been to see you in Philadelphia and he said he was pretty sure that you weren't going to be coming back to Boston. Since Maria mentioned you'd emailed her to see if she had any piano connections in Philadelphia, I thought maybe it was true?

Well, I don't know if you'd be interested, but one of my best friends is on the faculty at Curtis and I'd love to email intro you. Even if you're not interested in teaching, or they aren't hiring, Emmeline would be a great person for you to know in the city. She's a truly excellent musician and a kickass human being. I think you guys would get along.

Also...I don't really know how to say this so I guess I'll just say it and I hope you know what I mean. Jude, you and Kaspar were both my friends, but I wasn't a good friend to you. Over the years, I watched Kaspar act really badly sometimes. In front of us, or sometimes the way he talked about you when you weren't there. I saw it happen and I didn't say anything. I didn't call him on it because I told myself his relationship wasn't my business. But I also didn't say anything to you. I never told you that he was wrong to act the way he did, or that if you needed someone else to talk to I was there to listen. I guess I didn't want to make waves? Maybe I was just afraid of confronting a friend. But the way Kaspar's been talking about you since you left Boston makes me realize that he's not someone whose friendship I should value.

So I just wanted to say: I'm really sorry. I'm sorry I wasn't a better friend and I'm sorry I never stuck up for you. I should have.

Love, Timothy

I READ it three times before I put down my phone, and a warmth kindled in my stomach. There had always been some part of me that had thought since no one ever said that Kaspar treated me badly, it wasn't really true. That I'd exaggerated it in my head. Made him into the bad guy so I could feel better. Reading Timothy's email, something released inside me. His acknowledgment of reality set me free.

Faron stirred and I slid back into bed and kissed his cheek. His arms came around me and he pulled me on top of him without even opening his eyes. He'd fallen asleep last night without tying his hair back and now curls fell over his mouth. He wrinkled his nose and tried to blow it out of his face. He was so fucking adorable.

I gathered his hair away from his face for him since I wanted his hands to stay on me.

"Do you want a hair tie?" I gestured to the bedside table where he had bandannas and headbands and elastics.

"Boy, don't come anywhere near my hair," he grumbled sleepily, opening one eye. "You can't even handle your own."

He pulled me closer and ran his fingers through the knots in my hair. I melted against him as he started rubbing my scalp.

"Mmmm." I curled into him, trying to get closer, and he ran a hand up my spine under his sweatshirt that I was wearing.

"You're such a cat right now," he said. He rolled us so we were lying on our sides facing each other. "You look good in this color, baby."

The sweatshirt was a plummy color that he could probably name. I shrugged. I just bought everything in black usually.

"Thanks."

I traced the lines of his face, glad to see that sleep seemed to have erased the strain I'd seen yesterday, and the nightmare hadn't imprinted itself. I wanted to apologize for that nightmare, but I knew Faron wouldn't think it was my fault. And the way he was looking at me, I could almost believe it.

"Do you still—" I clamped my mouth shut.

"Hmm?"

I shook my head. I was a total goon.

"Jude."

I tried to kiss him to distract him and he caught my chin.

"Do I still what?"

My face heated and I closed my eyes, thinking of how I'd felt last night.

"Do I still love you?" Faron's voice was soft and serious and I opened my eyes. "Is that what you were going to ask?"

I cringed miserably but nodded.

"I love you." He said it soft and slow against my lips, so I felt every syllable. He said it like he felt it, and not like he was irritated that I already needed to hear it again. I closed my eyes because it was almost too much to feel. He kissed me and I fed the words back to him on my tongue.

We kissed until my stomach gave a loud growl. Faron would kill me if he knew how bad it had gotten before Christopher came over.

We made our way to the kitchen and I took my meds and ate a handful of dry cereal, but I felt woozy.

"Um, will you check your phone and see if Christopher texted you?" I asked.

He shot me a questioning look and checked his phone, then tapped out a text.

Faron sat me down on one of the stools and plugged in the blender. I couldn't meet his eyes.

His phone buzzed with a text and when he saw it, he tipped my chin up and kissed me.

"I'll make sure I have this stuff here. You make sure you have it at your house too, okay?"

"Christopher won't tell me what's in it."

"Does that help?"

"I don't know."

"Well I'm going to make this for you and you're gonna drink it. You're gonna see it makes you feel good. I'll make it for you again and again. Then, after a while, even if you know what's in it, you'll know you like it. Okay?"

"I'll try. But I'm not sure."

"Good." He kissed me lightly on the lips. "Go sit down so you don't see, then."

I sat on the couch and tossed a toy for Waffle as the blender whirred.

Faron handed me a cup and pulled my bare legs over his. He'd pulled on loose cotton pants that were soft against my skin.

I took a tentative sip of the smoothie. It didn't taste the same as Christopher's had, but it was close. I took another sip. Could I drink it? I thought I could.

"Chug it if you have to," Faron said, squeezing my knee.

"I am not a frat boy," I snapped, and Faron grinned.

"No. Of course not. You're very fancy."

I glared at him, but I couldn't keep the smile off my face when he blew me a kiss.

"So, Sabien's coming back," he said.

"What? Back where? When?"

"Keep drinking. Back to New York. He's getting discharged soon. My mom wants me to come to a family dinner for him."

"Is that why he emailed you all those questions before?"

He nodded and guilt washed over me that I'd forgotten to ask about it before.

I'll do better. I'm going to pay better attention.

"Are you going to go?"

He traced pictures in the freckles on my pale shins and nodded. "I told her I would. I can't believe it's been so long since I've seen him."

I reached for his hand and pulled him closer.

"Are you nervous?"

He thought about it and I finished the last of the smoothie and put the cup on the coffee table.

"Yeah," he said finally. "Little bit."

Before I could say anything, he pulled me even closer and my sweatshirt slid up, exposing my thighs. He *mmm*ed appreciatively and ran a gentle hand up and down the side of my thigh.

"So, I just got this email. From a friend in Boston. He said his friend works at Curtis and might have some connections for me."

"What's Curtis?"

"The Curtis Institute of Music. It's a conservatory. In Rittenhouse. You've seen it—it's right across from Parc." He squinted. "Oh, it's next to the Art Alliance."

"Okay, yeah. Is it a college-level school? Like Julliard?"

"Yeah, exactly. It's pretty amazing. I really would have wanted to go there if it was anywhere besides Philly. It's totally merit based, so the students don't pay. And you know how unusual that is for an arts school." He nodded. "I don't know, I don't want to get my hopes up because Timothy didn't even know if they're hiring or anything. But…maybe it'd be something? A contact, anyway."

"A contact is good. A contact is really good. Would you want to teach? You hate giving lessons."

I grimaced at the reminder that I'd have to get back to that this week.

"Working with musicians who are really good isn't like giving lessons to kids. It's kind of exciting, actually. More like collaborating on their playing, maybe? I worked with some Berklee students when I was in Boston for a few summers, before I started going to Tanglewood. They were really talented. It was cool to be an outside ear, point out things they were doing that they didn't even realize, or work on habits they were trying to break, and then hear them get better, or get closer to the kind of musicians they wanted to be."

"That sounds gratifying. I'm sure you'd be great at it."

I kissed his fingers but slumped against him.

"I'm so out of practice at this point they'd probably laugh me out of the building."

He turned me to look at him. In the morning light his eyes were the rich gray-brown of sea-touched driftwood and I never wanted to look away.

"Well, then," he said softly. "You better finish fixing that piano quick so you can get back to practicing, hmm?" He kissed me and stood up. "I'm gonna walk the dog."

CHAPTER SIXTEEN

I'D BEEN WORKING on the piano every day for a week, driven by the urge to feel the keys under my fingers again and the pedal at my foot. Each piece I put back into place was a promise to myself, from myself.

A promise that I could have the music again, on my own terms. A promise that anything that can be taken apart can be put back together.

In between working on the piano and giving lessons, I updated my resume and gathered a list of people to send it to that seemed like it included every person in Philadelphia and most of New York. I dropped twenty dollars on Ginger's station and printed my resumes on Small Change's printer, ending up with a stack so tall it looked like a manuscript. Ginger looked at me with big eyes, but then she held up her hand for a high five and said, "You got this, bro."

I was really coming around to the "bro" thing.

Phee, Ginger's backup-cum-part-time tattoo artist, was at his station, and his eyes widened at the stack of papers too. Phee looked really young at first glance, because of his messy hair and short stature, but his eyes told a different story. Still, he was certainly much younger than me because when he asked what the papers were and I told him they were resumes he gave me a strange look and said, "Uh, I'm probably the last person to talk about profesh anything, but...don't people, like, email that stuff now?"

Ginger started cracking up and tried to cover it by coughing.

"Thanks," I told Phee, and walked back to Faron's in a daze. It had become my home base this week because the piano was there, but every night I sank into Faron's bed felt more and more right, and my desire to finish the piano warred with my desire to stay. Sometimes while I was sanding keys, I indulged in fantasies of breaking pieces of it, Penelope-like, so that I ended the day no closer to completion than I'd begun it.

When he got home from walking Waffle, Faron rested his chin on top of my head and wrapped his arms around my waist. The pile of resumes loomed in front of me, and "Also sprach Zarathustra" as arranged for *2001: A Space Odyssey* played in my mind.

"I should email these, shouldn't I?"

He kissed my neck.

"Yes."

I groaned and turned in his arms.

"I just wasted a lot of paper and energy." I buried my face in his neck so I couldn't see the stack.

"We can use it for scrap paper. I'll make a sketch book."

He stroked my hair back, untangling it with his fingers.

"Okay."

We stood that way for a while, Waffle nosing around our knees and then trundling off to doze under Faron's easel.

"I'm gonna finish tonight," I said into Faron's neck.

"Yeah? You need any help?"

I shook my head. I had to do this on my own.

"Will you play something for me when you're done?"

"Anything."

———

IT WAS DONE. I'd tested every key, checked every bit of hardware. I'd halfway expected to end up with an extra pedal or a screw I'd forgotten, like the completion of Ikea furniture, but there were none. I had taken a broken god, torn it down to a pile of nothing, and built it back into something I could worship again.

Next thing I knew, Faron's hands were on my shoulders and he was pressing a kiss to my neck.

"You look like you're trying to play by staring at it."

"It...exists," I said.

"Play for me, Jude."

I repositioned a chair in front of the piano.

"What do you want to hear?"

"Anything. Everything."

He looked at me dreamily, eyes less focused than usual.

"You okay?" I asked, sliding a hand up his ribs.

"Yeah. I'm great. Play for me."

"Well, I could... Do you remember when I was telling you about black classical composers?" He nodded. "Samuel Coleridge-Taylor was the composer who got really inspired by meeting with poets and other intellectuals and... Do you remember?"

I was so nervous all of a sudden. Shaky and trying to stall.

"I remember."

"I, um. The other day I looked up one of his pieces. I thought you might like to hear it. Since you were interested. Or, since you were asking. Maybe you're not interested. I don't know if—"

Faron wrapped a hand around my hair and slowly tugged my head back. He leaned down and kissed my mouth. His kiss was so sweet, so gentle, so unexpected that I felt like I lost my balance. Felt like I was falling backward.

"Play it for me," he whispered against my mouth.

I forced myself to blink and to take a breath and let it out. I forced my fingers to touch the keys. Then I sank into the music. It didn't matter what it was—I was just glad that I was playing something for Faron. Glad to play something I had no history with except what I was making. When I finished, I couldn't look at Faron.

"That was 'Deep River,'" I said, eyes on my fingers where they rested on the keys.

"That was beautiful," he said. His voice sounded like it was coming from very far away. "Play something else." I felt his fingers in my hair, then at the nape of my neck. Light. Just touching and then gone.

So I played.

I didn't let myself think about it, didn't let myself decide. I played a note and then I played another note, and the music was there. I closed my eyes and felt the instrument beneath my fingers and knew that as long as I didn't stop, the notes would keep coming.

I played beginnings and endings and middles. I played my favorite bits of things and parts of popular songs I'd heard on the radio. I played like I could recharge myself as long as my fingers never lost contact with the keys.

And as I played, a sense of relief welled up in me, so immediate that it took my breath away. I let it spill over and I kept playing.

You didn't lose it. It's still here. You didn't ruin everything. There is still this. This is still good. There is hope, here.

I didn't know how long I played, but when I stopped it felt like I'd simply run out of notes to play and silence was the next one. It was how I'd often felt when I was performing and came to the end of a piece. As if there were three final notes: the last of the composition, silence, then applause.

I looked around, dazed, to find Faron watching me from his

easel, paintbrush in hand. He didn't say anything and I fumbled around for words.

"Do you need me to keep sitting here?" I asked finally, gesturing to his painting.

He shook his head.

"The piano doesn't sound great," I said, running light fingertips across the keys. It had a muffled, slightly flat sound. "Maybe the wood warped a little bit in ways that distorted it, or maybe it just needs to be professionally tuned."

"Come here," Faron said.

I walked to him on shaky legs.

He stood me in front of him, facing his canvas. I loved to watch him paint because he formed things in a way I couldn't conceptualize. He laid in paint in patches and layers that cohered into form and figure by way of contrast, but he didn't use any kind of outlines. It was all shade and shadow and highlight and gesture. There was a softness to his work—a dreaminess. And yet he painted boldly. On the canvas, the contrast coalesced into something beautiful and unique. He painted just as he was: strong and certain and gentle and open and captivated.

And tonight what he'd painted was me.

Me, pale skin flushed, eyes closed, hair a cloud of fire around me, its flames licking the dark creature I played. It was a piano, it was a dragon, it was a writhing, corbeau thing that I stroked with one hand and eviscerated with the other. It had scales that were the keys and eyes half closed beneath ridged brows. Its expression was part ecstasy and part pain. So was mine. It had dark wings that curled to touch the fire of my hair. They could have been protecting or consuming me, but its spiny tail curled around my ankles like a pet cat.

My freckles, which he always painted with flecks of metallic gold, spattered the whole painting, like I'd played and played until I'd pushed my outer membrane away and splattered it onto the world.

"Jesus Christ," I murmured.

"That's you," he said in my ear, voice low and avid. "You tame the thing you fear and you make it a part of yourself. You take the parts of yourself you fear and put them into the music. You live with all of it, swirling around you and draped on you and you curl into it like a blanket sometimes and sometimes banish it. That's you."

He pointed to my face on the canvas, pale and freckled and strange and always somehow beautiful as he rendered it.

"In love with the music and in love with the darkness. Terribly afraid and in love anyway."

My breath caught in my throat and my heart raced.

"Do you see yourself?"

He kept my face turned to the canvas. I nodded.

"That's how I see you."

He finally let me turn to look up at his face and I saw so much feeling there I almost gasped.

"Your battle and your love are the same to me, Jude."

He said it so low and rough I stared at him uncomprehendingly for a moment. He repeated it. He said it a third time. A fourth. I stared at him and he said it again.

Finally, like practicing a piece over and over, I got the shape of it. He said it again. He kissed me and said it one more time, and then he held us together, close, lips a breath apart.

He held me so I lived inside his words, and their shape became my shape.

He was answering my question. The one I'd asked a hundred times in glances or clutches, but never quite let myself put into words: *How? How can you love me? How can you, who are so magnificent, love me as I am?*

I couldn't find a single thing to say except "Thank you." It wasn't thank you for loving me this time though. It was thank you for helping me understand. Thank you for saying something I could believe.

I kissed Faron's chin and the bridge of his perfect nose. His eyebrows and his cheekbones and the swell of his cheeks as he smiled slightly. I pulled him down on the bed and we stripped our clothes off, but it felt like moving in a dream, every desperate motion rendered languid. I licked along the lines of his tattoos, over his shoulders and down his chest, taking his nipples roughly into my mouth until he arched his back and slid his fingers into my hair.

Down I went, over ribs and navel, and buried my face at the juncture of his thigh. He smelled like nighttime—amber and salt and something fresh like a breeze off the water. He was gloriously hard, erection straining against his belly even as his thighs were open and relaxed. His cock was a shade darker than his skin, the head ruddy, and I ran my tongue up the underside, tracing the vein. I wanted to play him the way I'd played the piano, the way he had played me so many times. I wanted him to feel how much I appreciated him. Every part of him.

I stroked his thighs open farther, enjoyed the contrast of rough hair and soft skin against my palms. I nuzzled at his balls and breathed in his scent. It was home. When I groaned and dropped light kisses along his balls and up his erection, Faron slid a hand into my hair and I shuddered. His hand in my hair always felt like an anchor, a connection, but tonight it felt like a consecration.

I knelt between his thighs and took him into my mouth gently at first, then deeper, harder. I fluttered my tongue at his frenulum and took his balls in my hand. I sucked him hard, licked teasingly, bore down and backed away. I wanted a story of feeling—beginning and variation; crescendo and plateau. I wanted to worship him.

Finally, he was moaning with every touch, and his hips jerked beneath me. His hand had never left my hair, and now his other hand fisted in the sheets desperately. I felt hot and achy and satisfied, my whole attention on the man in front of me.

"Jude, baby, please," he said unevenly, every muscle tensed, and his voice was raw with need for me.

I moaned and dragged my tongue around the head of his cock, then took him as deep as I could. I pressed my thumb behind his balls as I sucked, and he cried out. My skin thrummed with arousal and I could feel myself getting hard. It had been happening a little easier the last few days. I pressed even harder, and Faron bucked down my throat with a shout. I curled my tongue around him and he was coming in hot, seizing pulses, head thrown back on a silent cry.

His hand tightened almost painfully in my hair as he came and I moaned around his cock, licking him softly as he slowly relaxed.

He drew me up the bed and I settled half on top of him, kissing him. He swept his tongue against mine and hummed with pleasure.

"You look so hot between my legs," he murmured, and I shivered with lust. His fingertips running up and down my spine, creeping closer to my ass, made me thrust my hips against his.

"I love making you feel good," I said.

"Mmm. Now can I make you feel good?"

I whimpered and pressed against him. My skin felt hot and too tight and suddenly the evening felt like it caught up with me. I was overwhelmed and shaky. I grabbed for Faron's hand and he cupped my cheek.

"Or we can just stay like this," he said softly. I threw my leg over his hip and closed my eyes, breathing him in, taking note of the solid feel of his body around me.

"I want to feel good," I said. "I mean, I do feel good, but I could…" I broke off, annoyed by words because they were useless in the face of how I felt.

"I could make you feel a different kind of good," he said. He ran a hand over my cock so softly it felt like a whisper and I arched against him, moaning.

"Please," I said, eyes squeezed tightly shut. When he touched me like this, so gently, it did things to me. Deep, dark things that made me go inside myself and bring him there with me.

"I can take some things away," he murmured. "Help you focus on how I make you feel."

I nodded and he slipped something over my closed eyes. It was the bandanna he used like a headband to keep his hair back sometimes. His smell on it soothed me.

"Okay?" he asked, breath warm against my neck, and I nodded.

He moved away from me and I reached out for him automatically.

"I'm not going anywhere," he said. "I'm just getting something. Listen. Can you hear me moving around?"

I listened. I could hear him. I nodded because somehow I knew he was watching me.

The bed dipped as he sat back down and then I felt his mouth on mine, warm and familiar. He arranged me on my back, arms and legs starfished. He touched me, gentle and slow, over my ribs. But it didn't feel like his hand. I turned to look, even though I couldn't see what he was doing.

"Do you know what that is?"

He stroked along my stomach this time, and I shivered.

It wasn't the feeling of the thing that gave it away, it was how Faron wielded it.

"Paintbrush," I said. My voice sounded breathless.

He dipped into my navel with the brush and then circled my nipples, the bristles just rough enough to drag a gasp from me.

"More than one brush," I said, as a rougher, larger brush swept up my side and under my arm.

"Mhmm."

Faron wasn't touching me at all, only the brushes were. I never knew where they would touch me, or when, so each contact made me jump, and each caress made me moan. A brush snaked down into the crease of my thigh and electricity shot through my cock.

"Pull your knees up and let them fall open."

I did it, and tried to feel for him on the bed. I felt small and vulnerable in the middle of a vast space. For a moment, I had the sensation that the paintbrushes had worked like giant erasers and wiped me out entirely. I couldn't find him.

"I'm right here, baby. I've got you."

His voice came from the foot of the bed and I lifted my head up even though I couldn't see him. His hand closed around my ankle and I jerked at his touch. It felt like it had been forever.

"It's okay," he said. "I'm not going anywhere."

My head dropped back and I nodded.

The next touch made me arch off the bed. It was a feather-soft brush stroking my erection from root to tip. Faron stroked every inch of me with maddening pressure—too light to get friction but so deeply erotic and unfamiliar that it made my dick leak. He feathered the brush over my tip and I shuddered. There was nothing to press into; the bristles gave way with the slightest force.

"You look so gorgeous like this," he said. "You're flushed and your nipples are this hot, dark pink from the brush. Now you're desperate for contact but you can't get it. Jesus, seeing you try to fuck this paintbrush because you're so turned on?" He groaned low in his throat. "Exquisite."

I was practically choking on shame at his description, but it just ramped me up higher because I knew he liked it. Liked when I was open and wanton and desperate.

Then the brush dipped lower and stroked my balls and I whimpered, clutching at the sheets. It was too much and not enough and I felt like my whole body came alive with every light touch.

"Someday I'm going to paint you like this with these same brushes. Spread out, leaking and desperate. Mouth open, legs open, so eager to be touched that you strain toward every contact."

The image shot a bolt of lust through me and my hips bucked. The thought of him spending hours in the image of me as he'd described it. The idea that he could look at it whenever he wanted. I whimpered and Faron made a low, satisfied sound.

The brush tickled behind my balls, then swept over my hole. I clenched up, but then another brush took its place, short-bristled and slightly rough. It dragged over my hole like a tiny tongue and I tried to press back on it to get more contact, but it just kept circling my opening maddeningly.

Everything felt hypersensitive, swollen and dry and straining, except the line of precome I could feel sliding down my throbbing erection.

"Please, please," I begged, scrabbling in the sheets. "Please!"

"Relax for me," he said softly.

Shuddering, I forced myself to breathe and relax every muscle. Then ever so slowly, something slid inside me. It was slim and smooth, and didn't feel like much until Faron angled it and it brushed over my prostate.

I screamed at the contact as pleasure crackled through my whole pelvis. My thighs trembled.

"Is that... Oh god, is that the paintbrush?"

"Mmmm," Faron hummed. I knew which one it was too. A small, slim, plastic-handled brush he didn't use often. He angled the handle again and I clenched every muscle at the pleasure. Coming after all the light, barely there touches, it was so intense it almost felt like I was coming every time. But it was also impersonal and I ached for more.

I didn't even realize I was saying "Please" again, saying it over and over, until I jumped at a warm kiss pressed to the inside of my thigh. Then the brush slid out and nothing was touching me. I knew Faron wouldn't have left me, but I felt so profoundly alone that I started to cry.

Then Faron's voice was right there again, and one hand was back on my ankle.

"You need more, love?"

"Please, please, please, please, please."

"You could have touched yourself at any point. You could have touched me. But you didn't. Why?"

I was confused and so desperately on the edge between arousal and pain that it took me a minute to realize that what he'd said was true.

"I wanted... I wanted to have whatever you gave me," I said.

A kiss high on the inside of my thigh.

"Why?"

I was crying for real now, pleasure crossed with fear that I would never be able to come. That I would stay stuck here forever.

"Why, baby? Tell me."

"Because I wanted to be good for you," I said thickly, and heard Faron's breath catch.

"You were. You are. You're perfect."

Then Faron's hands were on me and I could feel his heavy cock at my entrance.

"You, yes, please, you, please, oh god, please," I was saying, and then he sank inside me and I sobbed in relief. Pleasure streaked through every nerve, but the hot, slick, human pleasure of Faron's cock and his hands and his balls pressed against mine was so different from the touches before that my brain almost couldn't process it. It felt like more, more, more, so much more that all I could do was feel it.

He was murmuring beautiful, sweet, hot things to me. Each powerful stroke of his cock inside me felt like completion. Every sweep and caress of the brushes over my skin had been the outline, the prelude, and now they coalesced into this throbbing, pulsing crescendo. Bass notes and high notes, muscular splat of paint hitting canvas. Squeeze and slide and harmony and thick minor chord all at once, and I was coming on his cock without even touching myself. Coming in shuddering waves that made me clutch at Faron and tensed every muscle in my body to a great explosive release.

Faron snapped his hips and groaned into my neck and I pulsed once more around him, my body totally overtaken by pleasure and release and then sweet darkness. I relaxed into the softness of the bed and drifted in outer space, stars floating past me, bright and safe.

"I'll be right back, okay?" I heard Faron say from somewhere back on earth. "Do you want this off?" He touched the bandanna. I shook my head.

I kept drifting and vaguely registered what sounded like water and then light switches flicking off. A warm touch to my shoulder told me Faron was back. He ran a damp washcloth over my stomach and back between my legs, and then slid into bed and pulled the covers up. I rolled into him, wrapping an arm around his stomach and burying my face in his neck.

"Hey," he said softly, stroking along my spine. "You back with me?"

I nodded.

"Can I take this off?"

I nodded again and the bandanna slipped off. It was dark, just the slight glow of the bedside lamp on one click. I blinked and Faron's face came into focus.

"Love and battle," I said, staring at him. At least, I tried to say it. It came out slurred and low. But I knew he heard me because his eyes went soft.

"Love and battle," he said.

CHAPTER SEVENTEEN

MY MEETING WITH EMMELINE, Timothy's friend who taught at Curtis, was at noon, and I had been up since five, when I'd started pacing around the apartment because I couldn't sit still. Waffle had thought it was a fun game and had begun walking beside me, but she'd taken to barking one single bark every time we reached the kitchen and turned around, as a gentle suggestion that while we were in there I might as well give her breakfast. The barking woke Faron up, and he took one look at me and dragged me back to bed where he proceeded to screw the living daylights out of me until I calmed down a little.

So. The morning wasn't all bad.

He'd walked with me to Rittenhouse Square, taking my cigarettes after I chain-smoked three, and said he was going to browse the work at Philly Art Alliance while I was meeting with Emmeline. He said he'd forgotten all about the place, but I couldn't help but suspect maybe he just thought I'd freak if I went on my own. I tried to be mad about that, but I did want him there. I told myself that he'd never hesitated to tell me the truth about his motivations before, even when they weren't flattering, so I didn't know why he'd hedge now.

I met Emmeline at Parc, the bistro on the corner, right across the street from Curtis, facing Rittenhouse Square. I was a little early, so I stood awkwardly at the corner, trying to keep far enough from the host's stand that they wouldn't try to seat me. It was always easier to let people find me, since all I had to do was tell them the color of my hair.

"Jude?" I spun around to see a woman crossing the narrow street. I waved and smiled, immediately struck by the picture she cut, striding toward me.

Emmeline was very tall with broad shoulders, and her dark hair was held up in a loose twist with a pencil. She had perfect posture and walked with her toes turned out like a ballet dancer.

"It's so nice to meet you," she said. "I'm glad Timothy thought to put us in touch." Then she looked right at me and somehow I knew that Timothy had told her the whole story. But instead of feeling shifty and resentful as I often did, I found myself immediately comfortable with her. "Well. Shall we get a table? Is outside all right? I'm positively starved for fresh air today."

"Outside's great."

She had us seated and drinks ordered so easily that I felt myself relax and sent up a silent *Thank you* to Timothy.

"So, first things first, I actually have a recording of yours, I realized after Timothy called me. It's from the Modern French Composers showcase in Tanglewood a few summers ago. Timothy sent it to me because I love that Miel piece so much and people rarely ever perform it. I like the live recordings so much more, you know? And I've listened to it often, but never realized who the pianist was. So, thank you, for many hours of great music."

She smiled easily, and I found myself smiling back.

"Wow," I said. "You've really got the whole 'charm them immediately and disarm them with flattery' thing going on, huh?"

She nodded sagely. "It is terribly effective. But in this case also completely accurate."

"Thanks. Seriously, thank you. I love that piece too. I'm so glad someone else listened to it. You know the Tanglewood crowds. You can never tell who cares about the music and who's just there to eat macaroni salad from the fancy food tent with their grandchildren and fall asleep on the lawn."

Emmeline grinned. "So listen, I hope you don't mind if I snarf food while you talk? I was running too late for breakfast today and I only have an hour before my next class."

"Of course."

She ordered food and I got coffee and I filled her in on my situation.

I'd sent my resume to the personnel managers of the Philly Orchestra and the opera orchestra, to see if they were in the market for a pianist to play with them when pieces called for it or if they needed a rehearsal pianist; contacted every faculty member at Temple, Villanova, Penn, and some schools I'd never heard of to see if they needed someone to accompany students; and contacted the best churches and synagogues in town to see if they needed an organist or someone to accompany the choir. The next step would be writing to the members of the orchestras to see if they were looking for collaborators, or if they had the need for a pianist in a trio. I was exhausted just thinking about it.

I told her I'd done a slightly more limited version of the same in New York and she nodded and agreed that was what she would do.

Then, for no reason I could imagine, except that she had her mouth full and couldn't talk, I found myself telling her about Faron.

"I could go back to Boston, but there's this guy here in Philly," I said. "And I really want to make it work."

She gave me a dreamy smile and nodded knowingly.

"Got it. We have to keep you here, then." She paused with a thoughtful look on her face, shoved the last bite of her food in her mouth as she was standing, and motioned for me to follow her with her mouth full.

"Don't we have to—"

"Put it on Curtis's tab, okay, Manny?" she called as she passed the host's station, and pressed a bill into his hand. "Thank you! See you next week!"

I jogged across the street after her, and up the stone steps of the building that housed Curtis. It was actually three large mansions that had once stood individually and that the founder of Curtis had bought and renovated into a single building that now made up the school. Or so Google had told me last night.

Emmeline bounded up the stairs and I followed her down a hallway. I could hear talking, laughing, and music coming from the left, but we turned right and it got quieter. Emmeline ducked into an empty office with a desk covered in files and a Steinway with notated sheet music on the music shelf.

"You know Bloch's Three Nocturnes?"

"Sure."

"You know the climax of 'Tempestoso' where the rhythm keeps shifting?"

"Yeah."

"Any chance you'd play the piano part for me? I'm trying to figure out a way to make it so the piano and cello don't over-power the violin, but I need an actual pianist."

I gave her an even look. "And you couldn't find one in this musical wasteland."

She smirked at me. "Will you?"

"Of course." I ran my fingers over the keys.

"Thank you. Once sec."

She popped out and came back with her violin a minute later. Her office must have been close. She shut the door and I felt my heart start to pound. Clearly she wanted to hear me play, but was this an audition? And if it was, that was good, right? Because maybe they had a position open? But also, that was bad, right?

Because I hadn't prepared anything and I was rusty as hell, even after a week of playing on the restored piano at Faron's.

"Can we just start from the beginning?" she asked. "I'm gonna play along, okay?"

I nodded. We both knew we could hear the cello even when it wasn't there, the bass notes rounding out our rangier instruments.

I closed my eyes. I'd performed the piece a handful of times over the years, and I knew it, give or take a bar here or there. But playing with another person was never about getting it note for note—not casually. It was about the way you sounded together, whether you melded well, interpreted the piece in compatible ways.

Just play.

I began to play, and the clear resonance of the Steinway after the shabby sound of the instrument at Faron's gave me goose bumps. I let myself settle into the melody, luxuriate in it like it was warm water.

When Emmeline drew her bow across the violin, the room vibrated with the sound, adding richness and texture. We vibed as well musically as we had energetically and I felt a thrill go through me. It had been far too long since I'd played with someone and I wanted to enjoy every second of it.

When we got to the part Emmeline had mentioned, I changed my posture so I could use the weight of my arm to transfer the pressure from finger to finger for my pianissimo. Fingers hovering right above the keys, I transferred weight gently from note to note to give the impression of a singing line. I could hear Emmeline's violin, and I knew that even the cello's lower notes would be perfectly audible.

We finished and she grinned at me.

"That was perfect. Thank you."

Perfect perfect perfect.

The word slid through my veins and lit me up. It had felt

perfect.

"Listen, I have to get to my class," she said. "But I'm so glad I met you, and got to hear you play. I'm going to think hard about who else to put you in touch with, okay? I'd love to actually get together sometime soon? When I'm not running here and there?"

"I'd really like that. And thank you. For taking the time, and for letting me play. I, uh. I just took apart this broken piano I found and put it back together, but the sound is...pretty much what you'd expect."

I moved reluctantly away from the Steinway.

"You rebuilt a piano? Never mind, there isn't time and I want to hear the whole story."

She walked me to the exit and when she said she'd call me soon, I was pretty sure she meant it. And I was even sad to see her go.

Faron was leaning against the wall outside the exit, looking like he was part of an impromptu photo shoot, and I slid an arm through his before he saw me.

"Hey, how did it go? Looks like good?"

He trailed a finger over my smiling lips.

"Great. Really great. Emmeline's great, the pianos are great. It was just..."

"Great?" Faron finished. He bent to kiss me before I could elbow him in the stomach.

———

I WAS home for the first night in over a week, my bare apartment feeling more and more pathetic with each night I spent in Faron's beautiful space. And Faron's arms. But Faron was working late tonight, and though he'd asked if I wanted to go to his place without him, I couldn't quite make myself say yes the way I wanted to. I didn't live there, and the last thing I wanted to do was wear out my welcome. Especially when things were going so well.

But something was eating at me and I couldn't shake it. I needed a reality check and I didn't want to ask Daniel and Ginger, since they knew Faron.

I chatted Maggie, knowing she'd tell me the truth.

Jude: *Hey, you around? I need your expertise in matters of the heart and your cutthroat honesty.*

Maggie: *hiiii <3 whose throat do I need to cut for you?*

Jude: *:) I'm convincing myself that Faron's upset with me and I can't tell if it's real or in my head.*

Maggie: *tell all leave nothing out.*

Jude: *Well, and upset isn't the right word, really. It's like he's... Okay, so: his brother has been in the military for a long time and is getting discharged next week. His parents and other sibs are in NYC and they want him to come for dinner when his brother gets back into town. They don't have the best relationship but F is going bc of course.*

Maggie: *yeah, hi, twins, obvi you gotta go*

Jude: *Exactly. But I know he's apprehensive about seeing his brother, and his parents too. They didn't love that he moved to Philly and all, and things've been strained.*

I paused, trying to think how to put it.

Maggie: *where's the problem, boo?*

Jude: *Well.*

Jude: *Faron didn't ask me to come to New York with him. Which is totally okay. It's soon to meet the whole family, especially when it's dramatic dynamics and Sabien's been gone so long. I totally get that. It's just...I kind of thought that F would've mentioned it to me. Like, told me that he wished he could invite me but it felt like too soon? Something?*

Jude: *Is that wrong?*

Maggie: *hmmm. well you said f is super communicative right?*

Jude: *He is. Well, he's very honest and clear. He's definitely not a share-every-thought kind of guy though. He's very quiet sometimes.*

Maggie: *are you sad he didn't ask you?*

Jude: *I totally get it—it's really early.*

Maggie: *not my q*

I sighed. As always, if I wanted to hear the music, I had to pay the piper.

Jude: *I'm...a little disappointed. Even though I really do understand why he wouldn't want me to. And also I'd be nervous as hell to go, no matter when it happened. But I guess, yeah, in my heart of hearts I wish he wanted me to come so badly that he threw all caution to the winds. Happy now?*

Maggie: *<3 yes*

Maggie: *k so i think you're very logical and right that its early. but also y'all are clearly super in love so idk if time matters much.*

Maggie: *its obvi what you have to do—you gotta just ask him*

Jude: *I was terribly afraid that would be your advice.*

Maggie: *if he's as honest as you say he'll tell you and then you'll know and knowing is much better than not knowing*

Jude: *True.*

Jude: *Another worry just occurred to me.*

Maggie: *of course it did. hit me*

Jude: *What if they know he's dating a white guy and they don't approve and he hasn't told me because he doesn't want to hurt my feelings?*

Maggie: *uh well if thats the case you DEFINITELY gotta find out bc its a much bigger problem*

Maggie: *or maybe its not idk if he cares what they think*

Jude: *He cares, but he wouldn't let himself be influenced by it. Certainly not by something like that.*

Maggie: *then yr fine. just ask him. tell him the thing*

Jude: *I hate the thing.*

Maggie *devil emoji* *the thing is useful even if you hate it*

Jude: *I hate you.*

Maggie: *i love you too*

———

THE NEXT DAY, I got to Faron's as he was getting out of the shower. I had been wandering around for an hour, trying to convince myself that I was not about to fuck up my relationship with Faron over something silly. Even though I knew intellectually that talking to him about how I felt was the right thing and that Faron would always rather know how I was feeling, my body was still reacting like I was about to be punished. I was vaguely sweaty and my stomach was churning.

Faron smiled at me as I walked in. He was wearing only a towel, and my churning stomach did a flip-flop at how gorgeous he was and how he smiled just for me, and that resulted in the conviction that I was probably about to throw up.

"What's wrong? You look sick," Faron said.

I shook my head. "Hi."

"Hi, baby."

And Jesus Christ, "hi, baby" was so much better than "hi, Jude" that I changed my mind about even bringing up the trip to New York.

Faron dropped the towel and ambled over to the bed, a bead of water sliding down his tawny skin, tracing the groove of his spine. I wished I could lick it off him, but I was frozen to the spot. He tugged on loose cotton pants and a tank top that was more armhole than fabric, and I got lost in watching his skin move over the landscape of his ribs.

"What's going on?" Faron asked, crossing to put his towel back in the bathroom.

"Nothing, I was just going to practice, if that's okay?"

He steered me to a stool and started making coffee and eggs.

"I meant what's up with you. You seem upset. Want a smoothie?"

I shook my head, stomach lurching threateningly.

I stared at the piano while he scrambled his eggs, looking back once they were solid.

"Coffee?"

I shook my head and he narrowed his eyes at me but just poured coffee for himself and ate his eggs, looking over at the piano.

Tell him the thing, Maggie yelled at me. *Tell him the thing*.

"I, uh. Can I tell you something?"

"Anything."

"I— It's— My brain is doing this thing. I know it's maybe not true, but my brain is doing this thing where it thinks that you don't want me to meet your family because you don't really want to be with me, so why bother introducing me to them. And logically I know that it's complicated, because Sabien's been away and of course no one wants to deal with a new boyfriend—or, whatever we are—and it's really soon, and...I know all that but still, my brain is. Saying you are ashamed of me," I finished miserably.

Faron came around the island and pulled me to the couch. He sat down and tugged me down next to him.

"What helps? Me telling you the truth? You telling me more?"

I blinked at him. "I guess it depends on if the truth is that you really are ashamed of me. Or that your parents will hate that you're dating me because I'm white. Shit, that was not the thing I meant to say."

Faron chuckled and I ducked my head.

"Yes, the truth. Please, tell me the truth. Sorry."

He caught my hand and kissed my knuckles.

"I'm not ashamed of you. Quite the opposite. My parents will not hate you because you're white. You remember my mom's a quarter white, right?"

I did remember that but apparently my nerves had overtaken my ability to think.

"They will tease you about things that they ascribe to being white, like for example you playing classical music. But it won't be mean-spirited. And then you can just tell them about Samuel Taylor Coleridge and blow their minds."

"Coleridge-Taylor," I murmured.

"Kalil's wife is white. They tease her for dipping her french fries in ranch dressing, liking horses, and being from Montana. They also tease her for having no sense of humor, which is slightly less good-spirited. But also—" He pressed his forehead to mine and spoke very seriously. "Lady straight-up has no sense of humor."

I laughed and he kissed me.

"Baby, honestly, I'd love you to come to New York with me. I've been debating whether to ask you."

"You have?"

He laced our fingers together.

"Yeah. It feels a little like bad timing though. I haven't seen Sabien in so long, and I don't know how things will go. Last time we got together he decked me and Mo kicked him in the nuts to get him off me."

"Seriously?"

"Oh yeah, don't fuck with Mo."

I smiled. "I meant him."

"I know what you meant." He got up and got his coffee and dropped back beside me on the couch, throwing his legs over mine.

Now that I knew he wasn't ashamed of me, my stomach had settled and I eyed his coffee greedily. He held it out to me and I took a sip.

"Sabien's angry, and honestly, he has every right to be. I fundamentally disapprove of what he's chosen to do with his life. I'd be mad as hell if he told me that painting wasn't an ethical way to live my life. Hell, I was mad when he was in a bad mood once and told me painting was pretentious."

He sighed and reclaimed his coffee.

"But he's out now. That might change his feelings. I don't know."

"You're so calm about it. It must feel awful to have that

between you."

He shrugged. "It helps that we know where we stand. Well, I used to, anyway. That's why I'm nervous about bringing you this time. I just don't know how it'll be."

I played with the hem of my shirt, trying to figure out why I didn't feel as much better as I'd hoped.

"If you don't want me to come because you need to focus on stuff with your brother and your parents then I understand that. I really do."

He tugged the elastic out of my hair and threaded his fingers through it. It was still a little damp from my shower and he spread it over my shoulders.

"I think I...I wish that I could be there for you because it's hard," I finally got out. "I don't want to make it more stressful. But if you're nervous about it, I guess I wish it would make you feel better to have me there. Instead of thinking of me as something that would make it worse. Or someone you have to take care of in case things go bad." I traced his eyebrows with my finger. "I want to take care of you this time."

He pulled me against his chest and wrapped his arms around me. We sat like that for a few minutes, and I thought he wasn't going to say anything else. Then he grabbed his phone from the coffee table and dialed.

"Mama," he said when someone answered. "I'm going to bring my boyfriend to dinner. That okay?" Then, after a pause, he smiled shyly. "Yeah." Then he darted a mischievous look at me. "Oh, and he's white." My eyes went huge and he grinned. "Wait, lemme ask him. Jude, do you like ranch dressing?"

I couldn't say anything and I shook my head in horror. Faron laughed.

"Nah, he doesn't like it. Okay, bye, Mama."

"Tell me that you just fake called your sister or something."

"Why?" he asked, and ducked when I tried to swat at him. He started laughing again. "Baby, you should see your face. Were you really this worried that my parents wouldn't want me dating a white man?"

I shrugged. I hadn't honestly given it much conscious thought, but apparently I had been that worried about it, because my heart was pounding.

He pulled me down on top of him and wrapped his arms around me.

"Why didn't you say anything before?" he asked.

"I… I don't know, maybe it seemed like one more check in the con column?"

Faron snorted and spoke in a melodramatic voice.

"Poor Jude. He found the one context in which being a white male might be to his disadvantage."

I laughed and pushed at his shoulder.

"They already knew you were white. My mom asked all about you weeks ago."

"You told her about me?"

He nodded, laughter gone, and ran a finger over my lips.

"What…what did you say?"

"I said that I met someone," he drawled, and kissed me. "And that he was amazing." Another kiss. "And talented." Another kiss. "And that I hoped I could introduce her to him some time."

"Oh."

"Okay?"

"Okay."

Faron rolled us so that we were leaning against the arm of the couch, and looked at me, hand back in my hair.

"How's your brain?"

I smiled at the question and did a quick scan. I was good.

"Well, now I'm cataloguing everything about myself to try and figure out which things other than piano your family will decide are white-person things to make fun of me for, but other than that, it's okay."

Faron smiled. "That's natural." Then he cupped my cheek.

"Thank you," he said. "For wanting to be there for me. I didn't know I wanted that, but I do. I'm glad you're coming."

"Me too."

I turned my head to kiss his palm, and forced myself to sit with this feeling. I felt needed, wanted, useful. I felt like part of a team. I didn't think I'd ever felt it before.

CHAPTER EIGHTEEN

FOR THE THIRD time in as many minutes, Faron put a hand on my knee and pressed down, stopping me from bouncing it. The train was just passing Newark and I was officially more nervous than I'd been since my first piano recital when I threw up in the wings before going on. I still couldn't hear Chopin's Mazurka in B-flat Minor without tasting vomit.

It wasn't just meeting Faron's family. The last week my mood had been up, which felt great. Things with Faron felt so good it sometimes took my breath away.

Unfortunately, my anxiety had been up too. I'd been right about Nate; Kira had called to say that he'd chosen not to continue with piano lessons, so even though I was glad Nate didn't have to spend time doing something he didn't enjoy, it was a hit to my meager earnings. I'd begun to hear back from people I'd sent my resume to and so far none of the responses had been positive. It was only a few people, but I'd felt the hit. Felt convinced that no one would want to play with me, that I'd have to go to Faron and tell him that I'd failed. That the person he somehow, miraculously, thought he wanted to be with was a total loser.

But this trip wasn't about me. This was about Faron, and I was supposed to be helping him instead of the reverse.

I crossed my legs and grabbed Faron's hand.

"Last time I was in New York I went to a contemporary opera with some very traditional opera fans and they hated it because they hate anything composed after 1890, but I thought it was beautiful."

I realized I was bouncing my knee again and made myself stop. I realized I was squeezing Faron's hand too tight, so I made myself loosen my hold.

"So, will we just take the subway from the train station? I should've brought them something—a bottle of wine, or... I could stop in a liquor store and pick one up. Do you know what they like? I don't even know what's going to be for dinner, and I don't want to bring something that doesn't go and then they feel obligated to open it but it doesn't go. Maybe whiskey? Do they like whiskey?"

I almost never did this nervous talking thing, but words were just leaking out of me. I didn't like being nervous in front of Faron. It made me feel like we hardly knew each other.

Faron covered my mouth with the hand I wasn't holding and looked deep into my eyes. He kept his hand there and kept looking at me, and it was like I could feel how much he loved me in the way he was looking at me. I felt my stomach unclench and my chest release and I took a deep breath through my nose and exhaled through my nose. Faron nodded and I did it again.

When he still didn't move his hand, I pressed a kiss to his palm and closed my eyes.

"I know you're nervous," he said, lips brushing my hair. "It's a lot. I'm nervous too." I snorted against his hand. Trust Faron to admit he was nervous only when I couldn't ask him about it. "Yes, you win in the competition of who is more nervous," he said, sounding amused.

He made his hand nothing but a gentle reminder against my

lips and I settled into the feeling of him giving me permission to just be quiet.

"So guess what," he said. I raised my eyebrows in question. "I got a call at work yesterday from the Art Alliance. Remember I went there when you had your meeting?"

I rolled my eyes and nodded. Of course I remembered.

"They offered me a spot in their next group show."

I shoved his hand away from my mouth.

"Are you serious? That's so amazing! Are you gonna do it?"

I couldn't quite read his expression. Pride, I thought, and apprehension? Or was that about going to visit his family?

"I told them I'd get back to them next week."

I tugged his hand into my lap and squeezed it. I'd learned to wait for him to gather his thoughts.

"I wanna do it," he said softly. "It feels like a good way to step back into those waters. But I have a lot of bad associations. And not a lot of trust."

I was so fucking proud of him, but I forced myself to put my pride on the back burner.

"A group show seems like not too much pressure, huh? It doesn't have to be just about you?"

He nodded. "It would be nice to meet some more folks doing art. Ginger's got her whole crew but it'd be nice to meet people on my own. And…"

I squeezed his hand and he licked his lips nervously.

"I thought maybe if things go well with Sabien, he would come. He hasn't seen my work in a decade. I've gotten a lot better."

My heart gave a helpless pulse of love for him.

"He'd be an idiot not to want to come. Your painting is out of this world."

A smile played at the corners of his lips. "No agents this time. No money. No bullshit."

"Whatever you want," I agreed. "You can do it however you want."

Faron nodded and pulled me against his shoulder. We both looked out the window and watched the city loom before us as we approached.

––––––

I COULDN'T KEEP my eyes off Faron. He navigated the crowds of the train station and the subway as gracefully as he did everything else, and watching him move with the swaying of the C train, one hand casually holding a rail above his head, the other relaxed at his side, was intensely hot. It felt like I was observing him in something closer to his natural habitat.

What I really wanted was to let my mind drift and hunch a little inside myself like I usually did in public. Watch people, watch everything, and listen to music so the whole world felt like it was happening around me and didn't include me at all.

But if I let myself slip away into the dark, gray place, I'd be of no use to Faron, either as a support system or as a boyfriend. He finally pulled me close to his side and I swayed with him until we got to our stop.

The Locklears lived in the Fort Greene apartment they'd been in since Faron and Sabien moved out, on the first floor of a large brownstone that faced a park. I bounced on my toes trying to calm down before we went inside, and Faron, glancing left and then right, grabbed me and kissed me, hard and deep. When he drew back, I grabbed at his shirt to avoid pitching forward and gave him what must've been a dopey smile because he ran a hand down my arm and squeezed.

The door opened and a woman leaned against it, looking down at us from five steps up.

"Saw you sucking face from the window so I thought I'd remind you where the door was," she drawled. But her expression was teasing and warm and when she smiled I couldn't help but smile back.

She had deep umber skin, close-cropped hair, and the same high cheekbones as Faron, and when she'd smiled her eyes had crinkled just like his did. She was wearing a high-waisted, knee-length skirt in a clingy deep blue, and a black short-sleeved top, but had stepped into slippers to come open the door. I knew she was in her early forties, but in the slippers, she looked really young.

"Hi, Mo," Faron said, and he bounded up the steps and hugged her tight. "This is Jude."

I held out my hand and she shook it, smiling a different kind of smile now. "Nice to meet you," I said, relieved my voice came out sounding relatively normal.

"Welcome, Jude," she said.

"He here yet?" Faron asked, glancing inside.

"Mhmm."

They exchanged a sibling look I couldn't read, but Faron nodded and reached back for my hand. It was the first time he'd reached for me naturally out of need and it made my chest feel so full I almost couldn't breathe.

The apartment was small and warm and very full. The Locklears had moved here from the three bedroom they'd lived in when their kids were at home, and the paring down was visible in the sheer amount of art, knickknacks, books, and picture frames on all the shelves and walls. There was a line of shoes at the door, and I toed out of mine when I saw Faron doing the same. Muffled talking and laughter came from what I assumed was the kitchen.

"You ready?" Mo asked.

Faron nodded resignedly.

Mo called, "Hey, look who I found," toward the back of the apartment. The voices cut out for a moment, then came back louder, and footsteps approached. Mo raised an eyebrow at Faron.

A woman came through the door first and she clearly saw nothing but her son. Gloria Locklear was in her seventies but she moved like a much younger woman, marching up to Faron and dragging him down to kiss his cheek and examine him. She gave him a once-over, clucked at his bleached hair, and then pulled him down again to hug him. "Hi, baby," she said as he squeezed her back.

"Mama, this is Jude," he said, hand at the small of my back.

She looked at me intently, and I warmed to see that she had the same brown-gray eyes as Faron.

"Nice to meet you. Thanks for having me." I didn't know whether to shake or hug, so I kind of half held my hand out, hoping she'd decide. I felt myself flush and she was looking at me so intently. "I'm ridiculously nervous to meet you all and it's either probably say dorky, embarrassing things or say nothing, so...I guess I've gone with dorky and embarrassing," I said, ducking my chin.

Soft laughter came from around the room and Faron's mom pulled me into a quick hug. "Call me Gloria," she said. "I'm glad you're here."

"Son," Faron's dad said gruffly, and he and Faron did a hand-clasp-slash-back-pat thing that was as uncomfortable to watch as it probably was to participate in. When I held out a hand to him, he shook it and smiled and just said, "Charles."

Clearly it was from Charles that Faron had gotten his height. His father was a large man, an inch or so taller even than Faron, and broad, with a barrel chest and stocky hips. He had deep brown skin and dark freckles, and his short hair and mustache were liberally shot through with white.

As soon as his parents had said their hellos, Faron got mobbed by two men who had to be Syrus and Kalil, but while they were fake-punching him—at least, I was pretty sure it was fake—and talking over each other, Faron froze, and I looked up to see another man standing in the doorway. Faron approached him and they stood, looking at each other.

Seeing Sabien was like seeing Faron aslant. They were the same height, but where Faron's muscles were lean, Sabien's were thick. Sabien's hair was shaved and he held himself with military bearing. They had the same high cheekbones, but where Faron's bone structure was beautiful, Sabien's looked too stark, his cheeks hollow, skin stretched just a little too tight. He had the same gray-brown eyes, but where Faron's were dreamy, Sabien's looked troubled. Sabien's nose was a little broader, his chin a little narrower, but their mouths were the most different. Faron's generous mouth always looked sensual to me—lush and inviting. But Sabien's lips turned slightly up at one corner, giving the impression that he was smirking, and it threw his whole face into chaos.

Those troubled eyes were fixed on Faron now, facing off.

"Brought a friend?" Sabien said without looking at me. It was Faron's voice, but harder, the same notes played on brass instead of strings.

"Boyfriend," Faron said softly. He'd told me Sabien had known he was gay since they were kids and never had any problem with it, so presumably this was just an opening gambit.

"Needed backup?"

"Wanted it."

"Scared I might kick your ass again?"

"Mo would take you down."

Sabien's voice had edged into warmer territory and Faron matched him.

"Didn't want to get stuck alone with me?"

"Thought maybe you wouldn't want to be alone with me."

I recognized the raw honesty in Faron's voice and I could see that Sabien did too. He rolled his shoulders.

"Been a while."

"Too long."

"I'm out."

"For good?"

"For good."

"You okay?"

Faron's voice trembled ever so slightly. Sabien rolled his shoulders again.

"Not really."

Then they were in each other's arms, clasped tight together. Sabien kept pounding on Faron's back like he wanted to get away, but he was holding on just as tight. They were talking in each other's ears too low for me to hear, but I heard Sabien make a sound like a choked sob and Faron hold him even tighter. They stayed that way for a minute and I couldn't look away.

Somehow, it soothed an ache deep inside me to know that Faron was generous and caring with all the people he cared about, not just me. It was a part of him, an essential piece of what made Faron Faron. What made him right for me. What made us right for each other.

He'd told me that he didn't love me in spite of my struggles but saw them as just a part of me, and I had believed him. But watching him with Sabien burned the truth of it into me.

This was how he loved. This was how he was made to love. Hardship and struggle were a part of it and he needed every shade to paint the picture. Needed them for contrast and harmony, for shadow and highlight.

I watched him with Sabien and I finally believed he wasn't going anywhere.

The brothers broke apart, wiping their eyes, with hands on each other's shoulders. Faron's eyes found me right away and his smile was so full of peace and relief that I felt it like a physical jolt. I smiled back at him, trying to put all of what I felt in my eyes. Faron reached out a hand for me and elbowed Sabien.

"This is Jude. Jude, Sabien."

Sabien looked me over, eyes narrowed. Now that I'd seen him embrace his brother, seen him cry, seen the armor he wore fall away like so many rose petals, his face rearranged itself for me. His eyes didn't look so troubled anymore—they looked curious, wary, but warm. His smirk didn't look cruel anymore, it looked playful, like he was daring you to do something you might not want to do but promising it'd be fun anyway.

He looked away finally and glanced at Faron. "Okay, okay, I get it, okay."

Faron just shook his head resignedly.

"Hey, Jude," Sabien drawled, and he pulled me in for a hug. It didn't feel like hugging Faron, but there was an undeniable resonance that fascinated me.

When Sabien let me go, he winked at me and elbowed Faron. "I think he likes me better." He turned to me, preening and slick. "Whattaya say, Jude. You wanna ditch him and hang with big brother?"

Sabien managed to sound filthy and completely playful at the same time, and I thought I could see how he got into a lot of trouble as a kid.

"Yeah," I said, making my eyes soft and wide and looking up at Sabien. "Gosh, I can't believe you feel the same way, but ever since Faron showed me your picture, I just...I can't help the way I've been feeling."

"Uhhh," Sabien said, and froze. His eyes darted around for a minute and I took pity on him, giving him a wink and sliding my arm around Faron.

Everyone started laughing and heckling Sabien, and Faron drew me tight to his side, squeezing me happily.

"Alright, alright," Sabien muttered, embarrassed, but he took the teasing good-naturedly.

Faron introduced me to Syrus and Kalil and we all sat around chatting for a while. I leaned a shoulder against Faron and listened to their family chatter, happy to be there and happy that no one seemed to want to ask me a hundred and one questions about me or my intentions for their son.

"Where're Mike and Sharon, and the kids?" Faron asked. Mike was Amo's partner and Sharon was Kalil's wife. Amo and Mike had a daughter and Sharon and Kalil had a daughter and a son. Faron had never mentioned Syrus having a partner or kids.

"Boy, we've hardly got enough chairs for all of you," Gloria said, flicking her hand at the room. But Sabien caught Faron's eye and gave a single nod, and Faron changed the subject.

Dinner was fun and chaotic with so many people in a small space, but it also served to distract people from the fact that I was talking more than I was eating. As Faron predicted, Syrus teased me about worshipping at the altar of dead white composers, but was interested when I told him about Chevalier de Saint-Georges, George Bridgetower, Samuel Coleridge-Taylor, Florence Price.

It was Sabien who noticed first. He leaned across Faron and said, "Yo, do you not eat?" Then he turned to Faron. "Seriously, bro, do you not cook for his skinny ass, or what?"

I knew he was just teasing and I wouldn't have cared if it was just us. But my stomach clenched and I glanced at Gloria, waiting to see that look of offense that my own mother got when I didn't eat what she'd cooked. The look that said, *This is how I show you I care and you reject it.*

But Gloria reached over and grabbed Sabien's wrist, her delicate fingers an iron grip.

"Did I teach you to make comments about other people's food at the dinner table?" she asked, her voice calm.

Sabien wilted immediately. "No, ma'am."

There was a beat of silence, then the conversation continued around us. I glanced up at Gloria, wondering if I should apologize, but she had already turned to Mo and was asking a question. Faron's hand pressed into my lower back.

"I told her," he murmured close to my ear. "Hope that was okay."

Relief flooded me and I nodded.

After we'd finished eating and cleared the table, Gloria said, "Faron and Sabien, do the dishes, please. I think the rest of us will take a little walk to help us digest."

Faron and Sabien looked at each other warily for a second before nodding. Faron walked us to the door and pulled me in for a kiss before he squared his shoulders and walked back to the kitchen like he was heading into battle.

———

AS WE SETTLED into our seats on the last train back to Philly, Faron took a huge breath and blew it out. I'd taken a cue from him and stayed silent the whole way from Brooklyn because he clearly needed some space to think, but now he seemed to relax for the first time all day.

There weren't many people on the train, so I turned to face him and threw a leg over his, and took his hands in mine.

"How did it go?" I asked.

Faron blinked dazedly for a moment, then he smiled. A sweet smile, full of joy and relief.

"Good. He sure liked you."

"Haha."

"No, really. He always used to play like that—did it with every guy I ever liked. Flirty and braggy. But he told me."

"He hardly got to know me," I protested.

Faron shrugged. "He knows me though."

I kissed his cheek and settled my shoulder against his, drawing his hands into my lap. "Did you guys hash it out?"

"Didn't really have to. He's done. He chose not to make a career of it because it's not what he wants. I don't need him to condemn it the way I do. We've never been the same person. But things will be different between us now that he's done. I think. I hope."

I rubbed my thumb over his hand. "I hope so too."

"I think he got scared," Faron said slowly. "Not of being hurt. He's been hurt and that isn't what scares him."

"What scares him?" I asked as the train pulled out of the station into the dark.

"Himself."

We left the city behind, bright lights and tall buildings glittering outside the scratched and cloudy windows. With the solidity of Faron beside me, they looked as insubstantial as fireflies.

"I get that," I said.

Faron nodded. "Thank you. For coming with me. For having my back."

"I'll always have your back," I said. "That...that's what partners do, right?"

Faron brought our joined hands to his mouth and kissed my knuckles softly.

"That's right, baby."

EPILOGUE

Three months later

I STOOD outside the open garage door, shivering as Waffle batted at the snow falling in fat, lazy flakes. It had just started, but the forecast predicted we'd have an inch or two by the evening and more overnight.

"Hey, baby, you should probably start getting ready," Faron called from inside.

"Hear that, Waffle? No more snow for you."

Waffle barked, her shaggy fur now crusted with snow. I nudged her inside and she pulled her leash out of my hand.

"Look out!" I yelled, and Faron came through the door with a towel and snagged Waffle's collar before she could get into the apartment from the garage.

"You muppet," I told Waffle, and Faron shook his head and dried off the dog.

Inside, the apartment was warm and cozy. We got a Christmas tree last week and I'd brought home a box of plain glass ornaments and given them to Faron, thinking he might like to paint them. I don't know what I expected exactly—I'd just thought he might enjoy it—but Faron had shattered any expectations I might have had.

Some were abstract swirls of color, some were fire and water, some were snowy. He said he'd painted them listening to me play the piano and had me guess which one was which piece of music. Then he'd painted an ornament of me, and, when I asked him, one of himself too. They gleamed on the tree and the colors glowed richly when we turned the white lights on.

It was so cozy that I almost wished we could stay in all night. But that was mostly nerves talking.

Things had been both incredibly good and incredibly hard since we'd gotten back from New York. I got a few bites from people who needed an accompanist every now and then, which I couldn't turn down since I needed the money, but was nothing like what I wanted to be doing. Mostly what I got was silence. And that was worse than rejection. I retreated to my apartment and wouldn't let Faron or Christopher in for a week as I lay in bed and nursed my wounds.

In the end, it was Ginger I'd let in. Ginger who'd sat with me, watching movies and eating noxious Chinese takeout I wanted nothing to do with. Ginger who'd called Daniel and told him to come over to my apartment and bring cake.

They'd sat there, mostly ignoring me, talking to each other, eating noodles and cake. Daniel graded papers and grumbled about students and Ginger sketched tattoo designs for her clients the next day. Around midnight they'd left, the half-eaten cake and the greasy takeout containers a constant reminder that someone had been there other than me.

I'd called Faron the next day and told him I needed him but I couldn't move. When I turned the lock and held the door open for him, I tried to say I was sorry but he just held me. He'd brought a smoothie in the cup I used at his place.

"I don't like your apartment," he'd told me after we lay together in silence for hours.

I'd told him I didn't like it either, and then I'd gone home with him and I'd kind of never left. A few days later, Faron came home from work late, wheeling my suitcase.

"I want you here," he'd told me. "I want you here all the time. Do you want to be here?" And I'd nodded and watched as he wheeled my suitcase to the bed and placed stacks of my black among his beautiful colors.

———

A WEEK later the call had come. Emmeline apologized for taking so long and invited me to join a piano trio with her and her friend Zoe, a cellist. They'd played for two years with another pianist, but he'd moved and wasn't playing much anymore. They were looking for a replacement.

They played chamber music as well as more contemporary compositions and even some piano arrangements of popular music, and when she said they were called Penny Candy, I realized I'd heard of them. Zoe played with the Philly Opera orchestra and when we all met up at Curtis for the first time, it felt like we'd been playing together forever. Zoe and Emmeline exchanged looks as we played and finally broke out into grins.

We'd begun practicing right away. They'd had some performances already lined up, so they were eager to get me up to speed. It was wonderful to be playing chamber music again, and I was impressed with Zoe's ability to take popular music and pull out the strains that would make it sing on our instruments. We added a Tom Waits song and a Riven song to our roster, as well as one of Thomas Groen's newer compositions, since, weasel or not, it was a coup to perform it.

Our first performances had gone well, and after one Zoe introduced me to a member of the board of the Philly Opera, who had later gotten in touch with me because their practice pianist wasn't working out. That had led to me filling in for the pianist who played with the opera when they needed one, who had an opportunity to play in New York. I had my fingers crossed that next season they might want me on a more regular basis.

The more I was playing, the happier I was. I was living with Faron, and got to share a bed with him every night. I got to watch him sink into his paintings for the group show at the Art Alliance and produce three times as much work as he needed. The night of the opening, he'd tried to hide his nerves, and I'd realized they weren't just about showing in public for the first time since he'd left the New York art world behind. They were also about Sabien seeing his work for the first time in a decade.

When Sabien clapped his hand on Faron's back and said, "Not bad at all," Faron's shoulders had relaxed and the smile that played at the corners of his mouth had been relieved and gratified. I maintained that Faron's work was by far the best in the show, even if I might've been slightly biased.

I'd brought him home to meet my parents, who'd adored him, and he and Christopher already got along. We'd been going to Ginger and Christopher's for dinner more and more often, and once we'd all gone to Daniel and Rex's place in North Philly, which was slowly being transformed into a space that promised to be amazing when it was done.

We'd gone to New York for Thanksgiving with Faron's family, and stayed over with Sabien, who'd gotten an apartment a few blocks from their childhood house. The more I saw them together, the more I saw their echoes with one another. But also the more I could see how each had become who he became based on his differences from the other. Faron had grown up comfortable with silence because his twin was always talking. Sabien felt comfortable to push and cajole because his twin drew boundaries in safe places.

I found myself more and more grateful to Sabien, because he'd had a hand in making Faron the man I loved today. And the man who loved me, against all odds.

Now it was two weeks until Christmas (and one week until Ginger's Chanukah bash that she told me I was familially obligated to come to but not required to stay at any longer than I wanted) and the night of Penny Candy's most important performance to date.

We were playing a show at the Perelman, the small theater in the Kimmel Center. My family was coming, and Christopher seemed to have gotten everyone else I'd ever met in Philadelphia to come too. The entire Small Change crew was coming and Ginger was taking particular delight in bringing Phee, the youngest and least predictable member of the Small Change family, and making him dress for the occasion. Faron had bought a ticket of his own and given the one I'd comped him to his friend Winston, from Mightier Than The Sword.

Ginger had also planned a little gathering for me at Small Change after the show, which she said was "definitely not a party, since you don't like parties, but a gathering of humans you like, booze, and snacks." I'd flared my nostrils at her, but was actually very touched. I was pretty sure she got it.

"You thinking about getting dressed?" Faron said, sliding his arms around me from behind. I'd gotten lost in looking at the Christmas tree.

"I can't believe we're going to have Christmas," I said. We'd been through this a couple of times.

"We are going to have Christmas," Faron said. "I can't wait." He kissed the side of my neck and then pushed me toward the clothes rack. "Get dressed, okay?"

I shucked my jeans and sweater and slid my suit on. It was a new one. Faron had brought it home for me last week.

"You hate your clothes and you don't feel comfortable in

them," he'd said, holding the garment bag out to me. "I think this might be better."

It was a black suit, yes. But this one had a subtle pattern to the knit, so it was matte and swallowed the light like velvet. The pants were cut slim and I thought they made my legs look like spokes, but Faron said they were supposed to fit like that. The jacket fit just like a suit coat, but the undersides of the arms, the armpits, and the sides of it were made of a stretchy material that made it feel like I wasn't wearing a jacket at all.

My shirt was a lavender so pale that it could almost look white at a glance, and my tie was a deep violet silk.

The matte black made my hair gleam like copper and the color of the shirt and tie made my complexion look creamy rather than stark white. When I asked Faron how he'd know what would fit me and what would look good, he'd simply smiled and kissed me.

When I'd tied my shoes, I stood in front of Faron and held my arms out to be evaluated. As he'd pointed out, I'd never cared about my clothes. But now. Tonight. In the clothes he'd chosen for me. I wanted to look good for him, and I flushed with that knowledge.

Faron ran assessing hands over my clothes and straightened my tie. Then he leaned in and kissed my cheek.

"You look beautiful," he said. Then, "Sit down."

It had become a ritual, and while I pretended to be long-suffering about it, in truth having Faron do my hair was one of my favorite things. He loved to play with it. When we were alone, sometimes he'd do elaborate braids and twists, and I let him, my mind drifting, happy to feel his hands on me, and just as happy when he'd take it down and brush it out again.

Now he brushed it in long, slow strokes that massaged my scalp and dragged fluidly through my hair.

"You purr like a cat when I do this," Faron said in my ear, and I hummed. We didn't talk as he worked. I was going over the program in my mind and hoping that the director of the Philly Orchestra might be there tonight. Emmeline had also invited a number of people from Curtis. Every contact was a good contact to have.

"Okay, all set."

Faron picked a few stray hairs off my shoulders and steered me into the bathroom.

He'd parted my hair in an imperfect diagonal and done the French braid slightly to the side, making the whole thing look cool and a little edgy even while it was neat and matched the suit perfectly.

"How the hell do you always know exactly the right thing to do?" I asked, staring at myself in the mirror.

Faron's smile bloomed in the mirror behind me and he pressed a gentle kiss to my jaw.

"I'm trying to decide about the mascara."

The stage lights always washed me out and turned my eyelashes invisible.

"Do whatever will make you feel most confident and most like yourself."

Most like myself. It sounded so simple and felt so complicated when myself wasn't always something I liked very much.

"I don't need it," I told him.

He squeezed me tighter and kissed my lips. Then he slid a tiny tin of lip balm into my jacket pocket.

"I'll see you after?" I asked, though I knew I would.

"You'll see me after," he said. Then he bent and whispered in my ear, though there was no one else there. "I love you, Jude Lucen."

I shivered. It got me every time.

"I love you," I told him. "I'll be playing for you."

Faron ran a gentle hand over my hair and smiled. "Play for yourself, baby. That's how you can play for me."

I PLAYED FOR FARON, I played for myself, I played.

The show rushed by the way really good shows always did and when we neared the end, I felt that subtle shade of loss that meant I was having a good time. We played the Tom Waits and the Riven songs to the delight of part of the audience and the mystification of another. I was pretty sure I'd heard Ginger whisper, "Holy shit, is that Tom Waits" a couple of bars in, and I'd winked. We finished the program off with Zoe's arrangement of "Carol of the Bells" because seasonal music never failed to bring the house down, and then it was over.

When we took our bows, I saw Faron sitting third row, center, with his hand over his heart, looking at me like I was everything. Tears sprang to my eyes and made the lights kaleidoscope magically.

Zoe, Emmeline, and I hugged in the wings, falling into our typical post-show debrief of this transition and that diminuendo.

The problem with the Perelman was that when you exited the theatre, you were directly out in the lobby. This was only a problem if, like me, you didn't want to have people pay attention to you after a show. But I tucked my shirt in firmly in the back where it always got mussed as I played, checked to make sure my hair was still in place, and hooked arms with Zoe and Emmeline to walk through the door.

We'd lingered backstage on purpose, so many people had left, but our families and friends were waiting for us and they clapped when we emerged. Zoe and Emmeline squeezed my arms from either side and went to greet their people. I only had eyes for Faron.

He was standing off to the side, next to Winston, and when he saw me he held his arms out. I tried to look decorous as I walked to him, but the second I was in front of him I hugged him so hard my feet almost came off the ground.

"My hair look okay?" I murmured into his neck.

"You were spectacular," he said. "And I really want to kiss you right now in front of all these people so they know my boyfriend is brilliant."

"Do it."

He tipped my chin back and kissed the bejesus out of me. Someone whistled—I thought it was Morgan—and I felt Faron smile into the kiss. When we broke apart, my parents were at my elbow.

They smiled and patted my back and complimented the performance. I searched their faces for the anxiety and worry and pity I usually saw there, but I didn't find it tonight. My mom kissed my cheek and my dad squeezed my shoulder, and they hugged Faron and Ginger and Christopher, and then they left.

"You were amazing, I expect to hear all about the Tom Waits at the shop, and I adore you, but I gotta go set up so stuff's ready, kay?" Ginger said.

"You didn't invite my parents?"

"To the after-non-party? No, what the hell do you think this is?"

Christopher hugged me. "You were great. You all were. I'm gonna help Ginger."

Emmeline caught my eye and gestured me over.

"Rob," she said, "I want to introduce you to Jude Lucen. Jude used to solo with the Boston Symphony Orchestra, and work with students at Berklee, among other things. Jude, Rob Pankhurst, a dean of Curtis."

Rob was complimentary about the show, and asked a few questions that made Emmeline raise her eyebrows pointedly at me where he couldn't see.

When he walked away, she said, "There just might be the need for another part-time piano faculty," she said out of the corner of her mouth. "Nothing official yet, and I don't know more, but." She winked. "Doesn't hurt to be on their radar."

I thanked her and waved to Zoe, and grabbed Faron.

"Can we get out of here and go to Ginger's party now so that we can get out of there and go home?" I asked.

"Absolutely. I invited Winston to the party. That okay?"

"Yeah, of course."

As we crossed the lobby I paused near the doors to the larger theater.

"Never thought we'd be back here like this," I said. We were standing in the spot where Faron had caught me when I ran out of the performance I'd brought him to months before. The spot where despair swallowed me and he just held me through it.

He swung me around to face him and brought his forehead to mine. "I did."

———

GINGER HAD DRAPED a long paper chain around the entrance to Small Change. It alternated white and black like piano keys and I was immensely touched that she'd gone to so much trouble. Inside, it was surreal to see the tattoo shop but hear a Beethoven piano concerto coming through speakers that usually played metal and punk.

"Yay!" Ginger yelled as I came through the door. "The conquering hero returns!" She slung an arm around my waist and pulled me inside. "Seriously, bro, you were amazing. Also you do know that Tom Waits is my all-time favorite musician, basically, right? Oh, good, Phee, thanks, put those over there."

She untangled herself from me and pointed to the table she'd set up near the front of the shop. It was half makeshift bar and half food.

Phee slid a tray onto the table and tugged at the collar of his shirt, glaring at Ginger. I could imagine the joy she'd taken in getting him out of his usual slouchy jeans and sweatshirts and buttoning him up. Ginger had a streak of the sadistic in her.

I looked at what Phee had just put down.

"Are those…"

"Yep," she said. "Christopher made them."

I turned around to see my brother smiling at me.

"I know, I know, you actually like the ones in the box better, but I couldn't bring myself to serve guests store-bought Pop-Tarts."

"Psh," Ginger said. "You just wanted to show off because you knew people would be all 'Oh. My. God. Did you *make* Pop-Tarts?'"

Christopher grinned. "Yeah, that too." He pointed. "Those are the brown sugar cinnamon ones, and the rest you won't like."

"What are they?" I asked. If he'd gone to all the trouble of making them, I was sure he wanted to tell me what they were.

"Okay," he said delightedly. "These are blueberry and those are cherry, but these are awesome. They're s'mores, and they have actual toasted marshmallow inside. I made the crust with part graham flour. I took the idea from a sandwich I made for Ginge once. I put it on the menu for a while but no one really ordered it. Too confusing that it wasn't desert but was a sweet sandwich. The world is not ready."

He shrugged and smiled.

"Chris. Thank you. For this. For everything. I… I love you a lot. You know that, right?"

He'd always been so painfully easy to read. Surprise flashed across his face, then a moment of fear, then such relief I almost cried.

"Yeah," he said. "Yeah, I know, man. I love you too."

He pulled me into a tight hug. It was clearly the night for them.

People drifted through the door in twos and threes. Marcus and Selene, Daniel and Rex, Morgan and Lindsey. Winston came in and went to stand with Faron.

Daniel took one look at the snack table, turned to Christopher, and said, "Oh my god. Did you *make* Pop-Tarts?" Ginger shot Christopher a raised eyebrow, and Daniel tried to be surreptitious about taking one of every flavor, but I was pretty sure later I heard him ask Rex, "Wait, could *you* make Pop-Tarts?"

After a little while, Ginger couldn't stand the music anymore and she changed it to something that sounded like orchestral music with metal vocals.

I felt light and a little fizzy, even though it was kind of a party. People were really complimentary about the show and seemed genuinely curious about the music. I felt even lighter and fizzier after Ginger brought me a gin and soda. After a while, I left Selene and Marcus talking with Rex about Blossom Dearie and went to stand with Faron.

"How are you feeling?" he asked.

"Really fucking grateful," I said, and grabbed his hand. Across from me, Christopher held up the bottle of gin and I nodded.

"Just tell me when you want to go," Faron said after a minute, squeezing my hand.

"You know what I want?"

"Hm?"

"I want to have this second drink, then I want you to take me home and fuck me in our bed."

"Uh, happy to assist on this end of things," Christopher said, overhearing. He handed me the gin and soda and departed quickly. Faron chuckled.

I sipped my drink with one hand and held Faron's hand with the other and felt the deep contentment that came from being somewhere I felt like I could belong. Winston was standing in front of the Pop-Tart table with an odd expression on his face.

"Is Winston okay?"

Faron sighed. I knew he would never break a confidence so I didn't ask, just said I was glad he was here.

"Yeah, he will be. Probably. Just a rough time right now. I wanted to distract him a little tonight."

I squeezed Faron's hand. Phee approached the table and stood next to Winston, pointed at the Pop-Tarts, and said something that made Winston laugh.

"Do you think we could sneak out the back?" I asked.

Faron gave me this look that I could now recognize as one borrowed directly from his mother. "If you must," he said.

"Ugh, fine." I gestured Ginger over. "Hey, listen. This was an amazing after-non-party. Thank you for doing all this for me. Now I desperately need to go home and make out with Faron and I don't want to say goodbye to everyone individually. Can you, like...party-fairy it for me?"

"My pleasure." Ginger handed us our coats and guided us to the front door, then faced the room. "Hey, everyone! Jude and Faron are leaving now and Jude loves you all. Everyone say 'Congrats' and 'Bye' to Jude on three, okay? One, two, three!"

A chorus of "Congrats!" and "Bye!" and "Congrats and bye to Jude" rang out, and I smiled hugely. I waved to everyone and called goodbye, and then Faron and I were outside.

"Damn, she's good," I said.

"Mhmm," he agreed. "You down to walk?"

"Yeah, the air feels good." I put my coat on and Faron slid his elbow through mine.

The snow was still falling and the city felt like it had been muted, every sound muffled and delicate, every breath fresh and new. We walked through the spangled dark arm in arm, and the snow collected on our hair and shoulders. I felt like I was floating.

At home, Faron took Waffle out while I changed into pajamas. I plugged in the Christmas tree lights and walked once around the tree, taking a tour of the ornaments. The lights reflected in muted pools in the top of the piano, as if I could dip my fingers in and they would come out dripping silver.

I plugged in the space heater near the bed and rolled the one from the living room in too, making a microclimate of warmth around the bed. Waffle's bark sounded outside the door, and in a split-second decision, I stripped my pajamas off and dropped them beside the bed just as the garage door opened. The sounds of Waffle shaking off and getting rubbed down played in the background, but all I cared about was seeing Faron when he came through the door.

He was a shadow among shadows, in his black overcoat and dark scarf, but I could see him freeze as he stepped through the apartment door, and warmth gathered in my belly that had nothing to do with the space heaters.

He patted Waffle's dog bed and unlaced his shoes, hung up his coat, all without looking away from me. I imagined what he saw: me, splayed naked, skin pale against the midnight-blue sheets, lit only by the fairy lights from the Christmas tree.

He was out of his clothes and on me almost as soon as he crossed the room. His hands were chilly, but his mouth was hot and we kissed until we were both writhing and his hands had warmed.

My head spun with desire and a little bit with gin, and I stretched out on the bed so I could feel the soft mattress beneath me and the hard man on top of me. Most nights I loved how slow Faron built our pleasure. How he played my body and our desire like laying paint on the canvas. How he edged me until I was so desperate for him I felt like I would die if I couldn't have him.

But tonight I wanted to feel only the simple, animal pleasure of him. Of life.

"Sweetheart, I want you so much," I said. "Please, I want you now, just like this."

"Anything," he said, and with a swipe of lube and a swipe of his tongue against mine, he buried himself inside me, deep and endless. I clung to him as we moved, our hips seeking the rhythm that was just ours. My pleasure built and built until each stroke felt like I was unspooling from somewhere deep in my belly, and every touch was electric.

Faron seemed touch-drunk, his hands roaming everywhere, his mouth latching onto every inch of me he could reach. When he closed a hand around my cock, I spilled immediately, like he'd coaxed the pleasure from the deepest parts of me. I shook as wave after wave of orgasm crashed through me and as soon as mine ended, Faron's began. His chest was a dreamscape and his throat a fantasy, and he shook above me and inside me like we were one creature made of tinder and fire and drowning in each other.

He gasped my name as he came and when he shot inside me I clenched up around his offering like a devotee and trembled with it.

"My love," he murmured, and kissed my neck and face. My arms around him felt barely big enough to contain all that they held.

In the warmth of our bed we clung to each other as our breathing evened out. I almost couldn't look at him because when I did, my heart threatened to overflow. But I held tightly to his hands until we met in a kiss.

After a few minutes, we made our way to the shower and rinsed off quickly. Faron ran his fingers along my braid. I hadn't taken it down before because I wanted to keep the evidence of his hand on me. But now I nodded at him and he unbraided my hair slowly, kissing my neck as the strands fell free.

I felt so very on the edge of something that was beautiful and frightening and huge.

We dried off but didn't get dressed again because we kept reaching for each other, kept needing the comfort of skin on skin. Faron rolled a space heater over near the piano.

"Will you play for me?" he murmured against my lips.

I'd bought a bench for the piano months before, and I sank to its silky surface and touched the keys.

Faron knelt behind me, arms wrapped around my waist, and rested his cheek on my back.

"Don't let go," I murmured.

"Never."

I played. I drifted from piece to piece and movement to movement because it didn't matter. Faron's arms held me tight, and he pressed kisses to my back every now and then. Sometimes he hummed along and I felt the vibration up and down my spine. Mostly, he drifted with me, anchoring me to him as I sent my music up into the night.

THE END

DEAR READER,

Thank you so much for reading *Invitation to the Blues*! I hope you enjoyed Jude and Faron's story.

If you did, consider spreading the word! You can help others find this book by writing reviews, blogging about it, and talking about it on social media. Reviews and shares really help authors keep writing, and we appreciate them so much! The power is in your hands.

Thank you!

xo, Roan Parrish

Want to get exclusive content and news of future book releases? Sign up for my newsletter at **roanparrish.com**!

ACKNOWLEDGMENTS

Deepest thanks to my first readers, Jenny and Anni, for your feedback on all elements of this story.

To Jude Sierra, for your passionate encouragement, and for being such a champion of what is a personal story for us both.

To Julian Winters, for your astute and generous feedback.

To Natasha Snow, for another beautiful cover. And to Julia Ganis, whose strong editorial eye saved me from my complete lack of temporal reality (among other things) yet again.

To Maury Okun, whose input on the workings of the classical music world were essential to understanding Jude's story.

Forever thanks to my parents, for your unwavering support, in my life and in my work.

And the warmest thanks to my amazing readers. Without you, none of this would be possible.

ABOUT ROAN PARRISH

Roan Parrish lives in Philadelphia where she is gradually attempting to write love stories in every genre.

When not writing, she can usually be found cutting her friends' hair, meandering through whatever city she's in while listening to torch songs and melodic death metal, or cooking overly elaborate meals. She loves bonfires, winter beaches, minor chord harmonies, and self-tattooing. One time she may or may not have baked a six-layer chocolate cake and then thrown it out the window in a fit of pique.

———

MORE INFORMATION

You can keep up with all my new releases and get exclusive free content by signing up for my **NEWSLETTER** at **roanparrish.com**.

Come join **PARRISH OR PERISH**, my Facebook group, to hang out, chat about books, and get exclusive news, updates, excerpts of works in progress, freebies, and pictures of my cat!

You can follow me on **BOOKBUB** and **AMAZON** to find out when my books are on sale.

You can follow me on **PINTEREST** at ARoanParrish, to see visuals of all my characters, books, and settings.

And you can follow me on **TWITTER**, **FACEBOOK**, and **INSTAGRAM** at RoanParrish.

SMALL CHANGE

You just met Ginger and Christopher in *Invitation to the Blues*. Read Ginger and Christopher's story in **Small Change!**

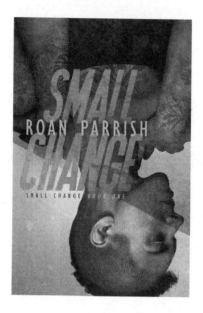

Ginger Holtzman has fought for everything she's ever had—the success of her tattoo shop, respect in the industry, her upcoming art show. Tough and independent, she has taking-no-crap down to an art form. Good thing too, since keeping her shop afloat, taking care of her friends, and scrambling to finish her paintings doesn't leave time for anything else. Which ... is for the best, because then she doesn't notice how lonely she is. She'll get through it all on her own, just like she always does.

Christopher Lucen opened a coffee and sandwich joint in South Philly because he wanted to be part of a community after years of running from place to place, searching for something he could never quite name.

Now, he relishes the familiarity of knowing what his customers want, and giving it to them. But what he really wants now is love.

When they meet, Christopher is smitten, but Ginger ... isn't quite so sure. Christopher's gorgeous, and kind, and their opposites-attract chemistry is off the charts. But hot sex is one thing—truly falling for someone? Terrifying. When her world starts to crumble around her, Ginger has to face the fact that this fight can only be won by being vulnerable—this fight, she can't win on her own

IN THE MIDDLE OF SOMEWHERE

You just met Daniel and Rex in *Invitation to the Blues*. Read Daniel and Rex's story in **In the Middle of Somewhere**!

Daniel Mulligan is tough, snarky, and tattooed, hiding his self-consciousness behind sarcasm. Daniel has never fit in—not at home in Philadelphia with his auto mechanic father and brothers, and not at school where his Ivy League classmates looked down on him. Now, Daniel's relieved to have a job at a small college in Holiday, Northern Michigan, but he's a city boy through and through, and it's clear that this small town is one more place he won't fit in.

Rex Vale clings to routine to keep loneliness at bay: honing his muscular body, perfecting his recipes, and making custom furniture. Rex has lived in Holiday for years, but his shyness and imposing size have kept him from connecting with people.

When the two men meet, their chemistry is explosive, but Rex fears Daniel will be another in a long line of people to leave him, and Daniel has learned that letting anyone in can be a fatal weakness. Just as they begin to break down the walls keeping them apart, Daniel is called home to Philadelphia, where he discovers a secret that changes the way he understands everything.

OUT OF NOWHERE

MIDDLE OF SOMEWHERE #2

The only thing in Colin Mulligan's life that makes sense is taking cars apart and putting them back together. In the auto shop where he works with his father and brothers, he tries to get through the day without having a panic attack or flying into a rage. Drinking helps. So does running and lifting weights until he can hardly stand. But none of it can change the fact that he's gay, a secret he has kept from everyone.

Rafael Guerrera has found ways to live with the past he's ashamed of. He's dedicated his life to social justice work and to helping youth who, like him, had very little growing up. He has no time for love. Hell, he barely has time for himself. Somehow, everything about miserable, self-destructive Colin cries out to him. But down that path lie the troubles Rafe has worked so hard to leave behind. And as their relationship intensifies, Rafe and Colin are forced to dredge up secrets that both men would prefer stay buried.

WHERE WE LEFT OFF

MIDDLE OF SOMEWHERE #3

Leo Ware may be young, but he knows what he wants. And what he wants is Will Highland. Snarky, sophisticated, fiercely opinionated Will Highland, who burst into Leo's unremarkable life like a supernova... and then was gone just as quickly.

For the past miserable year, Leo hasn't been able to stop thinking about the powerful connection he and Will shared. So, when Leo moves to New York for college, he sweeps back into Will's life, hopeful that they can pick up where they left off. What begins as a unique friendship soon burns with chemistry they can't deny... though Will certainly tries.

But Leo longs for more than friendship and hot sex. A romantic to his core, Leo wants passion, love, commitment—everything Will isn't interested in giving. Will thinks romance is a cheesy fairy tale and love is overrated. He likes his space and he's happy with things just the way they are, thank you very much. Or is he? Because as he and Leo get more and more tangled up in each other's lives, Will begins to act like maybe love is something he could feel after all.

ALSO BY ROAN PARRISH

The Middle of Somewhere Series:

In the Middle of Somewhere

Out of Nowhere

Where We Left Off

The Small Change Series:

Small Change

Invitation to the Blues

The Remaking of Corbin Wale

Heart of the Steal (with Avon Gale)

Available for Preorder:

Riven

Short fiction:

Mayfair (in *Lead Me Into Darkness: Five Halloween Tales of Paranormal Romance*)

Company (in *All In Fear: A Collection of Six Horror Tales*)

Made in the USA
Lexington, KY
21 January 2019